BLOOD
— FOR —
BLOOD

BY

D. S. ALLEN

Contact Information: www.dsallen.org

First paperback edition May 2014
Editor: Finish The Story
Publishing History
First Edition, 2014
Second Edition, 2019
Print ISBN: 9781796417838
Published in the United States of America

To Sonja

TABLE OF CONTENTS

Foreword

The Historicity of Blood For Blood.

The foundation for Blood For Blood came from two main ideas. The first of which was to include a witchcraft trial in the novel. Secondly, I wanted the plot to be driven within the backdrop of historical events. In other words, to weave the plot through historical events, which acted as a catalyst in the lives of the fictional main characters. Some (there are others, but I won't include them because of potential plot spoilers) of these historical events include:

1. The Battle of Worcester, 1651— The Battle of Worcester ended in victory for Cromwell and ended the Civil War. Charles barely escaped Worcester and only after weeks on the run, managed to find sanctuary on the continent. Thereafter, Charles worked through his loyal agents as they plotted the downfall of Cromwell. Charles was also in constant danger of assassination during these years.

2. Witch trials –The last witchcraft trial in England that resulted in hangings was in Bideford in 1682. I wanted to highlight the terrible and unbelievable injustices perpetrated against women—and sometimes men—during these sad times.

3. Penruddock's Uprising as part of Charles' rebellion of 1655.

4. Cromwell's new government of the Major-Generals— introduced to protect the protectorate against rebellion, and to introduce 'Godly reform' after the failure of the Western Design in the Caribbean.

5. The Earl of Rochester's participation in Penruddock's Uprising as the king's representative.

Sometimes history is stranger than fiction!

Chapter 1 – A Necessary Visit

Worcester, September 1ˢᵗ, 1651

With his men accounted for and safely billeted outside the city walls alongside the Duke of Buckingham's other English regiments, Daniel Davenport skipped through the bustling streets. Time was short, and the crammed streets presented only obstacles as he wove through the crowds. He had been rendered temporarily speechless when Colonel Harrington told him of his sister's arrival and request to see him. He hadn't seen Johanna for months, and now, of all places, she had arrived in Worcester. For months she had pleaded for him to return home, but he had ignored all invitations, vowing to never set foot in Father's home again. Her pleading then gave way to a warning: if he didn't come home to visit her, she would come to him. And now Johanna was in Worcester as Cromwell's Parliamentarian army prepared to do battle.

"Captain, it's quicker when we make toward High Street," Private Templeton called from behind him.

Daniel halted to let his guide catch up, and a white-haired ancient stumbled in front of him. Daniel gave the old man his arm and pulled him to his feet.

The old man dusted himself off before eyeing Daniel from head to toe. "I thank you. They're bloody everywhere. Even climbing the bloody walls."

Daniel nodded sympathetically.

"I tell ye—" the old man trembled "—these bloody Scots will bring these walls down even before Cromwell arrives. Mark my words."

"I hope you're wrong." Daniel smiled. "For without these

walls and those Scots, we're not going to give Cromwell much of a fight."

"Mark my words," he muttered as he hobbled off.

Since King Charles II had arrived at the end of August with his Scottish army, the population of Worcester had doubled. Worcester, a strategic gateway with good roads linking London and Wales, also provided the King's army with strong walls and thriving agricultural land to feed his hungry army.

Daniel swiveled around and took a moment to observe the comings and goings of the tide of humanity rumbling through the streets. The old man was not far wrong: compared to the Scots, Buckingham's English regiments seemed no more than a drop of water in a deep Highland loch. As soon as the king had left Scotland and made known his intention to gather support in the South West and Wales, small pockets of Royalists all over England converged on Worcester to fight for him. But overall, the number of English Royalists was insignificant.

"When you count our numbers, Private, Buckingham won't have much of a say in the matter."

"I'm sure you're right, Captain."

"And how have the locals reacted to our Scottish allies?" Daniel enquired as a company of Scottish foot trudged past.

"Aye, the locals are none too happy, Captain. There was plenty mutterin' after the Scot's last visit when they took all and sundry. But what can we do?"

"Sure as hell, I won't ask them to move on."

"There's just not enough room on the east side of the city. Billetin' their tents where they can."

"Has there been much trouble?"

"I think they're too tired, Captain."

Close by, exhausted men and women washed their grey rags and mended their shoes after the long march from Scotland. "An army of grey ghosts," Daniel muttered to Templeton.

"But see here—" Templeton pointed to the market square "—only three hangings so far. Thievin', Captain."

"They've been up a while?"

"Three days," Templeton replied, screwing up his nose.

Daniel grimaced as three bloated corpses swayed in the breeze. "A stench like that can only bring us disease."

"Aye, Captain. But it's not as bad as the stench of the whores."

Daniel bristled at the comment, but he bit his tongue. The private was still young, and all soldiers masked their fear behind bravado. The women, vulnerable and alone, had arrived in droves since the Royalist army had reached Worcester. Young women and girls were taken advantage of and abused on street corners. And when the war came to Worcester, then heaven help them, for they would be at the mercy of brutalized men, and no hand would be raised to help them. As an officer, wearing the garb of a gentleman, Daniel had been inundated with propositions as soon he'd stepped foot into the city. He'd chatted with a young woman, not more than fifteen, telling her to leave Worcester before it was too late, but she only lamented the fact that so many Scots had brought their wives with them.

As he reached High Street, Daniel slowed to regard the commotion before him. Camp wives scrubbed clothes in dirty water; groups of soldiers played at dice, while others lay outside their tents, waiting for officers to tell them which part of the defenses needed bolstering. Carts trundled past, moving supplies through the city. A horde of armories and smithies was busy fixing weapons and molding breastplates, while others melted lead into musket balls and shot.

"The field hospital is close to St Martin's Gate, on the north-east, Captain."

They continued onward past Town Hall, and then made a right toward Cornmarket. Just north of Cornmarket, a group of haphazard tents marked the field hospital.

"I can find my way from here, Templeton," Daniel said. "No loitering, Private. And conduct yourself like a soldier of the king."

Templeton nodded, but his mischievous grin suggested otherwise, as he wandered back toward High Street.

A number of Scottish soldiers rested outside the closest tent, their feet wrapped in linen. Daniel skipped past them, ignoring their scowls.

The smell lingering about the field hospital was worse than that on High Street. The heavy air was suffocating; a heady mixture of human waste amid the enduring smell of decay assaulted him as he lifted the flap and peered in. With little enough

11

space, men lay where they could. After his eyes adjusted to the gloom, Daniel spotted his sister, Johanna, assisting a physician with a patient. Her usual lissome movements were cumbersome with the strain of the heavy work weighing upon her.

"I told you not to come to Worcester," Daniel said from the tent flap.

Johanna whirled around, but she couldn't entirely mask her smile. She set her hands on her hips. "And I warned you I was coming."

His measured steps avoided the injured and dying strewn across the ground. He embraced his younger sister, and then nodded at the soldier who was slipping in and out of consciousness. "Fever?"

"Typhoid." Johanna wrung out a rag and dabbed the man's forehead.

Daniel lowered his voice. "This is nothing but a plague pit, and Cromwell is coming, Johanna. I can't fight Cromwell and trail after you at the same time."

She cradled the soldier's head and helped him drink a little. "I know."

"Does Father know you're here?"

"Of course not."

"You came alone? That was insane."

"Don't worry yourself," she tutted. "I met soldiers from a General Mass-Mass—"

"Massey."

"Yes," she said, "Massey. I was safe with them. It's your fault. I warned you."

"I could order my men to take you home."

"You could, *Captain*, but I'd never speak to you again. Anyway—" she twirled a length of her fair hair that had escaped her coif "—Colonel Harrington introduced himself to me this morning. He complemented my work."

"And I have no doubt Colonel Harrington has *no sister* to worry about. Johanna," Daniel whispered, "the king is outnumbered. Where are the English armies flocking to his banner?"

"They will come, Daniel."

"I see my efforts are wasted on you."

12

She reached out for his hand and clasped it tight. "I stood with you all those years ago, because I believed in you. I believed in my heart that you had the right to choose and to follow your convictions. Father had no right to force you."

"I know, and you've suffered for it ever since."

"It was worth it. But let me also choose, brother, as you once did. I need to help, to be of some use."

He fixed her coif back into place. "And now you will suffer all the more for it if you stay here. You do not know what is coming, Johanna."

"I sometimes watch Father as he stares at the fire—"

"Changing the subject won't halt Cromwell's advance."

"Father will forgive you. It's time for you to come home. He's softened. He's old. He talks about you. After Worcester, come home with me."

Daniel frowned. "He won't even forgive *you*. He only tolerates you as his housekeeper—you know it. All my life, I did as he asked, but...the price would be too high."

"We can be a family again. Talk with him. Give him a chance, Daniel."

"You saw his face, the hatred and shame. There can be no forgiveness from either side."

Johanna stamped her foot impetuously. "Well, I'm not giving up."

Daniel smiled despite himself as the many memories of his sister's willfulness flooded back to him. "Stay in the city, but don't get trapped here. If it is in danger of falling, *promise me* you'll leave before the end?"

"I'm not leaving unless you promise to take me home."

"If—*when* we win, I will take you home. But I will not stay. Promise me you will leave before the city falls?"

"I promise." She lifted off his hat, smoothed back his fair hair, and then embraced him. "I always pray for you, Daniel. But be careful."

Daniel laughed at the remark and wiped away the trace of a tear that appeared on her cheek. "Always. And never stop praying for me."

He stepped out into the air and the faint trace of his smile disappeared. He had already neglected his sister, by leaving her with their father. From day to day, week to week, the bitter old man would set about crushing her spirit—her spark of independence. Cold, calculating submission—that was his way. Once Daniel had saved enough money, he would free her from him. He would give Johanna the life she deserved. But first, Cromwell and the New Model Army had to be dealt with.

He wandered back toward High Street without Johanna, weighed down with the dread of Cromwell's approaching Roundheads.

Chapter 2 – Time Heals All Wounds

Hereford, September 1ˢᵗ, 1651

Manfred's chestnut destrier, Smithy, stumbled into another pothole, and Manfred lurched forward in the saddle. His curse sounded like a pathetic whimper in the gale. He shook the water off his heavy riding coat, giving his cold, rigid body some freedom from the sodden material, and pulled the horse steady at the top of the hill. Scrutinizing the steep track leading down, he squinted through dawn's half-light and the slick, dark rivulets of mud snaking down the path. He moved Smithy forward. The horse expertly shifted its weight back, testing each step until it reached the level ground. Why did it always seem to rain when he journeyed back to Glenview? If he had his way, he would have traveled directly to Worcester, but his elder brother, John, had insisted that he meet him. Obviously, his unexpected transfer to Colonel Hacker had something to do with it.

Manfred patted the horse's muscled neck, and Smithy snorted, sending droplets of vapor into the air. He peered into the trees, hoping to see the song birds, but even they hid from the deluge. The wind's shrieking whine and the beat of the spattering rain as it slapped through the trees were all that remained.

"I should have left yesterday!" he shouted into the gale.

But the prospect of hearing his brother's insufferable monologues on tactics, and of his prowess in the saddle had been enough to persuade Manfred to stay an extra day. Now, with the going slow, there was little enough time to reach Glenview and then later, their regiment by nightfall.

The path widened, and his horse balked when Blackford Bridge came into view. "Ssshh, be still, boy."

After hours of continuous rain, the river ran deep and fast. Manfred dismounted. A jarring shock shot through him after hours in the saddle. He patted Smithy again and guided him over the bridge. Midway, Manfred stopped and leaned over the wooden rail. The white water roared below and sprayed the riverbanks with grey foam. "That's the quick way home," he said to Smithy as the horse pulled away from him. "As you wish. I believe we'll take the long way this time."

By the time they left the track, the sun was high, and the fog had belatedly thinned out. Oak trees bordering John's land came into view, and he straightened in the saddle. He removed his sagging felt hat and gave the sun a chance to dry his hair.

"Three years, Smithy. The trees have grown," Manfred said.

The lines of trees were soon replaced by an old stone wall, and five minutes later, they reached the lane to Glenview. Straight ahead, about a hundred yards farther down, John's country estate loomed between the procession of magnificent oaks bordering the path. On the right, the familiar apple trees were shriveled without their fruit. Old memories gripped Manfred, and he drove Smithy forward again.

A boy he didn't recognize came running from the stables that bordered the west side of the house. Gangly and with wild brown hair, he stopped at Smithy's shoulder and patted the horse.

"The master said you'd come, sir," the boy said.

"What's your name, boy?"

He lowered his head. "Larry, sir."

Not convinced the floppy-haired lad knew the backside of a horse from the front side, Manfred continued. "Where's the stable hand, Larry?"

"William? He joined the militia, sir."

"I'll leave within the hour. Make sure the horse is fed and watered. And check his shoes."

"Shoes, food, and water. Aye, sir," he said, counting off with his fingers.

Manfred left Smithy with Larry and made for the house. His sister-in-law, Sarah, waited before the steps. His heart jumped into his mouth. Had it really been three years? Three years without seeing her. Old feelings, too long suppressed, rushed over him. Her gaze was heavy, even as her smile crinkled the edges of her eyes. Was it as difficult for her as it was for him?

She embraced him, and he held her for a second too long before releasing her. "A smile? For me?" He teased.

16

Sarah closed her eyes as a sigh escaped her lips. "John and Francis are waiting for you."

"It's been years, Sarah," he said stiffly, "have you nothing more to say?"

"I...no." Sarah shook her head and bolted inside.

Manfred traipsed behind her, ignoring the housekeeper's greeting, and followed Sarah to the drawing room. In his haste, he had forgotten to remove his sword, and he held it close to prevent it from clattering against his leg. He stopped at the threshold as John fumbled with Francis' sword belt.

"John, Manfred has arrived," Sarah said.

John and Francis grinned. "Ah, the drowned rat is here at last." John winked at Francis.

"The drowned rat with his perfectly fixed belt. If you need help, John, you have only to ask." Manfred pointed to his own fixed belt.

John rose from his seat and opened his arms like two giant pincers.

Manfred prepared himself for the bear hug which never failed to impart some injury on his tired body. He clasped his brother in return and ran his hand over John's beard. "It gives you the philosophical look."

"Huh." John frowned. "I will get rid of the damned thing then."

Manfred smirked. "No, the beard suits you well enough."

"Well, you always were the *pretty* one anyway. You know I'm all thumbs." He wiggled his fingers.

Manfred embraced Francis, and then scrutinized the belt. "But it's fixed perfectly?"

"I had help." John gestured toward Sarah.

Francis straightened and removed his gleaming rapier from its scabbard. "Well, Uncle, how do I look?"

Manfred groped for words. He felt uncomfortable seeing his young nephew kitted-out for battle. Francis was as tall as John but built like a reed and needed to fill out with a few good meals. There was also tenderness in his eyes that didn't fit with the uniform.

"You are a man!" John glared at Manfred. "Isn't that right, Manfred?"

"Yes." Manfred nodded. "A finer picture of a young gallant I have not seen."

Francis waved away the words and sheepishly ran his gaze along the length of the sword, admiring the workmanship.

"Francis, I need to speak with your father and uncle," Sarah said.

John's eyes shifted to the blade. "Aye, that blade's dull—sharpen it outside."

With a nod, Francis sheathed the weapon and left the room.

Sarah paced until the back door closed. "He's only sixteen, John. He's not old enough to fight battles."

John groaned, but his eyes never left her. "He's a man. I wasn't much older."

"Make him understand, Manfred," she pleaded. "You know he's too young!"

Manfred flinched as John's stare bore into him. John knew as well as he how young men lost their innocence on the battlefield. "If you speak to the colonel, John, I know he will sympathize. Leave the boy here. He is too young for Worcester."

John scowled and flicked the words away. "We'll finish Charles this time. There'll be no more war left after Worcester."

"He's my son!" Sarah said.

"He's a soldier in the New Model Army. Besides—" John put his arm around Manfred's shoulders "—he'll have the two best soldiers in the field looking after him."

Sarah took John's hands. "Please, John."

John pulled his hands from her grasp.

"Please, John, don't make me beg you."

"No!" he thundered. "That's my final word on the matter."

Defeated, she stumbled out the door. Manfred had to stop himself from following her. He shook his head. Still the same boorish John. No reflection nor consideration. "You should go after her."

"She doesn't understand." John planted himself in his chair and glared at Manfred. "Running after her will not change anything." His eyes narrowed. "Maybe you should run after her?"

The question caught Manfred off guard. He broke from John's stare. *Does he suspect?* The love he'd carried for her for sixteen years. The love that had made each journey to Glenview almost unbearable. "What do I know of marriage?"

"Exactly. Sixteen years—I've given her everything. My name. My son. She wants for nothing."

"Her only son is going off to war, John. What do you expect?"

"He's my son. He's been mollycoddled enough with me being away." John rose from the chair. "Come, let's take a walk. I need some air." He motioned for Manfred to follow.

Manfred followed John outdoors, and together they made toward the apple trees. It was turning into a nice day, and he took in a deep breath of late summer air. "As I rode down, I saw the shadows of our childhood games. Here we defeated the Spanish, and Achilles would battle the noble Hector. Do you remember?"

John's countenance clouded over as he regarded his brother. "You have questions. I know you do."

"You're bloody well right. I was going to leave it, but you had no right to transfer my troop."

"Colonel Hacker transferred you, not I."

"Hacker has dragoons, and you didn't need mine," Manfred countered.

"One troop of dragoons is not enough. Anyway, Captain Price is a buffoon, and I want you there for my boy."

Manfred shook his head. "I don't understand. What has Francis got to do with this?"

"Francis will join your troop. Hacker owed me a favor, and now Francis is with the only man I trust." John paused a moment. "I thought you'd be glad."

"I'm just surprised." Manfred hesitated. "The troop is raw. I've only had a few weeks with them."

"It doesn't make sense to me either. You know I wanted him for the cavalry. But that can't be changed now. I trust you. I trust you with the life of my boy." John clasped Manfred's shoulder and drew very close to him. "He's going to make Colonel one day, and Worcester is the first step."

"Yes, a colonel commanding dragoons," Manfred said to rile his brother. Francis was a sweet boy, with a good head on his shoulders. And John was right about Price, but the responsibility would be a burden nonetheless.

"Yes." John sneered. "Well, at least he didn't choose infantry. Better he's not in the thick of it this time. After Worcester, I'm going to join Cromwell's army in Ireland. I want Francis with me."

"Ireland? You're not serious?" A graveyard of English soldiers, where the pestilence was as dangerous as the Irish—what was John thinking?

John stroked his beard. "I told you he's going to make Colonel one day. He's not going to do so by sitting behind a desk."

"Well, you're on your own. I won't be volunteering for that hell-hole. "

"I know that." John sneered again. "But you can at least persuade Francis to join my troop."

"Don't risk everything you have, John."

"I need money."

"You have money."

"I need more. I will need it when I run for Parliament."

Manfred's jaw dropped.

"There's money and land in Ireland, Manfred. I will return and with Sarah and Francis leave this God forsaken place. London, Manfred. I will take them to London."

Sarah in London? It would kill her. "And what of Glenview?"

"I will hand over the running of it to you. You're the farming type."

And you the selfish bastard type! "I will do what I can." Manfred stroked the rough bark of the apple tree. Was this the tree they'd fished for apples from when Sarah had first visited Glenview with her father seventeen years before? The announcement of her engagement to John had cut Manfred in two. Her father had been as proud as a peacock when their father had finally consented. John might be in Ireland for years. Sarah would be alone.

"Now, go and talk to her. She won't listen to me, but maybe you can convince her that Francis will be safe with his uncle. Don't mention Ireland."

Manfred nodded. He would be sure *to* mention it.

"I'll make sure your nephew is ready, Captain!" John bellowed to Manfred as he reached the steps.

"You do that!" Manfred called back as he felt for the locket in his waist pocket. It was all he had left of Sarah and their time together: a reminder that all other women were second best to her, just as he was second best to John.

He returned to the house, let himself inside, and knocked on Sarah's bedroom door. "It's me, Sarah."

No reply came, but he heard soft footsteps approach. The door opened, and she regarded him with a pained stare.

"May I come in?"

"No, of course not!" Sarah's eyes darted to the stairs.

"He's outside with Francis," Manfred whispered. "Would you rather we talk on the landing?"

Sarah stood back to let him pass. "What more is there to say, Manfred? You were quiet enough when John humiliated me. You barely opened your mouth when he ordered my son off to war."

Her cold words stung. She was desperate. "Francis will be by my side, Sarah. God as my witness, I will let nothing happen to him. I will keep him by my side. Believe me, it's better he's with me."

Sarah wiped her eyes. "You should have said more, insisted Francis remain here."

"It would have made no difference. He's not my son. You married John, not me."

"Why must we go over this again? You can still stop this."

"If it was my decision," Manfred said bitterly, "Francis would never leave your side. But it is not my decision. You saw to *that*, Sarah."

Even before her engagement to John had been announced, she had met Manfred in secret. Cold and severe, she had told him that she no longer loved him. Then she walked away, leaving him with only memories and a locket. But Manfred had known her words were hollow lies—as much for her benefit as his.

"Yes, my father consented, and I followed. You know I had no choice. He's your nephew, Manfred. Stop this!"

"I have no influence over John. And, anyway, Francis wants to fight."

"Only because he listens to John's lies. He knows nothing of the reality of war."

Manfred shook his head and headed for the door.

"Wait!"

Manfred stopped.

"I loved you!" Sarah cried out. "I broke my vows for you! Adultery is a sin, Manfred. I sinned for you."

"A sin?" Manfred clasped her shoulders. "No, marrying him was the sin. He never loved you, and you never loved him." He banged a fist against the wall. "True love can never be a sin, Sarah."

"I loved you," Sarah cried out, "and I broke my vows."

"And then you broke love's vows by staying with a man who's married to the army."

Sarah hid her face in her hands. "You don't see the truth. What I've lived with all these years."

"Do you think that you alone have suffered?" Did she know nothing of his feelings? Of his years of sacrifice and what it had meant to cut her from his life.

"No, you don't understand…it's Francis…he's…"

Manfred lifted her chin. "What?"

Her troubled eyes held his. "Francis is your son."

Manfred stumbled back. His head whirled. It had to be a lie. She would say anything to stop Francis from leaving her.

"He is your son," she insisted.

"You can't be certain," Manfred gasped. He swayed as the blood throbbed in his temple.

"A mother knows. He's nothing like John. He's a gentle soul."

"*He takes after you*! He can't be mine."

"He is your son. But one son was never enough for John. He tried for years. Believe me, I know. Listen to your feelings. Seek the truth—look into his eyes."

Manfred flopped down on the bed. His wiped his damp forehead. Memories of Francis' childhood flashed through his mind. He had seen so little of the boy. "John would know if it were true."

Trembling, Sarah sat down beside him. "John? He is the last person who would suspect. No, he gave up on me a long time ago when he realized I was barren. It would never have occurred to him that he was the problem." Sarah grabbed his hand. "He would have killed me if he'd known."

"Why did you not tell me?" Manfred asked, groaning.

"What would it have accomplished? What would have changed?" she asked, pleading. "He would have murdered us all, Manfred. I'm sorry. I would never have told you, but now you need to know you will lead *your son* into war."

Ireland! Manfred's eyes widened as John's plan pushed back into his memory.

"What is it?"

"He's taking him to Ireland, Sarah."

Sarah gasped. Her hand covered her mouth. "No!"

"We have to stop it, Sarah."

Sarah jumped up from the bed. She rubbed her forehead as she circled the floor. "I must confront him!"

"No!" Manfred clasped his arms around her. He brought his mouth to her ear and whispered, "No, Sarah. It will change nothing. You're right, Francis is no soldier. I will speak to him at Worcester, when I have him alone. Francis will listen to me. He will never leave for Ireland."

"John will force him!"

"John is reckless. Perhaps he won't make it make it back from Worcester," he whispered.

Sarah's eyes widened, and a deathly paleness overcame her. "Bring Francis back. Bring him back to me!"

He wiped her tears from her cheeks. "I promise you I will bring our son back. We will start again, my beloved."

Chapter 3 – Crowning Hope

Sidbury Gate, Worcester

The news of Cromwell's reserves being brought to battle south of Worcester at Potwick Bridge, against the stubborn Highlanders of Montgomery, gave the Royalists back the initiative. Daniel's commanding officer had ordered an immediate attack against Cromwell's weakened center east of the city. Daniel's company was to join the attack against Red Hill, with orders to secure the high ground.

With all haste, his men readied for the assault. Ammunition was distributed and field signs of colored ribbons were affixed onto hats and sleeves for identification. Shouts of "crowning hope" uttered from man to man spread through the company. Michael Tierney, Colonel Sinclair's runner, said he had heard the king call out the same words as he rode past Sidbury Gate.

King Charles and his retinue rode up and down the columns as they advanced through Sidbury Gate. With each cheer from his men, he sat a little taller and straighter in the saddle. Daniel had heard the stories, but here was the fabled king in person. He was indeed unusually tall—well over six feet in height. He rode down the lines, sitting his horse superbly.

Daniel had been told Charles had acquired extravagant tastes from his time on the continent; that he had Catholic sensibilities and enjoyed life too much. But here was a king of regal deportment, wearing simple, soldierly clothes. Only the Garter Sash, which he wore over his breastplate, made him stand out from the rest of his retinue. As the men roared as one, an indescribable enthusiasm gripped Daniel. The fear within his breast dissolved before the mighty thunder reverberating across the field.

Daniel led his company through the gate, and a barrage of cannon fire from Fort Royal opened up on the enemy, who was well dug-in on the surrounding hills. Even if the salvo did little damage to the Roundhead defenders, at least it kept the enemy pinned down for a time while the king's men advanced on Red Hill.

"Wallace," Daniel called his Sergeant forward. "Speed will be the key to victory. Keep the company moving forward."

"I don't want to see Cromwell's reserves anytime soon, Captain." Wallace's eyes darted over the rank and file.

"Their position is strong, but they're only militia." A flash of cannon fire erupted from the Parliamentarian held hill and interrupted Daniel's instructions. "When we take those gun emplacements, the city will be safe. And with Perry Wood at our backs, Cromwell's cavalry will be useless."

"Yes, Captain."

"Standard formation, Sergeant."

Wallace shouted out the commands, and pikemen marched forward in rank and file, with the musketeers on either flank.

Daniel steadied himself. His company knew the entire battle hinged on the king's counter-attack. He clamped his jaw shut as he regarded the men marching forward with both victory and defeat etched upon their features. He cast his eye further north. The force of General Middleton and the Duke of Buckingham assembled outside the city walls. Middleton and Buckingham would lead the 4th Cavalry Brigade, along with a column of foot, against Perry Hill. The pincer would close and crush the Parliamentarian forces of General Lambert and Harrison, knocking their gun emplacements out of the battle.

King Charles now rode down the line toward Daniel's company. A cannon shot hit the turf ten feet from the king's horse, spraying muck into the air. The men cheered and hollered as he brushed the muck from his gleaming breastplate with a flick. Every eye fixed on the man they were fighting for.

His Majesty stood higher in the stirrups and shouted. "Your King rides with you! Your King rides with you! Now we drive them back!"

Daniel cheered with his men and walked to the head of the pike formation. "Forward with the king! Forward with the king!" he bellowed back to his men.

The company roared the same and followed Daniel toward the Roundhead lines. The ground was heavy and trampled, and their short, steady steps stuck to the turf with the weight of their kit. There was no fear, but the enemy was still far enough away. Just lines of men, standing stock still and unwavering. No doubt they were like his own men—from veterans to soft faced youths. What kept those Roundheads from running? Their prayers? Their faith? How many old friends were standing amongst the enemy ranks? How many men would die this day as the unholy echo of war swirled about them?

Chapter 4 – The Battle of Worcester 1651

Manfred's horse, Smithy, pawed the ground while his troop of Parliamentarian dragoons waited five hundred yards east of the boats that formed a bridgehead across the river Severn. After the order had reached him to hold his men back, Manfred had halted his troop at the base of a small hillock, which afforded a measure of cover from any stray shot. Together with Lieutenant Strafford, he now ascended the hill to get a clearer view of the troop movements and the fighting beyond the bridge.

On the west side of the Severn, Fleetwood's and Deane's forces were bogged down in heavy fighting against Charles' stubborn Highlanders.

Earlier, Cromwell himself had led the attack to relieve the exhausted western force. The Highlanders proved too slow and too few in number to counter-attack the bridgehead once Cromwell and his Lifeguard had stormed across the Severn. Perhaps the Highlanders knew that behind Cromwell's Lifeguard another two regiments were being brought to battle. Cromwell had consolidated the bridgehead, avoiding the error of rushing into General Dalziel's reserves. Cromwell had his distracters. But while some mocked his caution, Manfred commended his common sense and his ability to leave nothing to chance. One should never disregard the practicalities of battle.

"Captain, should we not push forward with the vanguard?" Strafford grumbled.

"Leave that to the heroes," Manfred snapped back. "You're a dragoon, so get used to dog work. We flank them or hit from the rear. That's how you stir up fear." He didn't volunteer the remainder of his orders that stated the officer in charge might use his discretion. Better to wait for things to quieten before leading his inexperienced troop into the battle. His vow to Sarah rang in his ears: *I promise I will bring him home.*

"There is no need for dashing military maneuvers and heroics when your army is stronger and has every advantage brought to bear upon the enemy," Manfred noted as another troop of cavalry crossed the bridge.

"But, Captain, why give them a chance to dig in when we can keep them on the run?"

"The ground's not good for cavalry. Each day the Scots are here, the weaker they become. Nothing wrong with attrition, Lieutenant."

Strafford's half-hearted nod reflected the troop's desire to get at the Scots.

Before the enemy appears, it's the long wait that drives a man insane. "Now, my brother would tell you differently."

"He's a brave man, Captain."

"Aye." Manfred snorted. "Heroically leading his men into the mass of musket fire with his sword flashing through the air. Brave? There will be no need for heroics, Lieutenant. Common sense will achieve all. We have the numbers, and the right sort of men. It's just a matter of time."

Strafford nodded. "Aye, the bastards won't come back to England in a hurry, Captain,"

"After we cross the bridge, Hacker's orders are to follow the river north. Once we flank the enemy, they will have no time to regroup. The north side of the river is marshy in places. I don't want any horses stuck fast."

"Anything else, Captain?"

"Keep an eye on my nephew. Now rally the men, Lieutenant."

Horse and rider shimmied down to the waiting men. Strafford passed on Manfred's orders, and then the sergeants rallied the men.

Francis mounted and checked that his sword and carbine were in place. He then checked again. His face was taut and stretched with nerves: the shadow of the paralyzing fear that squeezed every soldier's guts before a battle. Manfred turned his gaze skyward. "Lord, God, hear my prayer. Keep my son safe this day."

The troop galloped up the hill, and Manfred led the dragoons down toward the chaos.

The sergeant bellowed above the roar of the battle, "No king, but King Jesus!"

The rest of the men chorused in turn, and the troop's pace quickened toward the pontoon bridge.

A sulfurous fog obscured the field of battle, but the clamor of war fought its way through the grey mass to reach Manfred. His troop, impatient for action, cursed the company of pike that had just reached the bridge before them.

After a long, hot summer, the water level was significantly lower, and he considered taking his men across the river. Private Samson waded out a few yards, but he got stuck in the heavy silt, and it took three to pull him out.

After the company of pike crossed the bridge and marched toward the unknown, Manfred led his men across the bridge and then skirted the Severn's edge as close as possible. Although the ground was heavy and marshy as it sloped toward the river, it was free of the numerous hedgerows surrounding the main battlefield.

A horse screamed, and Manfred spun back as a cob buckled over and tumbled down the slope. The cob writhed on its side, and its rider, Masterson, apparently unhurt, scrambled back to the horse. He patted the poor creature to calm it.

Strafford, already there, shook his head. "The leg is broke, Captain."

"Put it out of its misery. Quietly," Manfred said.

"And Masterson?"

"He can walk. Let him watch the rear."

Thereafter, the company moved north as silently as a troop of horse could. Not one soldier carried bandoliers on their person. They were to flit across the battlefield as ghosts, and the rattle of bandoliers announced their arrival from miles away. The men had complained when he'd ordered them to remove the 'Twelve Apostles' as they referred to them. Instead, they were issued with cartridges, which they carried in their pockets or on their belts.

They had grumbled when he took away their bandoliers, but it had been different when he issued them the latest flintlocks, allowing them to move in the dark when needed. John had mocked and dubbed Manfred's troop 'the Silent Sisters,' but even he had admitted they were second-to-none as a heavy scouting force.

After half a mile of hugging the river, Manfred brought the troop to a halt. It was quieter now. They had passed the main fighting, but the crack of musket and cannon fire, along with the heavy blanket of smoke further south, indicated the fighting was still heavy. Without a word, the troop dismounted.

29

Manfred waved his officers over. "I want to split the troop, but we stay within eye-shot. It'll be easier to ambush from two sides. Lieutenant Furse, take the second column south. Leave three men with the horses. Travel quietly, and use your scouts. I don't want to be surprised."

Furse led his men a hundred yards back down the river and then moved inland.

Manfred's men fanned out and marched toward the battle smoke to the southwest of their position. He nodded encouragingly to Francis. His son's movements were jittery; his smile practiced and glazed.

The men gripped their muskets tight. They were too frightened to breathe, holding on to their last breath as if their fading courage depended on it. Peterson—until this morning the cockiest of the lot—crept along with his mouth wide open, catching flies, gulping for saliva to wet his mouth. For many of them, this was their first battle, and enthusiasm for the war had drained from their faces.

They marched for ten minutes before they reached the hedgerows. Further south, Furse's men marched forward, still in view.

Manfred motioned to Sikes, and the scout crept up to him.

"I don't want to walk into an ambush. I need to know what is behind those hedgerows," Manfred whispered. "The whole area is littered with hedges for half a mile. If you spot Royalists, I need numbers."

Sikes set his musket down and moved off as silently as he had come. The men crouched behind the hedge but stayed alert. Manfred moved up the ranks, checking that they had everything they needed.

After thirty minutes, Sikes had still had not returned, and Manfred cursed his scout. Something must have happened to him, and they would have to crawl through those hedges blind.

Sergeant Bruen crept over, his fingers drumming on his musket. "What are your orders, Captain?"

"We have to move on. Send a man to Furse and tell him to move in five minutes."

Bruen made to leave, but Manfred stopped him. "Send Francis to me."

A moment later Francis appeared. "Yes, Captain?"

"Stay close to me."

"Yes, Captain." Francis beamed.

"The uniform suits you well. I couldn't be prouder, Francis."

"It's an honor, Captain."

"When we win this damn war, I promise to spend more time with you and...your father."

"I look forward to that, Unc—Captain."

"Perhaps John will hire me as a farmer." Manfred winked.

Francis raised his eyebrows. "You would leave the army, Captain?"

"Why not? When you get older, the soldier's life becomes wearisome. You are too young to understand. John will need help, for farming is not in his blood."

Francis nodded, and the corner of his eyes crinkled with his smile.

"Your father is planning to take you to Ireland."

Francis raised his eyebrows again. "Oh...Ireland?"

John hadn't told him. Only the most desperate would volunteer to fight there. Not a place for a boy of sixteen. "Most won't come home. Your mother's worried, Francis."

"I can imagine, Captain." Francis' jaw tightened. "But father said fear's a weakness. It's a soldier's duty to stamp it out. The quickest way to end a war is to kill the enemy."

John had once said the same to Manfred verbatim. "It would kill your mother, Francis."

"She worries too much, Captain. Father believes in me. I won't disappoint him."

"I believe in you, Francis." Manfred clasped his shoulder. "One day, the estate will pass to you, and you'll need someone to help you. If you need my help, I'll be there for you, Francis."

"Not for a long time yet, Captain."

"True enough." Manfred patted Francis on the arm. "But first, we've got to relieve a king of his head."

Maybe Sarah was right. Deep inside, Francis was nothing like John. How could he have not noticed before? The dear boy wanted to please him and to earn the respect of his men. But not because of his name. He wanted to be one of them. John had indeed filled his head with the glories of war. Soon Francis would experience the reality. And Manfred would be there for him. He would never let Francis leave England for those disease-riddled Irish bogs. *I promise I will bring him home, Sarah.*

* * *

The hedgerows provided a measure of cover, but sometimes Manfred had no option but to crawl through them. It was too far to skirt around them, and with the wind picking up, the battle mist crept closer. Furse's southern column was still in view, but the mist would soon overtake them, and he would lose sight of the group. Manfred waved them forward, and Sergeant Bruen's scowl helped the men to their feet.

Eventually, they found a path through the hedgerows. One hundred yards ahead, running north toward Worcester, they came upon a stone wall.

Manfred held up his hand and the column halted. "If there are musketeers behind that wall, we're in trouble," he said to Bruen.

Bruen frowned. "If we stop now, Captain, I might not be able to get them moving again."

"No cavalry signs," Manfred said, casting his eyes over the ground ahead. The mist slithered forward, increasingly engulfing the expanse. The wall was about four feet high, and all seemed quiet behind it.

Bruen pointed north. "Can we flank it, Captain?"

Manfred shook his head. "It keeps going to Worcester. I believe there's a road on the other side."

"It sounds like the fighting's nearly stopped."

"Aye, that's what worries me. We must be close to their reserves if they haven't retreated into Worcester. The smoke will give us some cover, but we need to reach the wall."

Manfred dismissed Bruen back down the line. Ensign Cutler gripped the company flag under his arm, making sure it didn't flap in the breeze. All eyes were fixed on their objective as they edged toward it.

With about fifty yards to the safety of the wall, the crack of musket fire rang out. Men dropped to the ground. No powder flashed, and no enemy raised their heads. Manfred hunched down on his knees. No screams from his men, no casualties; only the sergeant's roar to move forward.

More shots rang out, and the mist lit up with powder flashes.

Screams of the wounded reached him. "Furse! Furse is in trouble!" Manfred bellowed.

Bruen sneered at the cowering soldiers behind him. "Move, you bastards!"

Manfred waved his men toward the musket shots. They were slow in rising: some rooted to the spot, staring dumbly into the mist. The sergeant's face contorted in fury as he dragged a young private to his feet.

They stumbled into the mist. The sulfur caught in Manfred's throat. More shots rang out. Furse's men cowered behind the wall. The shooting stopped, and the groans of the injured echoed about them. About twenty yards from the wall, three of Manfred's men lay dead. He bolted forward again and lunged for the wall. He grabbed the nearest of Furse's men. "Where is Lieutenant Furse?"

The soldier shook his head. "I saw him fall, sir."

Manfred wiped the sweat from his brow and cursed Furse's stupidity. "Are you ready to kill some Scots?"

The soldier closed his eyes and lowered his head.

Manfred sprang up; his carbine trained ahead. In the same movement, he flung his head back, expecting a claymore to take it off. His eyes flitted through the mist, seeking the enemy behind the wall.

Nothing!

But Manfred caught shouts from up ahead. He fastened on the sight of the fleeing Highlanders' grey forms until they were engulfed by the mist. "Get at them!" he screamed.

He clambered over the wall and then fired his carbine into the mist—a hapless act of defiance. With broadsword drawn, he charged forward with his men.

And then the thunder of a gallop surrounded them.

"Cavalry. It's a trap," he muttered.

More shots rang out from the mist, echoing about them. And above the screams of the dying, the shouts of "Cromwell" and "God and the right" reached them.

His men, buoyed by the sweet sound, and as a precaution against an unfortunate trampling by the charging cavalry, shouted the same in turn.

Manfred slowed his pace and came upon the dead and dying Highlanders encircled by the Parliamentarian cavalry. About twenty Highlanders lay dead, with less than half that number wounded. Their white ribbons were soiled with dirt and blood. Their heavy, grey woolen coats were scorched with powder burns or falling apart from wear. A Highlander with his jaw blown off tried to talk, but all that came out was a pathetic whimper. Manfred unsheathed his dagger and held it to the man's throat. The Highlander's eyes begged him to finish it, but Manfred sheathed the blade and backed away. Why should he put him out of his misery? He wouldn't have extended the same courtesy.

"No prisoners!"

The order pierced the mist. One cavalryman aimed his carbine at a wounded Scot who clutched his leg. The Highlander raised his hands in surrender, and the blood pumped from a vicious hole in his thigh. He pleaded for his life. He wanted to go home to his wife and son. But before the soldier fired his pistol, the officer barked out an order.

"Don't waste your shot!"

A few cavalrymen dismounted and proceeded to cut the Highlanders' throats. The Scots didn't plead for their lives. Some glared into the eyes of the Parliamentarians even as the blade slide across their throats. Others found peace as the light left their eyes.

Manfred, like his men, stared dazed at the slaughter. A tinge of sympathy welled within him as the men's necks were opened. *Foolhardy, but brave.* And then his thoughts flew to Francis.

Francis stared open mouthed. His eyes were two slits, rebelling against the brutality. Manfred had to take him away from this life. He wasn't a soldier. He was kind-hearted like his mother.

"Captain Hugo."

The gruff voice of the officer rang clear and true. Manfred and Francis turned to each other when they recognized the bark of the officer.

The cavalry officer removed his lobster helmet.

"John," Manfred said, "once more to my rescue."

"We've been ordered back with all haste," John blustered. "Red Hill is close to collapse."

Manfred cursed the news. If Charles managed to take the high ground of Red and Perry Hill, they could actually lose this battle.

Francis saluted John, and they exchanged a few words. Bile stuck in Manfred's throat as he watched them together. Now he would have to lead his son into the thick of the fighting. Their new life would have to wait.

Chapter 5 – Red Hill

The Roundheads opened fire from a hundred yards out, and at least six of Daniel's men fell. It could have been much worse if the Roundhead militia had been drilled to countermarch their ranks, keeping up a continuous fire.

"They are panicking—firing without discipline!" He waved his men forward. Each breath caught in his chest as he ascended the steep hill.

All along the line, the enemy formed into blocks of men six deep. Company after company ascended the fifty yards toward the summit of Red Hill.

"They have the fear of God in them! They're militia! They will break!" Daniel encouraged his men.

His sergeants bellowed the same, and the company marched forward with more resolve.

Sergeant Wallace's face screwed up. "Keep to rank and file, damn you! Keep it loose; dress the file leader!"

Only thirty yards from the Parliamentarian lines, the terrain slipped away to the south—perfect for an enemy counterattack. Daniel's men were positioned on the far side of the line, and their flank was exposed. A decimated troop of Scottish lancers held in reserve was all that stood between them and annihilation if Cromwell's reserves decided to show up.

"Hold! Call the muskets forward!"

Wallace passed Daniel's orders down the line. "Muskets to the fore!"

The musketeers came forward in three lines on either side of the pike center. One group advanced with Sergeant Wallace on the left flank and Sergeant Pierce on the right. Most of Daniel's musketeers still carried the cumbersome Matchlock muskets, and their match cords smoldered in the light breeze. Musketeers in the back lines fumbled with their bandoliers, trying not to spill the precious gunpowder.

The Roundhead musketeers concentrated their fire on the advancing Royalists. Harry Price fell to his knees as a musket ball ripped through his shoulder. Sergeant Pierce dragged him to his feet.

Further down the line, grapeshot tore into Captain Lewis' pike block, and the screams of men mingled with a medley of curses, blasphemies, pleading oaths, roars, and screeches: the quintessence of a battlefield song.

The first ranks on either side kneeled, and behind them, the next ranks fired a volley above their heads. The volley tore into the Roundhead musketeers. The next three ranks moved forward to take their place as the first unit moved back to reload. Their ceaseless drilling over the past weeks had not been popular with the men, but the fruits of their labor were now clearly evident. Even as men fell, Daniel's company maintained its discipline. Discipline under fire could unsettle an enemy more than firepower.

"They will break! Maintain formation!" Daniel hollered.

Another Royalist volley pierced the enemy's formations. The Roundhead Captain flailed his arms as a section of his musketeers edged back in disarray. Then the Parliamentarian pike moved forward, ready to engage, relieving pressure from their hard-pressed musketeers. Straight as reeds, their pikes pointed to the heavens as they marched forward.

"Pike, in closest order, forward!" Daniel ordered in response.

His musketeers let off one more volley and withdrew for the Royalist pike to advance.

The enemy files tried to step around their wounded comrades, but in such close order it was hopeless, and they trampled them. Others tripped over the screaming injured and the silent dead, only to be crushed underfoot themselves.

The Royalist musketeers fell back in good order. Daniel's pike moved forward to check the enemy's advance. The company drummer kept pace for the advancing red-coated Lifeguard, and the ensign's flag with the cross of St. George and Crown fluttered in the breeze. The evil-smelling sulfur wrapped about them in thick clouds of smoke as the fighting intensified.

The air vibrated as a musket ball swept past Daniel's head. A cold sweat came over him as his earlier euphoria evaporated in the midst of the chaos. From the look on their faces, the Roundheads were as scared as he.

Another crack of musket fire, and the file leader next to him, Tam Telfer, a veteran of the Thirty Years War, fell stone dead.

"Double the pace!" Daniel bellowed to the drummer, Robert Hobbs.

He complied, and the company matched the new rhythm. The two columns came within twenty yards. The pikes lowered, and the heavy mass crashed together into a push of pike.

"Heed the—" Daniel shot a Roundhead pikeman at point blank range. The shot pierced the man's breastplate and put him down. "Forward with the drum! Heed the drum!"

The tip of the Royalist pikes slid off the enemies' breastplates. But the combined weight of the Royalist front ranks pushed the Roundheads back.

Many Roundheads lost their footing, and the Royalists stamped on them like they were stamping out a fire.

A Roundhead lunged at Daniel, but the pike tip caught in his heavy buff coat without piercing it. Daniel hacked the pike in two; the Roundhead then swiped at Daniel with his tuck. The attack fell short, and Daniel thrust his mortuary sword at his exposed thigh. The Roundhead parried the blow and swiped again. Daniel beat the attack, and countered, grabbing the man's hacking arm. With a swift strike, he rammed his sword into the man's neck. The pikeman dropped; his head lopped, barely attached to the neck.

The lines locked together with men tangled up in a hurricane of violence. Frightful brutality marked the skirmish as musketeers used their muskets as clubs. Others clawed and gouged, nothing more than biting animals bent on maiming and killing.

A pikeman fell in front of Daniel and twisted his body to avoid Daniel's sword thrust. He lunged forward again, but the pikeman, without a weapon to hand, cracked him across the face with his helmet.

The impact threw Daniel back. He fell beside Tam Telfer. He opened his eyes, expecting a flurry of blows to rain down, but the Roundhead's brutish face was nowhere to be seen. Blood lathered the right side of Daniel's face, and he couldn't see out of his right eye.

He lifted himself up and staggered forward. Sergeant Pierce clutched his leg. The Roundhead corporal raised his sword to finish him off, but Pierce's pole-axe cracked against the Roundhead's knee, and he crumpled to the ground screaming.

The Roundheads fell back but were still in good order.

If their pike formation broke they would be routed. Daniel's men fought harder as they surged forward into Parliamentarian lines.

"Forward in rank and file! Keep to rank and file!" Daniel spluttered, his throat raw.

Either his men didn't hear him or just ignored the order, each caught up in his own personal war with only the instinct to destroy or to save himself cocooning him. Daniel joined them in the bloodlust. His sword arm felt as light as air as it impacted flesh and bone.

The Roundheads fell back, but Daniel cursed them for not breaking. The battered body of the Roundhead Captain lay among the dead; the distinctive red sash he wore across his buff coat torn and soiled with dirt. His face was crushed. Beside him, his black felt hat lay untouched.

"They're finished!" Wallace screamed above the roar. "Push through them, damn you!"

Daniel tried to reach Sergeant Wallace but was hampered by a wave of men pushing forward. A shot from a saker mowed into a tangle of Royalists and Roundheads, killing them instantly. To fire indiscriminately at such close range smacked of blind panic. He tried to escape the skirmish for higher ground.

He shoved through his own ranks and reached Corporal Johnson. Johnson grimaced when Daniel addressed him. "We nearly have them, Corporal. Keep them moving forward."

"Are you hurt, Captain?"

"I can see nothing from here. Get them forward, man."

The corporal pushed onward, and Daniel staggered through the lines until he reached a small hillock. The smoke tainted everything. And then, with the rumble of cavalry reverberating through the clamor, he swung around as Scottish lancers emerged from the sulfurous mist, bearing down upon the enemy's flank.

As he followed the thunder of their charge, a dark grey mass further south took form. Daniel's shoulders drooped forward. His face screwed up in pain and exhaustion. Only his sword held him up as the distant Parliamentary cavalry headed straight for them.

Chapter 6 – Skirmish

With the crossings at Potwick Bridge and the Severn secure, and the enemy in full retreat southwest of Worcester, Manfred and John's troop, along with the rest of Cromwell's reserves, left immediately.

"Our first objective is to relieve the Militia on Red Hill before they're overrun. If Red Hill and Perry Wood are taken," Manfred said, "we lose the high ground, and the road to London will lie open before them. Understand?"

Manfred's officers nodded.

"Specifically," Manfred continued, "we are tasked with securing the southernmost wing of the Royalist counterattack and taking back any artillery that has fallen into enemy hands. The rest of Hacker's Horse, together with Fairfax's Foot, will attempt to link up with the defenders on Red Hill and Perry Wood and trap them in a pocket before they can scurry back behind Worcester's walls. Any questions?"

"And what about infantry support, Captain?" Bruen asked.

"The infantry is coming. Until then, the dragoons will do the dog work as usual, Sergeant. "

Side by side with John's troop, at a steady trot and in good order, they approached the southernmost edge of Red Hill. The fighting had moved farther up the hill, and a mass of dead and wounded—arrayed in a multitude of color—lay scattered about the fields. No quarter had been given by either side. A dead Royalist lay on his back; his face frozen into a contorted mask. Even in death he gripped onto the Royalist banner, which fluttered in the breeze. Manfred yanked the banner from the corpse and threw it into the quagmire.

The Royalists had already split their forces, and sections of the enemy pike had already wheeled around to meet them. Not even John would be foolish enough to meet their pike head on. They would flank them, or use skirmish tactics, discharging their carbines and then withdrawing to regroup. As he'd informed Manfred often enough, it was not a tactic John cared for—it was unmanly and fit only for dragoons.

The irony was not lost on Manfred as Francis rode beside him toward their objective. *His son*, the dragoon, who sat his horse straight and proud: his red coat pristine; his heavy buff coat, the best that money could buy, costing more than his magnificent horse.

A few moments later, Manfred's troop disengaged and veered toward its objective of securing the artillery on the southeast of Red Hill, leaving John's troop to remain with the main body of Hacker's regiment.

"We fire from our horses! Speed and surprise!" Manfred bellowed as they approached London road and the climb to Red Hill.

By now, the Parliamentarians had either retreated north to Perry Wood or had regrouped and were reforming to support Cromwell's advance. The rest were scattered corpses, twisted and broken in the afternoon sun, the injured left behind in their agonies. Both Royalist and Roundhead alike cried out for help as Manfred and his men rode past.

After they climbed the hill, an outpost of artillery manned by a rag-tag bunch of Royalists came into view. The Scottish Saltire flew from a pole wedged into a mound of canon shot. They were evidently not gunners from their attempts at firing the three Demi-culverins. As they fumbled with the priming of the three canons, a Royalist musketeer battered a prisoner. The prisoner curled himself up, protecting his head from the clubbing. But as Manfred's troop reached the level ground, not more than thirty yards away, the Royalist stopped his attack and gaped in astonishment as the three ranks of dragoons bore down on them.

"Advance at a steady pace!" Manfred bellowed to the trumpeter, who then sounded out the call. "Aim for the chest at close range! Have your tucks close to hand!"

The Royalists, about thirty in number, tried to form themselves into a defensive line, but it was already too late. Their pikemen leveled their weapons, and the small group of Royalist musketeers fired off a few rounds with stolen firelocks. Bill Castell's cob got hit, and both he and the horse went to ground.

41

Manfred took aim, balancing his carbine on his bridle gauntlet. The shot hit true, slamming into the pikeman's chest. The rest of the company fired a salvo, and that was enough for the Royalists. Those still standing threw down their weapons. Francis and Edmund Cole galloped down a few runners, crashing into them and knocking them senseless.

The Parliamentarian prisoners took their revenge on the Royalist musketeer. They held him down and smashed his head in with a five-pound cannon ball. The gunners then made for the others.

"Enough!" Manfred stopped them. "They made you no harm. You'll treat them civil or answer for it. Who has the rank?"

They shrugged, and then a thick-necked man with a heavy black beard stepped forward. "Edward Mabb, sir, first gunner."

With his unkempt appearance, he had the air of a bedlamite rather than a gunner. "Where are your officers?" Manfred asked.

"Over yonder, sir." Mabb motioned toward a pile of bodies a few paces away.

"You need to get these men—" Manfred pointed to the group of laborers and gunners standing beside Mabb "—and get these cannons firing."

Mabb gaped at Manfred.

"You know where the enemy is?"

Mabb nodded.

"Well, make sure to find him with your shot."

"Aye, Captain."

The gunners leapt into action, first dragging away what was left of the dead Royalist, and then set to priming the cannon.

Francis returned to Manfred's side, beaming from ear to ear. How was it possible to have lived without him? The regrets and the lost time weighed upon Manfred, but he pushed the bitterness away. Later, there would be time enough to set matters right. *I will bring him home.*

Manfred caught Lieutenant Laney's eye. "Form the troop. I don't want my brother to win all the glory."

As Laney barked out the order, the rumble of cavalry approached. Manfred's eyes widened as Scottish lancers galloped past, making west toward the main fighting. Evidently his dragoons were of little concern as they sped past.

Calling to his men, he pointed his carbine in the direction of the charging Lancers. "Ride them down!"

* * *

Daniel's company had stood firm when the Roundhead cavalry had attacked, but it had been nothing more than a gentle prod, hoping they would break without a fight. After firing a volley, they had withdrawn to regroup. Other attacks soon followed, but their skirmish tactics caused little damage to either side. The continuous harassment was a headache nonetheless.

In the meantime, other companies had joined the line, but their increased numbers would count for little when Cromwell's foot arrived in force. Then the Roundhead cavalry would wreak havoc on the flanks of the Royalist lines.

Daniel's runner returned, red-faced and sucking in air. "Captain…No supplies…Captain." He patted the knapsack. "This is all I could get."

Daniel peered into the knapsack at the limited supplies. "It's not enough."

"I'm sorry, Captain. They're hard pressed all along the line. I saw the king himself there."

"Make sure the front ranks get first. And be quick about it. Their soldiers aren't here to parley."

As the Roundhead foot marched closer, Daniel's earlier, guarded optimism evaporated as he labored among his men. They were outnumbered and running desperately low on ammunition. Runners told him of the king courageously rallying his troops, telling them victory was within their grasp. Obviously, Charles had not yet observed Cromwell's foot descending upon them like a vision of the apocalypse.

Daniel split the company. He positioned half his men to protect their flank and the small gains made at Red Hill. His fake smile and backslapping helped the morale of his men as he readied them for the Roundhead assault.

Then John Bruen arrived, wringing his hands.

"Spit it out, John."

"Captain, the militia have regrouped and counterattacked. We can't hold them for much longer. What are your orders?"

Daniel threw his felt hat into the dirt. He stroked his blood-caked hand through his damp, matted hair. His eyes shifted in confusion. "Cromwell's infantry will be on top of us any minute. Withdraw in good order. Retreat to Sidbury Gate."

Chapter 7 – Charge of the Lancers

Even at full gallop, Manfred's dragoons didn't gain on the lancers. The lightly armed lancers avoided the mass of retreating Royalists, who were now surging toward Fort Royal and beyond that Sidbury Gate. Hacker's forces pulverized a decimated Royalist regiment. And then, in the center of the milieu, John's banner flitted briefly before disappearing within the maelstrom.

Suddenly, the lancers changed their bearing and headed straight for John's troop.

The lancers were outnumbered, but the Parliamentary cavalry was still unaware of them. His son's face reflected the danger. Francis dug his heels into his horse's flanks and whooped it forward. Too late to stop him, Manfred followed, but Smithy dragged behind the faster mare.

The Scottish lancers slammed into their rear, flinging man and beast, broken and crumpled, to the ground.

It took only a few moments to reach the slaughter. Manfred's gaze flitted over the mass of fighting men, searching for John. The tremendous crack of discharged carbines rattled his ears. And then he saw it: in the midst of the hand-to-hand fighting, John's horse lay quivering on its flank. A few feet away, John floundered in agony.

"Father!" Francis cried.

John groaned as he lifted himself to his knees. His ashen face racked with pain. His shoulders rose and fell with each shattered gasp.

"Francis, stay on your horse!" Manfred yelled.

But it was too late. Francis leapt from his saddle.

Manfred's face knotted tight like the muscles of his fatigued body. A Royalist hacked at Francis with a backsword, but his son shot him in the chest. The Royalist plugged the hole with his hand, his eyes wide in terror as blood spurted through his fingers. Francis ran him through, and the Royalist fell dead, still clutching his chest.

In the infinity of those seconds, the battle and Manfred's men faded into the void as he latched onto Francis. He clambered off Smithy and ran through the carnage after his son.

* * *

Daniel stumbled through the pandemonium toward Sidbury Gate and the haven of Worcester. The Royalist rank and file had disintegrated, and the retreat had become a rout. A choking haze surrounded him, and he eyed a path through the fighting and the clutter of dead and injured strewn across the battlefield.

A Roundhead captain struggled to his knees. Bent of back, he pulled himself up with shaking groan. He gasped as he lifted his twisted face.

The man's face? Daniel's eyes widened in horror. "John!" The gulf of fifteen years was obliterated in an instant. He had heard that John had sided with Parliament, but not even in his wildest nightmares would be have imagined they would meet again. His childhood friend shattered and broken.

Hunched over dreadfully, John lurched forward like a drunkard. His sword, fused into his hand, kept him on his feet as he shuffled closer.

"It is I!" Daniel yelled.

John's mouth opened, but no sound came out. He hobbled closer—his eyes reflecting agony and confusion.

"It is I, Daniel!" Tears stained his bloodied cheeks as the monstrous figure of his childhood friend limped closer. "And this is war, John? Friend killing friend? Our families ripped apart. Let us finish it then!" Daniel dropped his guard and closed his eyes.

The air broke as a bullet hissed past him. It was a mere fraction of a second, but when Daniel opened his eyes again, John lay flat out with a hole in his temple. The horror of the picture gorged on his senses until a scream rattled him back into world. A young Roundhead dragoon charged at him. Instinct saved Daniel from a blow that would have split his skull. He parried the strike, and the Roundhead overextended himself. Daniel limped forward, but his attacker was on him before he moved more than a few strides. The dragoon unleashed a flurry of blows, and Daniel stumbled back. He parried and blocked the onslaught, but then a

46

dragoon officer joined the attack. The officer readied to strike a killing blow, but a spooked horse clattered into him, flinging him to the ground.

The young dragoon attacked again. His thrusts and cuts reverted to wild swings as he tired. He bounded forward and stumbled over a severed torso. Daniel swayed as his legs nearly buckled under him.

The dragoon regained his footing and lunged at Daniel with a guttural roar. Daniel enveloped the thrust, flinging the dragoon's sword arm to the side. With the dragoon's guard down and his middle exposed, he rammed his blade into the boy's chest. The dragoon was dead before he hit the ground.

Chapter 8 – The Field Hospital

Johanna shielded her patient as the shriek of another projectile filled the air. Mercifully, the explosion was farther away from the field hospital this time. She tutted and shook her head. If cannon shot hit the tent, it wouldn't matter whom she shielded. They would all be dead.

"The sound of Armageddon. When will the cannons stop?" she asked Dr. Spence.

"Mortar rounds. They must be close, Johanna," Spence replied as he worked on a patient's lacerated hand. "Open your mouth, son."

The soldier opened his mouth, and Spence inserted a strip of leather.

"I have to staunch the bleeding. Do you understand?"

The soldier nodded and chomped down on the bit.

Spence branded him, and the man's flesh sizzled amid his groans. He sank back moaning as tears slipped out of his eyes.

"You know, Johanna," Spence said, shaking his head, "I don't even smell it anymore."

She knelt beside her own patient, who had been stretchered in thirty minutes before. Whilst refilling his bandoliers, a spark from a musket ignited the powder, burning him terribly. Dr. Spence could do nothing for him, so Johanna comforted him. She massaged a salve into the Scottish soldier's black, cracked skin. He held her arm, gazing into her eyes. He spoke Gallic into thin air. She told him he would get better, but he would be dead by the morning. Before then, if he were lucky.

Another mortar round approached. She buried her head in her hands. Her heart's pounding drowned out by the scream of the mortar round. It took all her self-control not to flee from the confined space.

The explosion rocked the tent, and she fell onto her knees. A cloud of dust swept inside. When she opened her eyes, Spence was still on his feet, shaking his head.

Light flooded into the tent as a young soldier from Colonel Grant's foot peered in. "That was close! God's truth that was too close!" He shook the dust off his uniform and coughed it from his lungs. His face screwed up when the stench hit him. He removed his helmet and nodded to Johanna without speaking. The soldier scanned the tent, and then hurried over to Dr. Spence as he directed two nurses bandaging a leg wound. "Sir, Colonel Grant said the city will soon fall."

Johanna gasped. So it was true, the Roundheads were close. Surely the King's army would retreat behind the safety of the walls. Why hadn't Daniel come for her? He wouldn't have left her alone.

The surgeon waved the young soldier's words away and continued his dialogue with the nurses.

"Sir," the soldier repeated much louder this time, "the city cannot be held."

Promise me you'll leave if the city falls! No. The king would rally his troops and defend the walls. Daniel would want her to wait with Dr. Spence.

Spence rubbed his eyes, and then studied the young soldier in much the same as he would a gangrenous leg. "And?"

"Colonel Grant ordered me to escort you from the city before it falls." The soldier's drawl spelled it out for the surgeon.

Spence lifted his head and rubbed his chin. "Miss Davenport, you will leave with this soldier."

"I will not! We have work." Daniel had promised to take her home. How could she leave him here alone?

"Daniel left me a note, and you promised him."

"But we still have time."

The soldier shook his head. "Fort Royal is in Parliament's hands. We don't know if the king is alive or dead."

"I am staying." Johanna folded her arms. "That is final." How could she leave not knowing if Daniel was alive or dead?

Spence ignored the remark and took the soldier's arm. "I am a close friend of Colonel Grant's. You will take this woman to safety outside the city. Clear?"

"I was ordered to take you, sir."

"We—" Spence waved his hand in a sweeping gesture "—are

from this fine city, and we will remain here. And if she refuses, I give you leave to take her by force."

Johanna stuttered for words. She paced about in a thither. Daniel was to come to her. That was the plan. She had consented to leave, but only because she was sure the King would win. "I can't leave. Please don't make me."

"I could never forgive myself, Johanna."

"Please, Daniel will come to me. Let me wait for him?"

Dr. Spence shook his head. "It's all arranged, Johanna. You can't stay, my dear."

Johanna pursed her lips.

"Go. If not for yourself, then for Daniel." Spence stroked her arm. "I promised him I would keep you safe. Promised. Don't have me break my word, child."

"He might be injured? He might be—"

"He'll be fine, Johanna. Especially when he knows you are safe."

Johanna cast her head down. She breathed in and then straightened herself. "Thank you." She embraced him. "No heroics, please."

"Not from me. The spirit is willing, Johanna, but the flesh...Well, you know the rest."

"If you see Daniel..."

"Yes, yes. Now go before it really is too late!"

Johanna skulked toward the flap but stopped. "What if he needs me?"

"My dear, the best way you can help him is to leave this city alive. Now be on your way."

Johanna nodded and crouched through the tent flap. She shielded her eyes from the sunlight beating down upon the devastated city. Soon, the Roundheads would be trampling through Worcester, burning, looting, and bent on revenge. Perhaps even women and children would not escape the carnage. The king would be captured and Parliament would be victorious. Would her father gloat? Would he forgive? "Come back to us, Daniel. Please, Lord, let him come back to us."

Chapter 9 – The Walls and Beyond

The cacophony of conflict drifted into Manfred's consciousness piece by piece. He attempted to lift himself up, but crumpled back down into the dirt, howling as the spasms racked through his body.

Francis!

The remembrance jolted through him. *Where is Francis?* He had been fighting the Royalist officer.

He groaned as he lifted himself onto his knees, and then to his feet. "Francis!" His gaze shifted from corpse to corpse. "Francis!" He tore at his hair in desperation. "Oh, Lord, give me the strength! Let him live! I will give you all that I am!" he pleaded.

He stumbled forward, wringing his hands. "John?"

John lay on his side four feet from him; his left arm impossibly twisted below his body. Dark blood stained his shattered temple.

"John," Manfred whispered, "where's my son? *My son.*" John lay silent—his eyes sunken into his skull. "No last words, John?"

Deaf and dumb to life. He wouldn't take Sarah away from Manfred again. He wouldn't take Francis to Ireland. His own foolishness and lust for glory had gotten him killed. He would take care of them.

"Francis!" Manfred slapped his head and forced the memories back. The Royalist had stumbled toward the city walls. Manfred hobbled forward, following his memories. His son hacking at the Royalist, forcing him back. Manfred had lifted his sword to strike him dead. And then..."My boy's tasting victory within the city walls."

And then, beneath a shroud of mangled flesh, a crown of black hair jutted through. His son's hair.

Pain filled every ounce of his skull as he dragged away the corpse lying on top of Francis. He heaved his son onto his back. Blood pooled around the hole in Francis' chest. But Manfred ignored the mortal wound, for Francis' face was unblemished. His son's half-opened eyes were fixed and dilated. He clasped his son's ashen face. "Francis! You're fine! Not a scratch!" He stroked his son's hair. "It's all right, Francis. You're safe now." He shook his son, but still he slept in deepest slumber.

Manfred doubled over and gagged as memories tortured him. Sarah's confession in her bedroom. His resplendent boy riding beside him. The Royalist's face, mocking him. His promise to bring their son back. He clawed at the dirt. He gripped his chest and wept over the body of his son.

He had failed them—Francis would not come home.

* * *

The unrelenting battle cry of Parliamentarian drums pursued Daniel and the rest of the fleeing Royalists past Fort Royal and then toward Sidbury Gate. He no longer commanded a company of foot—his men were dead or scattered amongst the hoard of retreating King's men. But he no longer cared. He had to reach Johanna.

He followed the tide of retreating men scrambling to enter the city. By the time he reached Sidbury Gate, the enemy had stormed Fort Royal. The Scottish Saltire was ripped down, and when the Commonwealth flag flew from the ramparts of the fort, cries of despair echoed through the terrified troops. Daniel shuddered as the screams of slaughter drifted to them from the fort.

"Poor bastards!" a musketeer shouted as he pushed past Daniel. "They're done for."

Panic turned to horror as the cannon from Fort Royal bombarded the city. The canister shot ripped into the retreating Royalist's backs. Helpless, they had no option but to flee. Their ammunition was all but exhausted, and with only swords and muskets—which were used as clubs—they were ineffective against the enemy cavalry. The crush of hundreds of men swarming through the gate killed more than the Roundhead cavalry that had harassed them for the past hour. Only the city walls gave them a glimmer of hope.

Daniel eyed the streets ahead, searching for landmarks, trying to remember the way to the field hospital. The Cathedral rose up, and he stumbled toward it. Scores of injured sought the safety of the sanctified grounds. They huddled together, praying for a miracle, waiting for the storm to come. Royalist officers encouraged them. But their shouts of "stand for the king" were lost in the wails of the camp wives and their children. Hundreds of soldiers piled north toward St. Martin's Gate, following the rumors of safety and escape through the only part of the city still in Royalist's hands.

Onward along High Street, Daniel forced his way through the crush. Soldiers threw off their uniforms and banged on doors, pleading for admittance. Distracted, he hadn't noticed that the Parliamentarian artillery had stopped bombarding the city. But the choking clouds in the fading light couldn't hide the dreadful sight of the Parliamentarian cavalry joining Main Street from the west side. The sea of people, whether soldier or civilian, woman or child, panicked and trampled around blindly. They were knocked aside like pins in a game of skittles, crushed under the weight of the Parliamentary Iron Sides.

Royalists threw up their arms in surrender, only to be shot in cold blood. The bloodlust was terrifying: houses were looted and burned; women were stripped naked and passed around, defiled by their assailants. Daniel shuddered. What if…what if she hadn't made it out of the city? He pushed the hellish pictures out of his mind and hurried onto a side street. There wasn't time for pity, just the need to reach the field hospital and Johanna.

Now the side streets filled with fleeing Royalists. They discarded their armor and weapons. Blue cloth bonnets were tossed aside and littered the cobbled streets. A Scottish musketeer threw an old Morion helmet through a window and climbed in. He collapsed when the owner of the bakery stabbed him in the face. Packs of soldiers broke down doors, searching for places to disappear, but the civilians, who had never wanted the Scottish army, vented their rage on the exhausted troops.

Gasping, Daniel staggered on. He mustn't get cut off from Johanna.

He headed east, staying within eye-shot of the city walls. Then the familiar sight came into view. The field hospital appeared untouched, and he lifted his eyes to the heavens. He drove his battered body forward. The dead were laid out against the city wall. He gagged from the smell as he reached the tent. He opened the flap, and it took a moment for his eyes to adjust.

"Daniel?"

A few paces from the tent flap, Dr. Spence slumped on a stool. The old man tried to lift himself up but sank back down again. Daniel helped him to his feet and embraced him.

"Where is she?"

"I sent her away, an hour past. She should be out of the city—on her way to my sister's home."

"Thank you!" Daniel rubbed his eyes. His body sagged, and only now did the splitting headache pound his skull as he relaxed.

"Sit," Dr. Spence instructed.

Daniel sat on a stool. He trembled and wrapped his arms about himself for warmth.

Spence held up a candle and studied Daniel's face. "Ah, your cheekbone is cracked."

Daniel winced as Spence examined his cheek. "I have to go." He gripped the old man's arm. "Come with me?"

Spence hesitated for a brief moment. "No. I'll slow you down. Don't worry, I'll be safe. They'll need a surgeon."

"That they will."

"You'll be safe at my sister's. Go now, before it's too late."

"I hope one day I can thank you properly, my friend."

"I hope so too," Spence said. "And remember, Daniel, you can't thank me if you get yourself killed."

Daniel peered through the opening. Two Roundheads trotted toward the tent. Spence pointed to another opening at the opposite end. Daniel gingerly stepped around an unconscious woman with a bandaged neck. Each breath caught in her throat, making a horrible hacking sound. A soldier lay dead across the exit. Daniel stepped over him and used his sword to pry open the flap.

Ten yards away, a Roundhead cavalryman was prying the ring from a dead soldier's finger. Daniel weighed his options. Without his pistol, he wouldn't stand a chance against the two out front. But the other was busy looting.

He stepped back into the tent and sheathed his sword, and then removed a dagger from his belt. The iron wire grip felt cool. Daniel peered out. The Roundhead cursed as he struggled to budge the stubborn ring. He spat on the corpse's finger and worked the spittle around the ring. Engrossed in his work, he didn't hear Daniel creep toward him. It would have been easier if the

Roundhead had given him his back, but he was kneeling sideways to Daniel.

Measured and light on his toes, Daniel made it to within a yard and then sprang forward. The Roundhead yelped with shock before Daniel's blade dug into his neck. The Roundhead, his eyes wide in terror, held his hand over the spurting wound. His mouth gaped, but all that escaped was a brief gurgle as blood filled his throat. A moment later, he slumped forward, dead. Daniel strained to listen for other soldiers, but all was quiet on the other side, and he headed for St Martin's Gate.

As Daniel turned onto Sidbury Street, the Royalists were forming a piecemeal defense against the advancing Roundhead foot. The Roundhead infantry had slowed its advance, not so much from the Royalist resistance, but more so from the widespread looting. The more disciplined cavalry had maintained its formation and had continued to harass the retreating Royalists, probing for weaknesses.

The decimated Royalist foot moved aside for a detachment of cavalry led by the Earl of Cleveland. They trotted past Daniel, knowing it would be their last charge.

Frank Harley, a burly pikeman who had volunteered for Daniel's troop a few weeks before, marched over. "Captain, the king lives!"

"The king has already fled." Daniel didn't try to hide his annoyance. "Save yourself before it's too late." He trudged off, leaving Harley behind.

"You're a coward, Captain."

Maybe, but he'd killed enough this day, and the king wasn't going to save his sister. Daniel had a promise to keep.

Moments later, the thunder of a charge reverberated toward him. A troop of Roundhead dragoons raced down Mealcheapen Street toward the Royalist defenders. Harley and a few others rushed to meet them, but Daniel did not wait to witness the outcome of Harley's heroically futile charge.

He reached New Street, where a group of Royalists stood outside a small townhouse. A tall man in the middle of the throng was fiddling with a breastplate. It took a few seconds for Daniel to realize the man was the king, surrounded by his guard.

Then the clatter of hooves on the cobblestones echoed through the street, and the Roundhead dragoons appeared. The dragoons charged the king, who was still unaware of the troopers.

Daniel drove his battered body forward and yelled out a warning. "Dragoons!"

The king's guard spun in alarm. King Charles threw aside his breastplate and was hurried off into the townhouse opposite Daniel. As he disappeared through the door, the dragoons galloped harder. A few of the King's Lifeguard stayed behind to block the entrance.

Just as Daniel reached them, the Royalists fired a volley over his head. He spun around to meet the dragoons, but they were already on top of him. He lifted his sword, but a musket ball tore into his right shoulder. He stumbled back groaning, hitting his head on the cobblestones. Before the prayer escaped his mouth, the butt of a musket cracked the side of his head, and all went black.

Chapter 10 – Johanna's Guide

For all intents and purposes, Johanna and Harry were brother and sister, civilians fleeing the battle like so many others. They had left the main roads, which were clogged with refugees, and instead took the quieter country lanes and fields. In the quiet of the countryside, even the thunder of battle seemed to fade away.

But the solitude of nature could not alleviate the terrible uncertainty of Daniel's fate. She paced beside her guide as he fingered over Spence's haggard map. Each step led her farther away from Daniel.

The stiff breeze of the afternoon had fallen to nothing more than a gentle breath. Johanna shielded her eyes against the setting sun. "I hope you can see in the dark, Harry?"

"Don't worry, Miss. We're close now." Harry's gaze shifted down the drover's path.

The ash trees grew luxuriantly on either side of the path. But the spectacle of nature was lost on her. The madness of the war had reduced them to nothing more than good cover if someone approached.

"Once we reach Lyppard Fork, I know the way."

With quick, clipped steps they continued on. About five hundred yards ahead, the fork in the road came into view, at last.

"That's it, Miss. I knew it was close."

"I never doubted you, Harry, even if you doubted yourself."

"Only around a mile, Miss, after we turn for Lyppard."

"I'm thankful to you…leaving your family."

"There's only my mother." He ran a hand across two-day-old stubble. "I brought her to my uncle when I heard Cromwell was coming."

"My brother is still in Worcester."

Harry gave an understanding nod. "I hope he makes it out, Miss."

Daniel would come for her, and take her back home. He would

see the change in their father, and then all would be forgiven. *He's not dead.*

From behind, branches rustled. Three Roundheads emerged from the trees and approached. A lecherous brutality marked their faces. The middle one's smirk darkened his face, his smile as rotten as his teeth.

Johanna quickened her pace.

Harry's gaze darted back as he walked. "No king but K-k-ing Je-esus," he stammered. His words were hollow and practiced, smothered with fear.

Contempt echoed in their laughter. Ahead, two more Roundheads emerged from the trees and blocked the road. From the other side a horseman—not cavalry from his uniform—appeared. They must be common rogues or deserters. *Stay calm.*

"I'm sorry." Harry's gaze lowered to the ground before he bolted for the tree line.

"Harry!" Johanna's heart sank into the pit of her stomach.

The soldiers ignored him.

Johanna shuddered as their stares bored into her flesh. She picked up a rock. "Stop!"

They laughed at her attempt to defend herself. Their leader closed in on her—a smirking horror of a man rubbing his hands. "You're not goin' to like this, Miss."

Johanna gripped the rock tighter to stop her shaking hand.

Still they stalked closer.

She hurled it with all her strength.

He threw up his arms to protect himself, but the rock had already hit him square on the forehead. He cursed in pain.

The others threw themselves at her. She hit the ground hard, gasping for breath with their weight crushing her. Her screams were smothered by a hand gripped over her mouth. They would violate her and then kill her.

The leader rubbed the bump on his forehead, wiping a trickle of blood with his dirty hands. He knelt down before her, his face contorted, bearing his teeth like a snarling dog. He ripped off her coif and breathed in a fist of her fair hair. He straddled her and wriggled his white-pasted tongue.

The others laughed even more when he licked her face.

The smell of his fetid breath made her choke. She twisted her head away. Damn him, but he would not see her despair.

He gripped her jaw and held her head still. She whimpered as his fingers dug into her jaw. He licked her cheek again, performing for the others.

Johanna gagged. She kicked out at them, but the more she struggled the tighter they gripped her. They wanted her to fight. The harder she fought the more they enjoyed it. She wouldn't give these animals the satisfaction. Panting for air, she stopped struggling. "God will not forgive you."

The brute punched her, and her head thudded against the ground. Dazed, she tasted blood. Johanna closed her eyes before the braying animals.

"Open your eyes, bitch!"

Her face stung as he struck her once more. She opened her eyes. Hot tears trickled down her cheeks, even as the blood trickled from her swollen lips.

He sneered. "I want your pretty eyes on me as I have you." He ripped at her petticoat, his hands burning her with their ferociousness. The others, with heavy, excited breaths, ripped at her bodice.

She mouthed the Lord's Prayer, but the words faded as the sound of approaching riders meant more agony. *Take me, Lord! I beg thee!*

The soldiers stopped their fumbling, and their grip relaxed. A large patrol of Parliamentarian cavalry halted. They had the look of real soldiers—discipline and self-control emanated from them.

An officer rode to the front and surveyed the scene. "Let her go, or I'll hang you all from the nearest tree," he snapped.

The ring-leader spat on the ground. "She's a Royalist!"

"She doesn't look like a soldier to me." The officer stared at the man in disgust. "Where is your regiment?"

The animal was lost for words. For he was a raper of women. He wasn't an animal, but something unnamable and evil. A coward at heart, except when backed up by his pack of scum.

A short, stocky man with pockmarked skin stepped forward. "We're with the Surrey Militia, sir."

"Deserters?"

"No, sir." The ring-leader stepped back from Johanna. "Ordered to find escaped Royalists."

"Get out of my sight."

Johanna blinked. How could he just let them leave? No punishment, not even a slap on the wrist.

The men slunk off toward Worcester.

Unsteady, Johanna held her ripped bodice together as she staggered to her feet. She snatched up her coif, which lay a few feet to the side.

The lieutenant dismounted. "Can I offer you my assistance?"

"Your men are animals." She stamped, holding back her tears.

"I'm sorry, but they are *not* my men. You shouldn't be wandering alone."

"I wasn't, until they chased off my brother."

He raised his eyebrows. "Are you normally so ungrateful to those who save you?"

Johanna straightened herself up with as much dignity as she could muster. She trembled from the shock and did her best to conceal it from the soldiers. She glanced up at the arrogant officer. "I am grateful to those who deserve it. You did your Christian duty and your duty as an officer and gentleman. But you also let those animals go free to molest some other woman."

"Maybe you are a Royalist sympathizer? I could arrest you."

Johanna replaced her coif and fixed her disheveled hair. She walked over to him, ignoring the whispers of his men. She glared at him. "And what if I am? I am also a woman and a human being, one who was set upon by those scum, who are now free. Do as you will."

"Harper, escort Miss...?"

"Davenport!"

"Take Miss Davenport to wherever she needs to go. Oh, one more thing, one day when you relate the tale of how the gallant officer saved your life, you can tell them his name is Richard Leitham." He doffed his hat, and the troop carried on toward Worcester.

Johanna stomped off in the opposite direction as her new guide, Harper, trotted after her. She skidded to a halt and swung around. The Roundhead cavalry was almost out of sight. Dr. Bannister's map floated across the path and rested in the grass. Harry had dropped it. She bent down to pick it up. Johanna unfolded it, and then took in a deep breath to clear her head. A prayer of gratitude filled her heart completely. No words came, just a bursting of gratitude for the Almighty. The arrogant Roundhead had let them go free, but he had also saved her. Who was she to question how the Lord sent help?

She exhaled a ragged breath. When Daniel returned they would become a family again. The war that had ripped her family apart would now bond them closer than ever before.

Chapter 11 – Sarah

Hereford. Seven Days Later

The cart that carried John's and Francis' coffins followed behind Manfred. The click of its wheels droned as he rode through his fog of depression. Two men from his troop had requested the honor of accompanying him, but he had ignored them and rode on, leaving them to follow him with the cart. An unnerving pressure trailed after them like a storm cloud, and words were few and far between. Truly, it had been a dark and somber journey for all.

For hours, Manfred had muttered speeches to himself. What would he say to Sarah? He had fought to find words that would comfort her, offering hope amid the greatest sorrow. But the regurgitated euphemisms always ended with the crushing reality: "Francis is dead."

No journey had been more arduous, and with each mile, the burden had increased until they reached Glenview estate. If only it had been just John. John had lived his life. Francis' life had only begun. Soldiering had been John's choice. A soldier accepted that he might die in battle. It had been different with his son. He had never been given a choice. For no one refused John. Sarah had been right—if only Manfred had stood up for Francis.

Mrs. Benson, Sarah's maid, approached from the stable. She clasped her hand over her mouth when the coffins came into view. But as Manfred dismounted, the front door opened, and Sarah froze. Her gaze shot to the wagon, and she cried out.

Manfred ran to her, but she staggered back into the hall. She fell to her knees; her head buried in her hands.

"I'm sorry. I'm…sorry, Sarah!" He knelt and enfolded her in his arms. *I brought him home. I brought him home,* thundered through his brain. He stroked her auburn hair and cradled her head against his chest.

She glanced up. The spark of life had left her. Her blue grey eyes narrowed. "Wickedness," she groaned. "We killed them. Our sin, Manfred. Ours is the guilt!"

Her words burned into him. "I will never leave you again," he whispered, brushing her cheek.

"I need to see my son," she pleaded. With each word, her body shuddered in heartbroken desperation.

"No. It's been too long—nearly a week. I beg you, remember them as they were, Sarah." He caressed her hand. "We must lay them to rest."

Sarah nodded and wiped away tears. "Sixteen years old!"

He sank back, groaning.

"Manfred, I…I need to know. Tell me what happened to my son?"

He rubbed his eyes. "I've been trying to forget, Sarah."

"I need to know."

He clasped his hands together and closed his eyes. "Their lancers hit John from behind, and he was knocked from his horse. We were there in seconds…I told Francis to stay on his horse..." He shook his head. "He…ran to John. John stood, and a…musket shot killed John instantly."

Sarah shuddered. "Oh, Manfred!"

"Francis charged at the Royalist and forced him back. I ran to him, to Francis…and then…I can't remember the rest. A horse. I think I was hit by a horse. I…found Francis…he didn't suffer." Manfred's neck muscles constricted as he held back his tears. He must stay strong for her. "I promise—I promise…he didn't suffer. He was a good boy. He was innocent and good, Sarah!"

"Was!" She buried her head against his chest, clutching tight to him.

"I can't get through this without you," Manfred pleaded.

"I can't think, Manfred. I can't think about a future."

"I know—not yet." Manfred stroked her hair. "But we have our past. The love that filled us. Together, we can have a future. Only together can we survive this." He fished the locket from his waist pocket. "Do you remember this?"

Her eyes sparkled for a brief moment.

"It's never left my side in sixteen years. Each day I gazed upon your portrait. I look upon you now, and I see only the true love of my life. You are today as you were then. Everything! I see a beautiful woman whose glorious auburn hair I wrapped about my finger and whose smile was the sunlight of my life." He handed Sarah the locket.

She studied her likeness. "That's the past. We've changed."

He squeezed her hand. "The past is the present. It's living within us."

She gazed at the portrait, and he read the longing in her eyes. She stroked her picture. Her whole body trembled as she lifted her head.

"It is you, and you are her. Our love brought Francis into this world. Let this love sustain us and strengthen us for the terrible days ahead. I knew my son only for a few days." Manfred's jaw trembled. "And that boy changed my life forever. I can't imagine your loss."

Sarah snapped the locket shut and embraced him. He held her tight, and her warmth flooded through him. Hands entwined, they gripped the locket tight.

Sarah kissed him and then lifted herself to her feet. She trudged into the parlor. He raised himself up and followed her. Her Bible sat on a small round table beside a cane chair. She held it and bowed her head.

He pressed against her and put his hand on hers. "Too many years have been wasted without you. I will be here only for you—I will live for you."

"I love you," she whispered.

"I will never let you down again."

Sarah lifted the Bible. Manfred held out his hand, and he led her up to her room. He stopped with her at the door.

"Mrs. Benson should stay with you tonight."

"No…I need to be alone." She caressed his cheek. "I need time. Give me time, Manfred."

"I love you. I will give you whatever you need." They embraced again. Manfred kissed her hand and backed away. He waited until her door closed and then trudged downstairs. He stepped out into the cold night, and Private Mynard saluted him.

Manfred gave him a short nod. "Stable Smithy, and then lift the coffins into the stable. Find the Leaping Trout Inn. Tell the innkeeper I sent you. Get what you need and rest."

Mrs. Benson waited in the hall. "I'm so sorry, Mr. Hugo.

What can I do for Mrs. Hugo, sir?"

"She needs to rest. But please, call on her later tonight."

"And for you, sir?"

"I will stay in the parlor."

"A blanket, sir?"

"That won't be necessary. But thank you, Mrs. Benson."

Manfred closed the door and walked back to the table where Sarah's Bible had lain a few moments before. He rested his hand upon the table, imagining her hand was still there. He had wanted to say so much more to her upstairs, but he couldn't let the words pass his lips. He had to stay strong for her.

He fell to his knees and gripped his heart. "Don't leave me, Sarah. I need you. I beg you, forgive me," he whispered. He no longer held back his tears. The spasms of his lamentations gripped the pit of his soul. He was alone now. No one would see him cry.

* * *

Manfred jolted up from the floor. *Wailing?* He squinted through the darkness, then rose and bounded to the door.

Mrs. Benson clambered down the stairs wringing her hands. "Mrs. Hugo! Oh sir, it's Mrs. Hugo!"

Manfred pushed past her on the stairs, sprinting up. "Sarah! Please God!"

Sarah's bedroom door was ajar, and his heart dropped. He stopped dead at the door, hesitating, unable to cross the threshold; he gripped the doorframe. "Sarah?" Her name dribbled from his mouth. The soft glow of candlelight beckoned him to enter. "Sarah, please answer!"

Manfred swung the door open. Hanging from a central beam, she swayed above a stool. A forsaken cry burst out of him, shaking him to the core of his soul. He collapsed to the floor. Her hanging body caught shards of candlelight streaming from the windowsill.

"Sarah!" He crawled to her. He clasped her legs, his tears wetting her bare feet. "Why punish me! You—you were all I had left!"

He held his face against her bare legs. Slowly, very slowly, he slid up her body, his cheek sliding up her nightdress. Blue-black bruises crept from her neck to her face. He clasped her face. "Suicide! Even death cannot bring us together now," he groaned.

65

"You were sinless and pure!"

He cut Sarah down and carried her to the bed. He laid her body down. Her Bible lay beside her pillow. A slip of paper jutted from the pages. It had been ripped out. Manfred brought it to the candle. "Scripture. 'Thou knowest the commandments, Do not commit adultery…Do not kill…Do not…'" Manfred clutched his chest.

He removed her nightdress, and with loving reverence, washed her clean. Her final baptism. He slipped a clean nightdress on Sarah, and then dropped down beside her, resting his head on her stomach. He whimpered until the very well of tears dried up within. The candlelight was now a dying flicker. His breath was shallow and labored, an assault against his will. He shut his eyes to the world, praying he would never awaken to the light of day.

Chapter 12 – Fisherton Anger

Salisbury, England, 1655

The temperature could determine the measure of Lawrence Bodley's shuffling gait. Outside or inside made little difference, for the cold, bare walls of Fisherton Anger Gaol reflected the misery both inmate and guard felt.

Mr. Bodley's daily reports rarely consisted of anything other than the mundane, but he insisted on them being kept, if for no other reason but to antagonize Captain Shaw. Shaw wouldn't press the matter, for he enjoyed the quiet life, and left the running of Fisherton Anger Gaol to Bodley. Shaw would soon be on his way like the rest of them. They never stayed long at Fisherton Anger. And if Shaw and his ilk couldn't wait to leave, it was different for Mr. Bodley. He loved his work.

With the morning frost, Bodley stuttered along as he made for Shaw's office.

The guard straightened as he approached. "It's a cold one, Mr. Bodley."

Bodley didn't bother to reply, but hobbled on quicker than was his wont, wincing with each step. His limp troubled him more than usual with the unseasonal chill. The old war wound always flared up with the cold. But he never complained, for pain and life were old friends who kept each other company. Nothing was wrong with a little pain.

He knocked on the door of the Old Keeper's House and entered the captain's office at his beckoning. The heat from a fire warmed his face. Captain Shaw raised his head from his work and set down his quill. "Sit down, please."

Bodley took off his overcoat and sneered at the roaring fire. Shaw was weak. Warming his arse beside the fire while pretending to work. "Morning, Captain." He sat down and raised his eyebrows as Shaw drummed his fingers on the desk.

"Well, let's get it over with."

Bodley cursed him under his breath. "There's talk of escape, Captain."

"Escape? Your favorite topic, Mr. Bodley. What have you heard this time?"

"Well, not talk, but a feeling. It's too quiet, Captain. I know how they work."

Shaw rubbed his eyes. "I can't do much with a feeling, Mr. Bodley."

Bodley's eyes narrowed. "It's Davenport. My men know he's behind it. We can stir things up—take 'im down to the lower cells. Give 'im something to think about."

"Mr. Bodley, we have fourteen men, not including you and I. I'm not stirring anything unless there's proof." Shaw set his spectacles down. "Maybe then I can get more men. Give me proof, Bodley."

Bodley put his coat on. "I'll see to it, Captain." The flames danced in the hearth, licking the air. He didn't need a fire. He wasn't soft like Shaw. "I'll get your proof."

Bodley hobbled back to his Spartan office. Except for a table and stool standing against the wall and a mattress at the far end, the converted cell was shorn of comfort. He rested himself down onto a stool and took out a letter from his doublet. He laid it out on the table, and then smoothed out the creases so it lay almost flat. His thin lips curled up as he read it. "Someone doesn't like you much either," he muttered.

A knock at the door disturbed him, and he placed the letter face down. "Come in."

A bulky guard plodded in. "News, sir?"

Bodley slid a shilling across the table.

The guard, Cranic, pocketed the coin with a seedy smile.

"There's more where that come from. Hugo wants him alive…for the moment."

"More's the pity, sir."

"Davenport's been a bad boy. Seems like Hugo's goin' after kin first."

"Just tell me what you need, sir. It's always a pleasure." A sick grin darkened Cranic's face.

"Just keep your mouth shut. This is an earner. Let's keep it that way."

After Cranic had closed the door, Bodley continued to peruse the letter. Alive for the moment? Suited him fine. Davenport didn't deserve a quick, clean killing. Once he got him down into the lower cells, he would take his time and do it right.

* * *

Routine had become the object of their life at Fisherton Anger. Routine kept a man sane. And after four years, their routines had been so precisely set out and respected that they could have been chiselled into tablets of law.

Daniel Davenport paced his cell, while Robert White lay on his mattress, counting the ceiling cracks. There was just enough space for one to exercise at a time.

"You've had long enough now, old man," Robert said.

"I need more time than you. Anyway, you need all the counting practice you can get," Daniel said, taunting the big man.

"What I need is the shit bucket to be emptied. For someone who doesn't eat, sure as hell you fill that bucket quick enough."

Daniel scratched his matted hair and picked out a louse. "Even the lice are monsters." He walked over to the bucket and flicked the insect into the foul stew. "Anyway, you know what they say, it's the shit vapors that hold these walls up." He pulled his mattress down flat on the ground.

"They're late today." Robert patted his belly as it growled out a tune.

The guards also had their routine. After the slop was delivered to the cells, they would take their own food in the hall downstairs. Then it would be safe to talk at a whisper, knowing how the sound echoed off the cold walls.

Daniel straightened himself out on the mattress. It was easy to think about the 'what ifs' in Fisherton Anger. Most of English Royalists captured at Worcester had been released long ago. While the Scots had been shipped away to the New World, Daniel had been offered freedom at a price: fighting for Cromwell in Ireland. His refusal had sealed his fate, and for four years he'd wasted away in Fisherton Anger. Each New Year had brought new promises of release. But they came to nothing, and all that remained were the 'what ifs.' In the past, he'd dismissed whispers

69

of a break-out. But it was becoming more difficult to heed his sound advice with each newly broken promise.

Daniel exercised his stiff shoulder. The dull pain gripped deep into his muscle. He rubbed some warmth back into his shoulder as Robert exercised. The heavy-boned man had lost weight, but he was still strong and healthy compared to Daniel's malnourished and wasted frame.

Footsteps approached, and the other the prisoners ceased their talk. The cell door opened, and the sneering Sterling and Cranic appeared. Sterling, like always, swung his club like a pendulum, while Cranic dished out the porridge. He slid the bowls across the floor and threw over a few hunks of stale bread to complete the feast.

"Why's it always those two?" Robert asked after they locked the cell. "The other guards rotate, but not those two."

Daniel stirred the porridge with his finger. "To irritate you?"

Robert grunted.

Daniel stared at the ball of porridge stuck to his finger. "This definitely needs more water. You could build a house with this."

Robert shambled over to the bucket and relieved himself. "I'll give you some water if you want?"

"I dare say it would improve it, but no thanks."

"Better to be cursed by that weasel Bodley than to endure the dead-eyed stare of Cranic. You know he was second in the file, like me?"

"A pikeman through and through. Those heavy rounded shoulders would do some damage. Lucky for you, you didn't meet him in the field."

"Huh, I ate boys like him for breakfast." Robert slid over to Daniel. "What about Pierce?"

Daniel's meeting in the yard with Lieutenant Pierce had been all too brief. The man had hemmed and hawed, had been evasive and non-committal. Although they had both been captured at Worcester and had also refused conscription to Ireland in the New Model Army, cavalry officer Lieutenant William Pierce had little in common with Daniel. Among the Royalist prisoners, Pierce had his men while Daniel had his own followers. But as different as they were, they understood the guards could only be overcome when they worked together.

"He's nervous." Daniel dipped the bread into the porridge. "He thinks Bodley knows."

Robert wiped the remnants of the porridge from his beard and sidled even closer. "An excuse. With him, there'll never be a right time."

"Maybe he's right to wait." Daniel scratched his hair. "And the constable knows his business."

"Huh." Robert snorted. "What was it he said? It's simply a matter of time before we're released, he said. Six bloody months ago." Robert stuffed more bread down his gob. "The New World— the plantations, is where we're headin'," he mumbled.

Daniel pushed the bread into his mouth, barely keeping the contents down. He nudged the bowl over to Robert. "You're right."

Robert nodded as he pigged into the repulsive slop.

"If I keep eating this, it'll be the death of me anyway. But if Bodley sniffs a break-out, we'll be the first to visit the lower cells. And no one comes back from there."

Daniel reached over for his knapsack. All his personal possessions were squeezed in, and he fumbled through the clutter for Johanna's letter from the previous week. He waded through the words again, delighting in her description of the coming spring. She would soon begin with plowing the small field attached to the cottage and hoped that her fingers would turn a shade of green for the benefit of the anticipated crop. She had also spoken to the constable, and he would speak to the magistrate on Daniel's behalf. Despite everything, she still held out that justice would prevail, and he would be released sooner than later. She finished by admonishing him to use the solitude for grateful prayer and to never forget his dear sister.

Daniel folded the letter and placed it back in the sack. All he had left were his prayers and Johanna. *What if...what if...* What if he'd never fought for the king and had managed the estate instead? What if his father had accepted his decision to fight for his king? What if that hate-filled bastard hadn't sold off the land and then burned down the rest? Johanna refused to believe it possible. He had been murdered by lawless rebels, but the bitter old man had torched it himself because he knew that would hurt them the most. But, in the end, the cold reality amounted to choices that had destroyed everything they had known. Johanna had been innocent, but she had suffered more than anyone. He couldn't change the past, but he could pray for the opportunity to change her future.

Chapter 13 – Richard Leitham's Request

Taunton, Somerset

The ale helped Richard Leitham's nerves. If he was going to visit Johanna Davenport today, then the one ale wasn't going to hack it. Months of planning, and more than a little bit of luck, had brought him to this moment. But facing down a horde of Royalists would never be as nerve-wracking as the task before him. Over the past weeks, he'd thought of every possible excuse not to visit her. She wouldn't remember him and think him to be some madman or deviant to announce himself. Or, if she did remember him, that would be worse. How could she not hate the Roundhead who had let her attackers go free?

He gulped down the last of his liquid courage and held his tankard up. The landlord refilled it and slid it back to him.

"Do you know the manor house up past the Vale?" Richard asked.

"I do, sir. It belonged to a Mr. Daniel Davenport senior. He died in the fire that gutted the place years back. He once owned a lot of land in these parts."

Once owned? He'd heard whispers that Miss Davenport's father had sold everything just before the fire. Some said he'd torched the place himself. "And the present owner?"

"I suppose it's the son." The landlord scratched his head. "By the same name, sir."

"I heard he fought at Worcester?"

The Landlord sidled close. "Aye." He lowered his voice. "A Royalist. Fought for Charles."

"And where's the gentleman now?"

"I heard they locked him up. Now it's just the sister—a sweet girl, I remember. But I haven't seen her in a long time."

"A sad tale indeed." Richard reflected.

"Ah, but there's some still bitter they sided with Charles. They say the fire was God's reward. But I always thought they were good people."

War always brought out the worst in folk. The bitterness would linger for years to come. "People don't forget. I know Taunton had it harder than most with the sieges."

"True enough. But you're not a local?"

"I moved to Taunton six months ago. I've set up a new law practice near Main Street."

The landlord filled his own cup for a toast. "Best of luck to you then, sir."

"I believe I'll need it." Richard swigged down another mouthful before leaving the Golden Heart Inn.

The cottage was about fifty yards from the manor house, running perpendicular to it. The cottage had its own land, which was enclosed by a small hedge. A woman collected rocks from the partly tilled earth. Richard pulled his horse onto the lane leading to the cottage. She raised herself up from the backbreaking work with his approach. It was her—unchanged and beautiful. Her clothes were threadbare, but her bearing and frame remained the same. He had never met a woman who carried herself with such grace.

He trotted over to the small wooden gate, dismounted, and tethered his horse to it.

Her eyebrows furrowed as he wandered over. He took a deep breath and clasped his hands together. "Miss Davenport, my name is Richard Leitham."

"Good morning, Mr. Leitham."

She still didn't recognize him. *I'm not even a memory.* He cleared his throat. "You may recall we met at Worcester?"

She regarded him more closely now. Anxiety crawled across her face. "Worcester?"

And then the light of a remembrance darkened her eyes. Richard smiled and gulped in air.

"What do you want with me, Mr. Leitham?"

"I am truly sorry to come unannounced." He cleared his throat again. "I mean to say, I didn't know how else to go about the whole thing." He talked fast, hoping she wouldn't interrupt him. "I recently moved to Taunton and made partner with a local Attorney, a Mr. Biggs?"

"Yes, I know the man."

74

"Well...I wanted to apologize for what happened that day...the day I let them go."

She straightened herself and folded her arms.

"The truth is...I haven't stopped thinking about you since then."

Johanna steadied herself. "That was a long time ago. If you are a gentleman, you will leave me now."

"Miss Davenport." Richard straightened himself to the task. "I believe I am a gentleman, but I cannot leave until I speak to you. You must think me cruel or a madman to remind you. I know I am foolish, but forgive me...I expect nothing from you, but let me convince you of my earnest and heartfelt feelings through my deeds and not my poor and foolish words. Let me help you?"

Johanna stepped back. "Help me? I assure you, Mr. Leitham, I have friends enough, one of whom is Vincent Lucas, the constable."

"He is a good man, but I can send you a man to help. You needn't break your back in this field."

"You can't give me what I want, Mr. Leitham."

"Your brother?"

Her eyes widened.

Was that fleeting hope in her eyes? "I can help him. I still have friends in the army."

Her face froze over again just as it had four years before, encapsulating her proud, independent soul. "I have no money to give you, Mr. Leitham, and I will not be indebted to you."

"Very well, call it a loan, then?"

She hesitated. Her eyes reflected her inner struggles. "If you are in earnest about helping me, then I must be clear with you from the beginning. Do not dare to hope for anything other than my deepest gratitude, sir."

"I hope for nothing but to help you in your difficult circumstances, Miss Davenport. As any Christian would do."

Her features softened just a little. "Then I thank you for your help, Mr. Leitham. My brother is a threat to no one, and I have never received a suitable explanation why he still in Fisherton Gaol. I have done everything I can to secure his release."

"I will look into it. I can travel next week if you agree to it?"

"Yes—yes of course." She clasped her hands together. "I

thank you."

He mounted his horse and doffed his hat again. "Good day, Miss Davenport."

"And to you, Mr. Leitham."

Euphoric, he patted his horse as the torment of the past months lifted away from him. *She smiled at me!* "Now, if I can help her brother, her joy will be complete," he muttered to himself.

Even if Johanna could never countenance him, she should not struggle alone in that field. She needed her family. He would then confess his terrible guilt. She might even forgive him, and then he might be able to forgive himself. Perhaps someday she might even grow to care for him?

Chapter 14 – A New Beginning

Road to Taunton

The early morning sun was a welcome change from the heavy rains the night before. The gale, which had lashed the county for the past two days, had blown itself out to give the county a promise of the coming spring. The glistening hedgerows teamed with life, and the song birds darted into the hedge as Manfred ambled past. He glanced back at Edward Mabb, whose discomfort grew more pronounced with every sway of the horse. The man held the reins like they were vipers ready to strike.

"You will soon appreciate him." Manfred grinned. "We will have to travel, and a horse is essential if you are to assist me."

Mabb swiveled in the saddle and groaned.

Manfred filled his lungs with the sweet air. He reflected on the last years of tragedy, struggle, and self-conquest. The nightmare of the battle before Worcester's walls had tormented him night after night. It was only when he had embraced his nightmares that he found the message hidden within.

The Royalist officer who had attacked Francis had first spoken to John. For days, Manfred had pondered the answer to this strange occurrence. And when he had given up all hope of finding an answer to the riddle, the picture of John's boyhood friend, Daniel Davenport, flashed into his memory. The realization had stunned him. John's friend, the Royalist, who murdered his son. It had been easy piecing together the rest. But why had God taken Sarah and Francis from him, while Davenport lived?

Manfred had searched long for the answer. Only later, after hearing a sermon on the coming Fifth Kingdom, did Manfred realize he had placed his love for Sarah and Francis above all else. They had been his idols. Because of his sins, they had been taken from him. His love for Sarah had blinded him to the growing corruption festering within. The sins of the father were visited upon the mother and the son. With their deaths came his rebirth. Davenport and his Royalist family also had some part to play in Manfred's future, and all would reveal itself to him, even as before inspiration had enlightened him.

And so Manfred had become an eloquent advocate of the burgeoning movement of the Fifth Monarchists. Colonel Harrison, a champion of the movement, had heard Manfred speak to a group of soldiers on the subject. He wrote to Manfred, expressing his hope that England, through its humble, godly people, and with her army at the vanguard, would receive Christ as his devoted servants. England's destiny would be to lead the godly on earth.

Soon after, Manfred had reunited with Gunner Edward Mabb. Also a devoted adherent of the Fifth Monarchists, Mabb had followed Manfred with his resignation from the army in protest of the dissolution of the Parliament of the Saints. Manfred had returned to Glenview, intending to devote his energy to the running of the estate. But when Colonel Bradshaw wrote to him, offering a position as a Commissioner of the Peace in Cromwell's new Government of the Major-Generals, it was clear the hand of the Lord had guided him once again. The army had the strength to lead the people into the Fifth Kingdom. Now Manfred, as a servant of the new Government, would have the power to lead the people to Christ. He would use his influence to right past wrongs and to protect the weak from the influence of the scheming Royalists.

"I wish you had been there to hear Simpson's sermon." Manfred closed his eyes, trying to recapture the experience. "It was as if…I saw the Burning Bush."

"I have you to tell me, Captain."

"Yes, you have." Manfred nodded. "The Fifth Kingdom is at hand, Mr. Mabb. We need to be ready."

"Aye, sir—ready."

"False idols appear where you least suspect. To tear ourselves away from them is always painful. Always remember the words: Unless a man be born again, Mr. Mabb."

"Like England, Captain?"

"England?" Manfred was struck by Mabb's interpretation of the words. "Yes, indeed, Babylon has fallen. And Colonel Bradshaw and Colonel Harrison know that."

"Are the rumors true, Captain?"

"Bradshaw confirmed them to me." Manfred's eyes lit with enthusiasm. "England's time has come. Bradshaw related the imminent rule of military Government to help with the purification of England. The Major-Generals will be incorruptible and tireless in their efforts to transform our Nation into a Godly one. In advance, they will send out their Commissioners to every county in England to prepare the soil for the coming purification." He removed a roll of paper from his doublet and waved it at Mabb. "Here it is, Mr. Mabb, my commission. The promise I have waited for these last years. This promise allows us to fight against England's parasites."

"Aye, Captain."

Manfred glanced over at his ever quiet companion, who was still fidgeting in his saddle. "You'll toughen up to old hide, Mabb."

"I'm sure you're right, Captain." Mabb's pained expression suggested otherwise.

A horse from an adjacent field trotted over to inspect them.

"Colonel Bradshaw swung a favor for me, Mr. Mabb. Major-General Desborough has given me permission to return to Taunton. There, our great work of purification begins. The Royalist traitors and evil doers will be brought to heel. This I vow."

Chapter 15 - Henry Massie

Margate, Kent

Henry Massie held his horse close for the warmth. The oars thrashed into the breakers, and the row boat cruised toward the shore. The heavy swell had made progress slow, but the sound of the rowboat dragging along the pebbles woke him from his contemplations. Massie's men peered across the beach, watching for unwelcome visitors. They were nervous. But that was understandable. Nearly all the King's pieces had been strategically positioned across the great chessboard of England. And now the final move had been completed as the King's knight—or rather earl—readied for shore.

The Earl of Rochester waded through the surf, grinning. He reached the shore and inhaled a lungful of the sea air.

Rochester grasped Massie's hand with a hearty shake. "It's good to be home, Mr. Massie."

"Welcome home, my lord."

"Though, to be sure, I'm not certain home welcomes me so much."

"Perhaps not yet, my lord, but it will before our time is finished."

"How goes our enterprise?"

"To plan—more or less. With your permission, we will meet tomorrow with the others to finalize everything."

"Good. Now get me to a fire and a glass of wine."

It had taken another two hours of hard riding before they reached the safe-house. Massie escorted the earl inside. Rochester studied the furnishings in the humble dwelling.

"You must be tired, my lord?" Massie said. "I can show you to your bedchamber."

"I'm in no mood for sleep. I brought a few bottles of wine with me, and I hope you will join me." Rochester walked into the drawing room, and Massie followed him. "This is not the time for abstinence, Mr. Massie."

"I have no objections, my lord."

"Excellent. It's always easier to know a man when his throat has been well oiled."

Massie nodded. "As you say, my lord."

"Of course, I'm speaking to the converted. A few bottles of good wine are always useful in your work?"

Rochester's servant came in and poured the wine. Massie waited until he left the room. "Among other things, my lord." He winked.

Rochester raised his glass. "God save the King."

Massie toasted the King and sipped the wine. "A fine vintage, my lord."

Rochester nodded enthusiastically.

"May I speak freely, my lord?"

"Please."

"I was against your coming at first."

"At first?"

"I had my reservations. This type of work needs subtlety and careful planning. One wrong word can destroy months of planning, or destroy the endeavor completely, my lord."

Rochester raised an eyebrow. "As we're speaking plain—" he took another gulp of wine "—I don't trust you. I don't trust people I know nothing about. I don't trust Jesuits, because they serve their Pope first and foremost and not their King."

"I am Henry Massie." Massie raised his glass to the earl and took another drink. "And I took my vows with the Society of Jesus at Clermont at nineteen. Until five years ago, I led a quiet life in the service of the Jesuits. That was until my Sociuos relayed orders from the Father General, detailing His Majesty's request for assistance in regaining his throne from the regicide and the heretics." Massie paused but continued at Rochester's nod of approval. "Since then, I have returned to England three times in the service of His Majesty. On each occasion, I prepared myself that I might never leave England in one piece. I could relate to you many experiences of escapes and near misses, failures, and sometimes even modest successes."

"Take another drink, my dear Massie, and continue."

"As you wish, my lord." Massie took another sip. "As you may have noted, I am attired after the Dutch fashion." He raised an eyebrow. "So popular in England at the moment."

He waited until Rochester had stopped laughing.

"I find the dark colors imminently suitable for my line of work. I know how to fit in, my lord. I am as comfortable playing cards with the wastrels of a bawdy inn as I am mixing with the society of the aristocracy in the grandest European palaces. And, if I were an immodest man, I might also state I am extremely proficient at what I do. Not because of any great talents which set me apart, my lord, but the truth of the paradox lies in the fact my greatest talent is that I am not supremely talented in any one area. I can adequately turn my hand to anything, even if I master none."

Rochester knocked the table. "You are winning me over, Massie. I am even willing to overlook your being a Jesuit."

Massie inclined his head. "And, my lord, you need not tell me your story, for I know more about you than most."

"Bravo!" Rochester raised his glass.

"Three years of planning is finally coming to harvest. The threads have been woven, and the mantle of the greatest rebellion in England's recent history will soon adorn our shoulders. But there is little more I can do, my lord. I now know cold steel and the warrior to wield it is what is needed most."

They clinked their glasses. "Welcome to England, my lord."

Chapter 16 – The Venerable Sam Tripton

Daniel's routine of lice hunting was disturbed by a terrible wail coming from the corridor. Robert clambered off his mattress and brought his ear to the door. He grimaced as the cacophony of the guard's curses, banging of doors, and singing of the prisoners assaulted his ears. Daniel frowned as the beautiful words of the Psalm, "I will say of the Lord, he is my refuge and my Fortress: my God; in him will I trust," were butchered by the screeching man.

Robert fell on his knees and clasped his hands together. "Lord, let it not be so."

His prayer was not answered as the singer was thrown against their cell door and the wailing ceased.

Robert stepped back, and the guards pushed a man wearing black tattered garb into the cell. His weathered features suggested he had turned the wrong side of forty.

"Scoundrels! Give me my hat!" the stranger demanded.

The guards ignored him and slammed the door shut. The newcomer proceeded to dust himself off, while Robert backed away from him like he carried the Black Death.

The newcomer seemed oblivious to their gaping stares. "Well met. Sam Tripton, formerly of Ulster," he announced with a high-pitched countryside brogue. "Now wandering the shores of England, spreading the word of the Lord through his inner light!"

"We have been cursed." Robert bulled past the smiling newcomer. "Remove this Ranter, or I'll kill him!" he yelled through the cell door.

"I'm no Ranter," Tripton said, sitting down opposite Daniel.

"They'll bring the bedding soon," Daniel said.

"I thank thee, stranger."

"And what terrible crime has brought you to Fisherton Anger?" Daniel asked.

"It was no crime," Sam said. "I followed the light within, and it brought me into the Church. I felt compelled to preach the true message of Christ, but the bishop didn't seem to appreciate my efforts. I refused to swear their oath never to set foot in their Church again. Here I am."

It was said of Quakers that they were the most disagreeable of fellows and could start an argument with their shadow. Disdainful of all earthly authority, whether religious or political, they lived life as they saw fit to be moved. Only the Lord was entitled to obedience. No doubt, Sam Tripton would find himself in a bother when he finally met Mr. Bodley.

Robert glared at the small man with the dark curling hair. "Wandering the shores of England?" He snorted. "You'll not be straying very far here, Quaker."

Sam, not in the least intimidated by the big man, smirked. "Did not the Lord deliver Daniel from the lions?"

"I hope you're right, Sam Tripton. I am Daniel Davenport, and that snarling oaf is Robert. We have been here since Worcester."

"So long? Now I fathom why your friend is in such a temper."

Robert crossed the room and grabbed Sam by the throat. "Perhaps I'll use your head to batter down the door and make my escape?"

Daniel sighed. "Robert, let him be."

With a grunt, Robert let the man go. "There is no escape here. In time, you'll recognize that, Quaker."

"Ah," Sam spluttered, while wagging his finger at the snarling Robert, "ye of little faith."

Chapter 17 – The Sealed Knot

Henry Massie followed the Earl of Rochester into the drawing room. The guests stood for the earl, whose attention was drawn to the fire. Rochester stared transfixed at the dancing flames, while the others shrugged.

"Gentlemen, the Earl of Rochester," Massie announced in loud voice.

Rochester jerked around and walked to the head of the table, casting his gaze over the expectant assembly. "Gentlemen, at great risk you have come here this night. The king is heartened by your plans and sent me to assist you. However, time is running short."

Massie nodded in agreement. Perhaps the mere presence of the earl would be enough to unite the fractures; for the knot had been slowly unraveling over the past months. "We must bring forward our plans. We must be ready from early March. Cromwell knows of a possible uprising, and—" Massie arched his eyebrows "—we have heard talk of Major General's securing the Commonwealth. Cromwell will also bring soldiers back from Scotland."

The earl made himself comfortable before continuing. "Hence calling this meeting at short notice."

A hushed muttering moved around the table, and Baron Belasyse spoke first. "My lord, all here are committed, but surely it cannot be done in a few weeks."

"We have no choice." Massie rose from his chair and gripped the table. "Punitive security bonds are to be placed on all Royalists. When the measure is passed, many will be too afraid to act."

Lady Anne Farmer spoke but was drowned out amid the din of arguments erupting around the table.

"Gentlemen!" The earl raised his voice above the clamor, and the noise ceased. "I believe Lady Farmer has the floor."

"Major Generals? This may work in our favor. The people are already angry. Soldiers swamp the country and leave no one in peace. The taxes are crippling. Perhaps this new measure will push the people too far."

"True," Sir William Compton said, "but with more soldiers coming back from Scotland, they'll be as docile as lambs."

The earl hemmed and hawed his way back to the fire. "We must act before it's too late. This is our Majesty's hope."

"How many will we have?" Asked the Baron.

Success or failure would depend on their raising an army in the West. "We can muster three hundred foot," Massie said, "and Colonel Penruddock has nearly five hundred cavalrymen."

"It won't be enough." Colonel John Russell shook his head.

"We have support in the west," Sir Edward Villiers said. "People will march to the king's standard, and Colonel Penruddock will liberate Fisherton Anger Gaol."

Sir Richard Willis squared up to Russell. "Nearly one hundred Royalists are held captive at Fisherton, Colonel, many of them veterans of the war."

"The people respect you," the earl said. "They have not forgotten that infamous murder. They will welcome their king with open arms. And our victory will bring *him* to them. For this, you will not be forgotten. May God grant us strength to overcome this tyranny."

The room fell silent as they considered his words. But as Massie observed, their faces told him more than a whole raft of words: they believed. Without their commitment and belief, the uprising would be doomed from the off. With the power of conviction, one victory would lead to another—success begetting success. Surely then the West would rise and Cromwell's support within the fractured army would wane. His Majesty would remember those who remained loyal during the hard years. Even one such as he—a humble Jesuit thrust into the murky world of political intrigue.

Chapter 18 – The Yard

It was a fine morning, but almost too cruel to look upon. The budding of spring was freedom and renewal, but for Daniel, those necessities of life had long faded and he preferred the heavy grey sky for his morning exercise in the yard.

He and Robert followed the others as they paced the small courtyard, dragging their shadowy forms in circles. Robert nodded for Daniel to follow him to a quieter corner of the yard.

"They're soft," Robert whispered. "They talk of the past, of better days."

Daniel nodded. "We're all shadows of the men we once were."

Robert straightened himself to his full height.

"Yes, even you. These men are still dangerous. They're like those old iron swords that become as brittle as flint. Even flint can be sharpened to a point."

"Huh." Robert snorted. "We'll see soon enough."

"There's appetite enough for an uprising. I'm more concerned with what happens after we escape."

"We escape and we hide."

"You hide? I'd like to see that. I just don't want to lead these men to the end of a rope. Not after surviving this hell."

"I'll take my chances. Better to swing on the rope than this slow death."

Daniel cast his gaze over the yard. Sam swayed as he prayed alone. The prisoners had mocked him at first, but he had taken their insults and had given back a warm smile. Even Robert was warming to the Quaker. It was difficult not to like him with his friendly and natural demeanor—small of stature, warm of heart.

Lawrence Bodley bounded into the yard with Cranic and Sterling in tow. Bodley's black scowl meant a punishment would be administered. Men lowered their heads, avoiding his scrutiny. A heavy silence engulfed the yard.

"Tripton!" Bodley screamed.

Frowning, Sam opened his eyes, as the prisoners around him backed away.

Daniel shook his head, and Robert cursed Bodley under his breath.

"Tripton, I warned you about your prayers to the Devil. I'll not have your Devil worshipping in my yard."

Cranic and Sterling sauntered over to Sam and dragged him before Bodley.

"When prisoners don't listen to me," Bodley announced, "they get punished."

Sterling removed Sam's doublet and shoved him forward to face the prisoners.

Sam straightened himself up, and then stiffly froze.

A guard handed a whip to Cranic. He shook the whip free to its full length and steadied himself.

Bodley nodded.

The *crack* echoed over the yard. Sam's jaw clenched, but he never cried out as he swayed on his feet.

Daniel winced with each stroke. He counted ten before Cranic handed the whip to Bodley. Daniel had also suffered the burning of its claws when he had questioned Bodley's order to punish a young corporal for fighting in the yard. The experience had taught him a valuable lesson about Bodley's character. He was as cunning as he was cruel, and his weasel-like appearance belied a man who struck fear into the most hardened of inmates.

"Next time, Tripton, I'll give you twenty licks. And if there's another time, then it'll be forty. And if there's another time after that, well—" Bodley sneered "—it'll not matter anymore."

Bodley left the yard, and they hurried over to Sam. Sam straightened with a grimace as he attempted to retrieve his doublet.

Robert bent down and handed Sam the garment. "It's nothin', Quaker. I've had a few women scratch me worse."

"Please, can you help me with the doublet?"

Daniel slowly lowered it onto him, and Sam wriggled into it.

"It's a good thing you've lost weight," Daniel joked. "It'll sting for a few days, but you'll live."

"I thank you both," Sam said

"Don't trifle with him, Sam. He meant what he said," Daniel

added.

"I believe you, but when the spirit takes you, it takes you." Sam winced as he straightened out the material.

"Well, you tell the spirit to wait until you're in our cell. You hear me?" Robert said.

"I'll tell him."

A shout for Glover announced a visitor for him. A flicker of envy darkened Daniel's features as Glover left the yard.

"Does..." Sam hesitated, "your sister visit?"

"I don't want her to come."

Sam lowered his voice. "And what is her wish?"

The question caught Daniel off guard; it was none of Sam's business anyway. "This is no place for her. She has enough to worry about. And what of your family?"

"I had..." Sam lowered his gaze.

"I'm sorry, Sam. Perhaps another time?"

"Perhaps."

Daniel left Robert and Sam to their conversation. He had stopped Johanna's visits long ago. The long journey from Taunton to Salisbury was too dangerous and expensive. Perhaps Sam was in a similar position? In Fisherton Anger, it was often prayer that gave a man the strength to survive. If, in these dark days, a man were whipped for saying a prayer in the yard, then how much worse would it be for plotting a breakout?

Chapter 19 – The Laborer

At first, Johanna had been able to use timber from the wing of the house that had not been completely gutted in the fire. But she had not been the only one to plunder there, and soon the house was stripped of everything that could be used for fuel.

It had been convenient, but the early morning search for firewood was now the highlight of her day. She set off early and drank in the sounds of the awakening nature. It took thirty minutes to reach the secluded thicket of Hawthorn trees, but the journey was worth it, for here she usually found the best wood.

By the time she had returned home, the heavy dew had soaked her through, and her arms trembled from the weight of the wicker basket. She set the burden down and wiggled her fingers to bring life into them. She examined the wood. It was a little too green and still damp, but it would have to do. She set it outside. The sun would dry it out in a few hours. She then planted herself on a stool to collect her thoughts. She stretched her arms above her head and rolled her shoulders and neck.

A man approached from the lane. His boots scraped along the stones. He wore the heavy overalls of a laborer. She heaved herself up and met him at the gate. "Good morning."

The man removed his cap. "Mornin', Miss. I'll be startin' today, with your permission?"

Johanna shook her head. "Starting today? I don't understand?"

"The name's Russell, Miss. Mr. Leitham sent me."

"Mr. Leitham?" The strange man who had visited her and promised to help Daniel. "I thank you for coming, Mr. Russell, but there's been a misunderstanding. I cannot accept your help." She had expected nothing to come of Mr. Leitham's promises of help, but now his man was here. If she accepted Mr. Leitham's help, gossip would spread rapidly through the town.

He scratched his head while he struggled for a reply. "But it's all been paid for, Miss."

"Truly, I am sorry, but if Mr. Leitham wants to pay for your services then you shall have to work for him."

Russell cast his eye over the field at the front of the little cottage. He shook his head. "Miss, you'll miss the plantin' if the field's not finished soon."

Johanna folded her arms. But Mr. Russell was correct about the field.

"I'll miss out on a good wage. I'm a good worker, Miss."

She cast her eye over the field again, and then back to Mr. Russell's expectant expression. "Very well, I'm sure Mr. Leitham taught you the tactic?"

Mr. Russell averted his eyes.

"I can't promise you anything, but come tomorrow, and we will see how it goes. And tell Mr. Leitham—" her pursed lips broke into a smile "—I am still not indebted to him, and if he wants to waste his money, then so be it. But I thank him nonetheless."

Mr. Russell eyes twinkled as he said his goodbyes, before darting off toward town. They could say what they liked—the gossips weren't going to help her plough and sow. Maybe this strange Mr. Leitham would help Daniel after all? Her mother had often enough told her that help came from the strangest of circumstances. One must simply be open for the possibility.

Chapter 20 – Manfred Hugo's Arrival

They passed over Tome Bridge, and then rode down North Street toward High Street. For Manfred, the bustling scene was much the same as he remembered all those years before. He scrutinized the many inns littering High Street: the Lion Inn, also the Robin Hood and Falcon Inn further up, were still there, along with many others long forgotten. "How many inns will we close before we are finished, Mr. Mabb?"

Mabb's brow furrowed. "As many as need be, Captain."

"The locals view us with suspicion, but they have good reason to. They suffered greatly at the hands of the Royalists."

"Aye, Captain. That they did."

"It will take time to win their trust. But," Manfred continued, "whether they trust us or not, they had better get used to us, for Taunton will lead the way toward England's Renaissance."

His men were thirsty, and Manfred led them to a well by the South Gate, just a stone's throw from the vicarage. The well was still in working order. "Harris, bring up a bucket for the men."

Harris pulled up the bucket, and Manfred's men watered their parched throats.

"Mr. Mabb, find suitable lodgings for the men. Try the Lamb Inn—" he pointed the direction "—over yonder. Their stables should be adequate for our needs. I will find the constable."

Manfred turned off from North Street and made his way toward Taunton Castle. He couldn't think of a better place to begin his search. As he walked past a side lane, a vagrant pushed an old man to the ground. If he hadn't been disturbed by Manfred, the ruffian would have done more. The villain made off before Manfred could challenge him. Manfred knelt down and pulled the beggar to his feet. "Can you make it to the well?"

The old man nodded.

"My name is Commissioner Hugo. My men will help you." The deserving poor would be helped; the idle sturdy beggars would be carted off to the gaol.

The old man thanked him and then hobbled off.

After losing his bearings, Manfred arrived at the constable's office in the castle grounds. The administration building, one of the many outbuildings spread over the outer hold, was old and crumbling. The whitewash had spread thin, revealing the brownish grey stone underneath; the carpets were threadbare and wasted within an inch of their life.

The clerk led Manfred up the stairs and along a corridor with a number of doors. They stopped at the far door, and the clerk announced him. "The constable will see you, Mr. Hugo."

Manfred walked into the sparse office as the constable stood to greet him. He would have been a hard fighting man in his day, but now he was in his late forties, perhaps early fifties. His beard had largely whitened out, leaving a spattering of reddish tint running through it. His puffy, ruddy complexion and the deep lines spread across his forehead gave him a menacing appearance.

"Good morning, Constable."

"I am Constable Vincent Lucas. Rest yourself, Mr. Hugo." He waited until Manfred seated himself before sitting down. "How can I help you?"

"Well," Manfred said, "I hope I can help you, Constable."

The constable leaned forward and cocked his head. "Offers of help are few and far between these days."

"As a Commissioner of the Major-Generals," Manfred sat forward and rested his hands on Lucas' desk, "I will be overseeing this area for some time."

The constable's smile faded. "I'm not sure I understand, Mr. Hugo."

"It's quite simple, Constable. Our godly revolution starts here in Taunton."

The constable folded his arms and leaned back in his chair. "I heard fanciful rumors of some grand schemes, but nothing as foolish as this. Perhaps you'd show me some proof?"

Manfred handed him the seal of his commission. The constable shook his head as he squinted at the document.

"Everything is in order, Mr. Lucas. Commissioners of the Peace are being sent to every county in England as we speak."

The constable's face turned a shade paler.

93

"I will require an office. Are there cells nearby?"

The constable placed the letter on his desk. "Yes, but we have no need of them."

"I will also need a room for…questioning."

"All these things we have at the castle, but I must repeat myself—there is no need for you here in Taunton. This is a peaceful town."

Manfred nodded. "If it is as you say, I will not be here long. I will need full access to your records for the past year."

"Why?"

"It gives me a picture of this town. I will be inspecting inns and taverns for licenses. Any unnecessary inns will be closed. Gambling and cock-fighting dens will also be closed."

The constable banged his heavy fists on the desk. "You haven't got the authority!"

Manfred waved his commission. "I have."

"The Justice of the Peace and the Magistrates are the judicial authority in Taunton."

"Of course, we will work closely with the JP's and Magistrates. They will also cooperate in England's renaissance. I promise you, no stone will be left uncovered, Constable. We all have our part to play in the great purification before the Judgment."

The constable sank back into his chair, shaking his head; his brows furrowed even more. "Godly revolution? Purification? And now Major Generals? Huh, we'll see about that."

"It has already begun. Good day to you, Constable." Manfred nodded and took his leave. He had to expect some resistance from local government. Change, even for the betterment of all, was difficult for some to stomach. He would be patient and give them more time. It would be better for all concerned if they worked together, but woe betide if they set themselves against the new Government. For change was coming, with them or without them.

* * *

Manfred enjoyed how the constable's right eye twitched with his growing resentment. Since he'd ordered Lucas to prepare the Great Hall for a meeting in which to clarify the new government's position, the constable's tick had become ever more noticeable.

94

Still, he deserved nothing less. For it was obvious that new blood was needed in Taunton. Lucas was the embodiment of the town's lethargy—anything for a comfortable life. The town's folk were at last being roused and didn't like it. They would have preferred to sleep on, lukewarm and comfortable, but Manfred would give them what they needed and not what they wanted. If need be, they would be forcibly roused from their slumber and punished if it were that only way. And if the constable resented having to introduce him to the people of Taunton on a blustery evening, then so be it. And if the town was in an uproar, then so be it; for what was it to him, a Commissioner of the Major-Generals, if they resented his great work? Only the wicked could resent the coming of the new godly kingdom. And it was written that the wicked would be smote from God's great earth.

The Great Hall was full to capacity as the last of the stragglers filed in. Rows of benches had been removed to accommodate the mass of people, but still many had to stand at the back. Curiosity, resentment, suspicion, and fear were branded into their faces.

Manfred, with his men standing close in attendance, walked to the table in front of the magistrate's raised platform. He nodded to Lucas, and the constable, with his face as curdled as Mary Steele's buttermilk, raised his hands to quiet the crowd.

The audience fell silent.

"Rumors have been spreading, and a few of you may already know of Cromwell's plans for the Major-Generals. Commissioners are being sent to every county to help prepare for the new government. The Justices of the Peace and the Magistrates are to continue in their role as before. Manfred Hugo—" the constable gestured toward him "—is one of the commissioners for this County."

Manfred stepped forward and drank in the thrill that surged through him.

"Nebuchadnezzar in a dream foretold of the prophecy of the Fifth Kingdom. The Fourth Kingdom was destroyed with the execution of the tyrant, Charles Stuart. Our Lord Protector desires to lead England into a new golden age." Manfred paused as a murmuring swelled through the hall. Some clapped, while others protested. "In great severity, we will act to transform England. Anything promoting wickedness will be crushed. Only then can

England convert Europe and then the world in the true spirit of Christ."

Long speeches were useless, and, anyway, his message would be hammered home over the coming weeks through actions and not words.

Surrounded by his men, Manfred left the stage, and then made his way up the hall as the murmur rose to a racket. The Town Watch broke up a few scuffles, while others gesticulated, debated or just stared in bewilderment.

Manfred smiled: the poor constable's tick must be in a gallop.

* * *

Manfred set down the quill and rubbed his eyes. After wiggling his fingers, he lifted a candle stub, illuminating a mountain of letters stacked upon his desk. During the war, feeding off the fear and excitement, he sometimes needed just a few hours' sleep. Those days were long over, and he let out an almighty yawn.

A knock on the door and Mabb's return galvanized him somewhat. Mabb removed his hat and stroked his thick beard.

"I need more candles, Mr. Mabb."

"Yes, Captain. Everything is quiet with the inns and taverns. A few disputes but nothing serious. No suspicious deaths—mostly childbirth and natural causes. Oh," Mabb continued, "one recent murder in a tavern brawl, and a man was hanged for stealing livestock, but nothing else suspicious, according to the constable."

"Very well, but keep the men searching." Manfred fiddled with a button on his doublet. "Everything relating to deaths, whether suspicious or not, I want to know. Any names relating to Davenport, I want to know immediately."

"Anything else, Captain?"

Manfred ignored the question, and Mabb crept out. From the candle's illumination, spellbinding shadows wove across the wall. He had been disappointed to hear Davenport's parents were dead. But at least the man had a sister, and Manfred would soon get to know her very well.

Chapter 21 – The Scarecrow

Johanna grabbed at the rock, but it wouldn't budge. She knelt down and clawed the earth around it. Breathless, she threw her hands up. It would all be worth it in the end. If ever there was an end.

Mr. Russell appeared by her side, rubbing his hands.

"Now I know why this field had been left untouched, Mr. Russell."

"We're nearly there, Miss Davenport." He knelt and shifted the rock a little to get a better grip. With his hands underneath it, they managed to lift it out, leaving a mighty hole where it once rested. "That's a brute, Miss Davenport."

"One more brute for the pile then, Mr. Russell."

Russell carried the rock to the edge of the field and threw it down with the others.

Johanna surveyed their day's work. "I could never have done this without you, Mr. Russell."

"Aye, I imagine it might have taken a while longer, Miss." Russell pointed over to the left section of the field. "Those cabbages are a hardy crop. I think we'll have no trouble from them. The same with the turnips. But the potatoes…it might've have come too late."

"With luck—"

"Aye." Russell finished her sentence. "With luck, you'll get a decent crop, Miss. Now don't be worryin' about the rougher pasture down yonder. The clover is a good fodder crop. Anyway, when the ground is fertile you might have a cereal crop one day."

"If Daniel could see those furrows," Johanna said with a tinge of melancholy. With his hands clasped behind his back, he would march along the furrows with a frown. But it was just one of his games. She had always played along too; for the frown, she knew, would soon give way to a smile and a warm hug. That had been the old Daniel. Now she wasn't so sure how he would react.

"He'd be right proud of you, Miss."

"He'd never believe it, Mr. Russell."

Russell rubbed the sweat from his brow and stepped back to admire the work.

"Get yourself a drink, Mr. Russell, and I'll see you tomorrow."

"Thank you, Miss. Good day to you."

Johanna lifted herself up. Further down the field, the scarecrow hung lopsided on its cross. She tiptoed across and propped it up, tightening the string to keep it in place. A clatter of hooves came to a halt opposite her. A rider stared. With his somber dress, he had the appearance of a preacher, yet possessed the lean physique of a soldier. He had dark hair and intense eyes. His features were sharp and defined, yet still had a softness to them, which was accentuated by his mouth.

"Good morning," she said.

He removed his hat. "And to you."

Johanna spun back to the scarecrow, pretending to work at it as the heat pervaded her cheeks. A heartbeat later, a furtive glance revealed the rider had already left. He didn't seem to be lost. "More strangers, and I look frightful," she said to the scarecrow. "He probably couldn't tell us apart."

Chapter 22 – Spring Cleaning

Manfred had believed Taunton would be largely sympathetic to Cromwell's plans, especially as they had so valiantly held out for Parliament against the Royalists during the siege of 1645. But as his list of informants grew, so too did it strengthen his conviction that a sizable minority of the town's folk were indifferent to their Lord Protectorate's plans, if not openly sympathetic toward Charles Stuart. "The lukewarm are even more contemptible than the Royalists, Mr. Mabb. At least the Royalists believe in a cause other than filling their stomachs."

"Aye, Captain."

"The word of the Scriptures confronts me: 'I will spew thee out of my mouth.'"

"Aye." Mabb nodded. "They need straight guidance, Captain."

"They allow traitors and the wicked to live amongst them, and yet they complain? When the people realize the coming disruptions are caused by the corruption of the traitors living in their midst, it will be easy to turn neighbor against neighbor."

And now, using information from his newest informant, the Horse & Hound would be investigated first. Manfred ordered two soldiers to stop anyone else from entering while the rest ventured into the dingy inn.

The windows were small, and any light managing to push through the dirty cracked glass didn't disguise the wretchedness of the place. The foul odor of rotting food mingled with the damp added to the squalor. A few patrons slumped against the bar though it was still early. A mangy dog growled at the newcomers, but it hadn't the strength to lift itself off the floor. And then the landlord raised himself off a stool. The red faced, piggish man glared from behind the bar.

Manfred sneered in disgust.

The villain attempted to smile, but with only two twisted black teeth in his maw, the effect was more of an unsettling leer. "What can I get you?"

"Your license."

The landlord's mouth curled up at the side. "I can give you a drink, if you can pay. If you're not here for a drink, then get out."

"You must have missed the meeting?" Manfred asked.

"*Why in hell*—" he stressed each word with a jab of his fat finger "—would I go to some meeting?"

"Give me your license."

The man's face turned a shade of purple. "I'll frig you with it first!"

"Mr. Mabb, throw them all out."

The patrons spluttered as they gulped down their ale.

"Take this man to a cell, and board up the door and windows."

The innkeeper let out a deep roar, and the fool attempted to vault over the bar with a club in his hand. On his second attempt, the landlord managed to swing both legs over, but it was too late. Manfred cracked a stool over his bulbous head before his feet hit the ground. Stunned, and with a deep gash across his crown, the landlord mumbled a few more obscenities before Manfred's men laid into him and dragged him outside. With the demonstration over, the last remaining drinkers slunk out.

With the door and the windows boarded and nailed shut, Manfred stepped back to admire his day's work. A crowd had gathered, but it was the cautious approach of a laborer who caught his eye. Unlike the others, whose curiosity had gotten the better of them, this man had no interest in idle gossip. He was here to see him. The laborer coughed a few times to grab his attention. Manfred regarded him closely. He reeked of fear, but also agitation gnawed at him. "What do you want of me? Speak, man."

The man came closer. Manfred smelled the drink on him.

"Murder." The word hissed from his mouth.

"Murder?" Manfred asked casually, feigning interest.

The man's eyes narrowed. "Not two month past, my boy was murdered."

"What's your name?"

"Bide, sir, Stephen Bide."

"I'm listening."

"She poisoned my boy. Witchcraft." Bide spat on the ground.

"Who poisoned your son?"

Bide steadied himself. "A Royalist," he whispered. "My wife once worked for her: Davenport—Johanna Davenport." He spat again.

Manfred's head whirled. *A sign. At last a sign from the Lord.* "The Davenports. I might have heard the name mentioned."

The shadow of a smile crept across Bide's face. "Traitors—everyone knows them."

"A witch?"

Bide nodded. "A witch, sir. She used potions, and my wife needs justice."

"Your wife or you?"

"Both of us!"

"You must understand, I must be certain of this woman's guilt. I will need to interview your wife alone."

Bide nodded. "Of course, sir."

"Bring her to me after eight tonight."

"God bless you, sir," Bide called as he walked away. "I knew you were a good man."

"After eight, Bide…I will pray for your child."

Mabb pressed closer to Hugo. "Davenport?"

"A name from the past, Mr. Mabb. But at this moment, we have other works to attend."

* * *

The bell rang, and gamecocks were thrown into a pit. Money was still changing hands as the birds circled to attack. The raucous crowd, well-oiled from the ale, cursed and cheered as the birds leapt at each other, tearing with their spurs. Too engrossed with the sport, they hadn't heard Manfred and his soldiers enter the barn. But they did hear the musket shot, which sent the lot of them into the air. Thereafter, only squawks and the flap of wings filled the barn as the two gamecocks continued their gladiatorial combat.

"This," Manfred said to his men, "is the root of all evil."

A hook-nosed man laughed and pointed at the gamecocks still fighting. "They didn't hear you!"

A few of the braver patrons chuckled.

Manfred's men fanned out, waiting for the order to apprehend the fool, but Manfred ignored him and pointed at the gamecocks.

"Who organized this?"

A few of the spectators shuffled aside to reveal two men that were holding money.

"Arrest them."

The startled men made to run, but the dense crowd blocked their escape from the back of the barn. A few patrons, anxious about their money, made for them, but the rogues threw the money into the air, triggering a desperate stampede. Buying themselves a few seconds, they bulled through the crowd, seeking the sanctuary of Manfred's soldiers. Like dogs fighting over the scraps thrown to them, the spectators fought over the coins. Mabb fired another shot, and the crowd ceased their brawl.

Manfred grabbed one of the prisoners. "Gambling, cock-fighting, whoring, drunkenness, lewdness, profanity, and blasphemy are outlawed and will be met with severe punishment." He threw the prisoner to the ground. "Next time, you will all be arrested. Get out of my sight."

The spectators skulked past him with their heads bowed. *So this how it feels?* Of course, there had been a certain satisfaction fighting for Parliament against the tyrannical Charles and his Laudian repression, but nothing compared to this. The thrill of being able to defend and implement the principals of the Godly revolution filled him completely. And now Johanna Davenport would be delivered into his hands. A Royalist? Absolutely. But a witch?

Chapter 23 – Ruth Bide

Ruth Bide was already waiting when Manfred arrived at his quarters. She jumped up from the stool, fidgeting with her hands. Her rounded shoulders and bent back gave her a pitiable appearance.

"Please, rest yourself, Mrs. Bide."

She sat down again and pushed a lock of brown hair back under her bonnet.

Manfred lit another candle before he too sat. "I want to thank you for coming at this late hour."

She was about to speak, but hesitated.

"Feel free to speak your mind, Mrs. Bide."

"I appreciate that, sir, but the truth is I didn't want to come."

Manfred raised his eyebrows. "Mr. Bide came to me."

Ruth shook her head. "I want to forget."

Manfred moved the candle closer to her. He had not expected this, especially after his meeting with Mr. Bide. "Of course, I sympathize with your pain. But until justice is served, how can you ever expect to find peace of mind?"

She lowered her head.

"Do you know why I am here in Taunton?"

"Yes."

"Then you must also know of my responsibilities. I am here to help those who have suffered under the yoke of wickedness." Manfred paused, expecting a response, but the woman bowed her head and stayed silent. "Was it your first child?"

"My third—three I've lost, sir."

"I sympathize. Mr. Bide told me Johanna Davenport was with you. Tell me about her."

"Well…" Ruth lifted her head and stared at the flickering light of the candle. "She was a kind young lady. She dismissed us, but until then she always treated me fair and good, sir."

"She was with you during your labor?"

Ruth shifted uncomfortably in her chair. "She...she tended me."

"How?"

"Herbs—a tonic, she said. It's hard to remember. She said it was for the pain." Ruth shook her head. "Maybe Doris told me later. I don't remember much, sir."

Manfred moved closer to Ruth. His eyes caught hers until she lowered her gaze again. "Have you not considered the concoction may have been responsible for the death of your child?"

Ruth welled up. She dug her nails into her leg.

"Well? Answer me?"

"I trusted her. She knows about delivering, sir, just like her mother. I trusted her."

"You trusted her?" His eyes narrowed. "She is traitor from a family of traitors."

"She was always good to me, sir."

"You took the herbs—"

"Kind to me." Ruth interrupted him.

"Without knowing what they were or how they would affect you and your child? Your baby."

Ruth shook her head. Her hands were clasped together as if in prayer. "She's always been kind to me," she stammered.

"As you say, but I suspect her. I suspect dark motives. Witchcraft." He waited for her to speak, but still she said nothing. "We hang witches, Ruth. You couldn't have known her dark motives."

"I didn't! I loved my boy!" Ruth shrieked.

"If you are innocent, she must be guilty. You had no hand in this evil, Ruth. Did you?"

"No. Nothing." Ruth wept.

"Yes, perhaps she fooled you?"

Ruth opened her eyes and nodded.

"Witches play at being good to hide their evil deeds."

"I know nothing about witches, sir."

Hugo nodded sympathetically. "Of course, how could you? I will have her examined. If witch marks are found, you will testify against her."

"Yes...yes," she stammered, "I will...it's my duty."

"It is, Ruth."

Ruth hurried out. The poor woman had actually believed the Davenport's were good people. Manfred rested his hand under his chin. As a Royalist, the sister was already morally guilty, and who knew what the examination would find? He would need to proceed with caution, for the Devil always preyed upon a man's weaknesses. And a man seldom acknowledged his weaknesses until it was too late.

Chapter 24 – The Examination

The room was bare except for a table and two chairs. A small window, which was barred and too high to reach, let in a few glimmers of light. It was cold and damp in the cellar, but Johanna shivered more from the shock of the morning's events. Fortunately, Mr. Russell had just arrived at the cottage, and had left immediately to tell Mr. Leitham of her arrest.

Her initial shock had soon given way to anger. The soldiers had told her she would be questioned for murder. Incredulous to the whole farce, she had pleaded with them to explain the charges. Obviously a grave mistake had been made. But her cries had fallen on deaf ears.

Johanna paced to keep warm as the hours crept by. Each time footsteps approached, she thought it must be Mr. Leitham to take her home and tell her it had all been a terrible mistake. But once again, their sound faded away, and Johanna was left with her doubts and questions to keep her company. The silence wearied her, and no answer came to her but one: it must be a terrible mistake.

Footsteps approached again. This time someone stopped at the door. Keys rattled in the lock, and Johanna's heart pounded. She gripped the table as the door opened. "Mr. Leitham!" She swayed precariously.

He grasped her hand to steady her. "I'm sorry, but they kept me waiting." He led her to the chair.

Johanna clasped her chest. "I thought myself forsaken."

"The constable and I will see you released. I promise."

"They talked of murder, Mr. Leitham?"

"We are as confused as you. I will go to your brother, for I've heard whispers this new Commissioner, Manfred Hugo, knows Daniel."

A connection with her brother? Johanna raked her memories, searching for the name Hugo. "I do not know the man."

"You will—soon." Mr. Leitham tentatively reached for her hand. "May I?"

She hesitated but then reached out for him. Tears trickled down her cheeks. "I'm sorry, Mr. Leitham. It's just…"

"Please tell me?"

"It's just…it is difficult without Daniel."

"Of course." He took his hand away. "I understand."

"I didn't mean it like that. No gentleman has taken an interest in me before."

"It was thoughtless of me. What I mean is, ensuring your release is paramount. Nothing else matters, Miss Davenport."

If only he knew how often he had been in her thoughts.

Mr. Leitham's face clouded over. "They talk of…witchcraft, Miss Davenport."

"It's not possible." Her mouth quivered as she stared back confounded. A cold sweat came over her. Hundreds of women had been executed over the course of the war. Her father had told her of one trial in Bury St. Edmunds, in which eighteen women were hanged in one day. The story had haunted her ever since.

"They will interrogate and examine you. I may not be present. Hugo may try to trick you. Try to sleep when you can. Stay strong. Heavens, I know it's difficult."

The guard, who had not left the room, grunted and opened the door.

"I must leave, Miss Davenport."

Johanna clasped her hands together. "Witchcraft!"

"Enough! Your time is up!" The guard grabbed Mr. Leitham's shoulder.

Mr. Leitham's jaw tightened, and he spun around to the guard.

Johanna clutched his arm. "Not this way. I will see you soon, my dear Mr. Leitham."

"We will get your release."

The guard shriveled under Mr. Leitham's stare as he hurried past. The door was locked and Johanna was left alone.

Witchcraft? Murder? Was there a connection between Manfred Hugo and her brother? She buried her head in her hands. "Thank you, Lord, for Mr. Leitham," she muttered. *We will get your release.* Her heart skipped a beat. For it wasn't just his words, but the ringing conviction in his voice that inspired the first hope she'd known in too many long years of dismay.

* * *

It had been a disappointing evening for Manfred. The information regarding the Swallow Inn had proved false, and no evidence of gambling had been found on the premises. The strutting owner had even produced a license, leaving Manfred with no option but to leave him be. Before he left, he branded the name of Charles Shank into his memory. Soon enough, Shank would learn from bitter experience not to disappoint him.

"Obviously, Lucas is helping with the licenses," Manfred said to Mabb. "And now the gambling and cock-fighting has moved outside Taunton."

Mabb stood to attention. "There's news, Captain...I..."

Manfred set his quill down. "What is it, Mabb?"

"Sorry, Captain," Mabb said, blinking, "Yates let a lawyer speak to Davenport."

Manfred's mouth curled up. Even the gods themselves fought against stupidity.

"Leitham's his name," Mabb continued, "said he was entitled to see a woman who had not been charged."

"I know who he is, and he's entitled to nothing," Manfred hissed. "The guard was tricked. I want him flogged."

He would have to watch this lawyer carefully. Obviously the fool had developed some infatuation for Davenport. And he had been a Parliament man? Still, why should Manfred waste his time worrying over a commercial lawyer? It would go better for him if the man spent more time worrying over his own prospects. If the good folk of Taunton realized he was fraternizing with a Royalist and a witch, it could irretrievably harm his blossoming business.

"Will I administer the punishment, Captain?"

Manfred was about to agree, but then shook his head. "Garsten. He will do it right. Any other good news, Mr. Mabb?"

The sarcasm was lost on the bearded man. "I moved her to the basement. Posted extra guards on the door. That's her last visitor, Captain."

"Good. I want an end to people meddling in my affairs."

"Aye, Captain."

"I will interview her immediately. And Mr. Mabb, I am a

Commissioner—not a Captain."

"Yes, Commissioner."

"I will entrust you with her observation. Familiars will come to her. Observe and remember. It's our Christian duty to help this poor soul."

"A witch and a Royalist, Commissioner."

"Yes, her brother rots in Fisherton Gaol for his...crimes. He will also experience justice before the end. I would have been content to witness the sister live out her remaining years in poverty, debased and made low, as a warning to other Royalist families, but they lost everything anyway. Still, the charge of murder and witchcraft must be investigated."

* * *

The guard opened the door for Manfred, and Johanna lifted her head from the table. Though her eyes were heavy and strained, he was surprised by how beautiful she was. Also sometimes a sign of witchcraft, he noted.

Her gaze shifted to a heavy rope strung over a beam at the far end of the room. Her clear blue eyes flashed as he sat down opposite her. There was a glimmer of remembrance in her gaze.

"You have been accused of murder and witchcraft," Manfred said, "if you confess it will go better for you. If you do not freely confess—" he nodded toward the rope "—we may have to use...other means. Do you understand?"

"You passed my field the other day. Why?"

The question confused him. He had expected hysterics, or at least protestations of innocence. "Tell me you are a witch."

"I am no witch," she said, enunciating each word.

"You were with Ruth Bide on the night she lost her child?"

"Yes."

"You gave her a tonic during her labor?"

"Yes, to relieve her pain."

Manfred wandered over to the rope. He tested its weight. The two guards who had accompanied him hadn't move from the door. "Miss Davenport, there are two kinds of witches: those who willingly give themselves to Satan, and those who are possessed by a demonic being. I believe the latter applies to you."

"I am not a witch."

"Often the latter—"

"Why did you come by my home?"

"—are not conscious of their actions, so completely have they been taken over. Over time, the demon corrupts ever more of their immortal soul. Papists—"

"Who are you?"

"Papists believe an exorcism can drive the demon—"

"What are you?"

"*Away.*" Hugo paused to collect himself. Some demonic force may well indeed have taken possession of this beautiful creature. "It cannot. The temporal form, the body, must be sacrificed to save the immortal soul."

"Mr. Leitham told me that you know my brother. Who are you?"

Who had Leitham spoken to? Obviously the man still had connections in the army. "I want to save you! Confess to the murder of the child. The child was a sacrifice. Consider your eternal soul."

"You want to murder me. Why?"

"Ruth Bide will testify that you are a witch. If you do not confess, you will be examined for marks. I do not doubt witch signs will be found."

"Why do you want me dead?"

Manfred shook his head. He walked back to her and sat down again. She was beautiful, but she was a Davenport. A black-hearted beauty implicated in murder. A demon would desire to possess that which was beautiful.

He turned to the guards. "She has been corrupted. Tie her up. She is to receive no food or water before noon tomorrow."

* * *

Johanna trembled as the guard inched toward her. Demons and witches—insanity! Where were Mr. Leitham and the constable! She backed up against the wall. The guard grabbed at her petticoat. She pulled away, and fabric ripped off in his hand. He caught her hair and dragged her to the rope. Johanna kicked at him, but the other guard snatched her legs and bound them. With the heavy rope that was hanging over the crossbeam, then then bound her hands together. It burned into her flesh.

They pulled her off the ground. Her arms seemed to tear away from her shoulders. She had vowed not to scream, but her cries filled the room as they tied the other end to the iron ring. Suspended and hanging against her own weight, Joanna cried out for her mother. "Please—please, help me!"

They folded their arms.

Her chest seemed to drop through her ribcage. Her arms shuddered in terrible spasms as the seconds crawled by. She closed her eyes and pictures assaulted her memory: her father disowning Daniel. Their curses and hatred flooded through her.

"Daniel!"

Why had he left her alone?

Even her prayers were silenced in her agonies. The guards' faces became hazy, shifting into brutal demonic forms. Johanna screamed and her head flopped down, resting against her chest. She drifted away, groaning into unconsciousness, but even her dreams were filled with the agony of fire.

The pain brought Johanna back to consciousness, and she found herself on the floor. Her eyes stung from the salt of her dried tears, and with difficulty she lifted her crusted eyelids. "Please…water," she croaked. She would have given anything for water at that moment, the desire filled her completely.

The guards ignored her and told her to stand.

"Water!"

They dragged Johanna to her feet and pain gripped her wasted muscles. Her legs buckled under her, and she crumpled to the floor again. Still bound, they dragged her along the ground. The rough stone scrapped the skin from her legs. They lifted Johanna and laid her flat on the table. Two women watched her from the shadows. A thick bearded man ordered the guards to remove her bindings. The pins and needles stabbed her skin as the blood circulated.

The two guards left the room, and the two women skulked closer.

"Please—please give me water."

No reply came as their petticoats rustled on the floor. The younger, taller woman, who carried a candle, had a softer face, in contrast to the stern, matronly woman, who held authority with the matter at hand.

"If you struggle," the older woman said as she bent over

Johanna, "I will ask Mr. Mabb to hold you."

"Blindfold her," Mabb barked.

"Please...I beg you, water."

The younger woman handed her candle to the other woman, and then tied the blindfold. Johanna's bodice was untied, loosened, and then pulled from her.

Johanna forced memories of happier days into her mind. The dragonflies danced above the pond; she helped her mother stir the curds—the delightful, creamy smell; and laughed as her father scolded her for taking the lambs from their mothers. Daniel, still a young man, invincible and heroic in his uniform, leaving to defend the King.

They removed her stay.

Daniel had returned from Naseby. He was no longer the young hero; for behind him stood the shadow of Death with its bony hands resting upon his dropping shoulders. Only after months did the old Daniel, more or less, come back to her.

They pulled her petticoats off and removed her stockings.

That was the last time Daniel saw their mother alive. Mother died in bed, riddled with the pox.

The women lifted her shift, and cold hands examined her. Every joint and muscle burned, but she would take the rope a thousand times over, rather than this violation, this humiliation. Her body stiffened as they examined every inch of her. The heat from the candle glided over her skin. She imagined their cold, inhuman eyes searching for the Devil's marks. Wax dripped on her, and she gritted her teeth to hold back her screams. Would it never end?

"Lord, have mercy," Johanna muttered over and over as she endured the unendurable.

But, after a long time, they stopped their work.

"Dress yourself," the crone said. Her voice rang as cold as her heart.

Still blindfolded, Johanna fumbled with her clothes, and with a cry of desperation collapsed back down onto the table.

"Help her," the older woman croaked.

After they roughly dressed her, and her nakedness covered, Johanna placed her hands together in thanks. Someone tied her hands and feet again, and then the dying clips of footsteps told her they were leaving.

"You found nothing," Johanna said in a feeble act of defiance as the door creaked open.

"We always find something," she crowed.

The door slammed shut, and Johanna gulped in air. Pain racked through her, but at least she was alone. But then a stool scraped across the floor. She heard ragged, heavy breaths a few feet from her.

Mabb!

Johanna curled up and prayed.

Chapter 25 – The Constable Vincent Lucas

The constable led ten men of the Town Watch to Taunton Castle. Not as many as he wanted, but they would have to do. A few had also declined to follow him, and he couldn't blame them, for to take up arms against Hugo might be misconstrued as taking up arms against the Protectorate. But something had to be done. Johanna's arrest on suspicion of murder was ludicrous enough, but the charge of suspected witchcraft smacked of some personal feud. And Leitham's assertion that Hugo knew Daniel seemed to reinforce that theory. Hugo had spoken of a desire to work with local government. Well, the constable would soon find out if Hugo's honey-dipped words held any truth at all.

George Armitage caught up with Lucas, wheezing from the effort. "I'm not too old yet, Vincent."

The constable shook his hand and pulled the older man along with him.

"Where's the rest?" George asked after counting the crew.

"That'd be you, George."

"What?" Armitage shook his head. "If I'd known that! Anyway, we've bluffed our way out of worse in our time."

"I didn't want this, but when I give an ultimatum…"

"Aye, right enough."

They marched into the inner courtyard and past the Great Hall on the left. Hugo had already vacated the outbuilding in the outer courtyard for the Keep a few days past.

"He's in the Keep now." The constable frowned. "Arrogant prick. He's welcome to the drafty hole."

"Ah," George cleared his throat, "storming a Keep with twelve men?"

A couple of Hugo's men loitered at the Keep's entrance, but made ready as the Watch approached.

Blood pulsed through Lucas's sword arm. The dull pain that had tortured his hands over the past years melted away. About fifteen paces from the entrance, he held his men back and approached the guards alone. Their eyes widened and the white of their knuckles showed as they gripped tight their Mortuary-Swords.

"I will speak with Hugo."

"The commissioner is not here."

The constable stepped closer, and the guards removed their blades.

"Tell the commissioner he will admit me now. Don't make us come in after him."

That wiped the smirk off his face. The guard hoofed into the Keep before promptly returning with his message. "The commissioner will see you, but your men will remain here."

Mabb, with five men towing behind him, passed the constable at the Keep's entrance. The constable noted the trick steps as the guard led him up the winding steps. The soldier knocked, and he followed him in.

Hugo dismissed the guard with a wave. "Why don't you sit, Constable?"

The constable ignored the request. "You have taken Johanna Davenport into custody. On what charge?"

"You know what the charges are, Constable. She was examined, and my suspicions have been vindicated."

The constable bristled. "Insanity. And I'm supposed to take your word on that? I know her, and I know she is no witch. You will release her into my company."

"You're letting your emotions blind you to the reality, Constable. I have a witness. Ruth Bide will testify against her."

He snorted at the idea. "The very same Ruth Bide who was in the employ of Johanna. No, she will not repay the kindness shown to her by making groundless accusations."

"Not groundless," Hugo said with the faintest hint of a smirk playing across his face, "and she will."

"Grief has poisoned her mind."

"The magistrate will listen to the evidence, and a trial will be called."

"Huh, we shall see. But until Hart arrives, you will release

115

Johanna into my custody. Or I will take her by force."

"The Major-Generals control—"

"That's debatable!" The constable flared up. "Run along to your Major-Generals and whine like the dog you are! Until then, release her to me!"

Hugo's nostrils flared, and he banged the desk. The constable readied himself for an attack as Hugo leapt from his chair. But then Hugo's fists relaxed, and he sat down again.

"As you wish, Constable. Take her, but a trial will be called."

The constable stormed out, barely leaving the door on its hinges. His head lowered and jutting forward, he bulled down the steps. "Not so old yet." He snorted to himself.

Chapter 26 – Daniel's Visitor

In his four years at Fisherton Anger, Daniel had received a handful of visitors. Only immediate family was permitted to call, and then only after receiving formal permission from the local Justice of the Peace. Other than that, visitors were allowed to visit a prisoner at the discretion of the captain in charge.

After his capture, Johanna had come, but Daniel had pleaded with her not to make the dangerous and expensive journey. What little money remained must be saved to safeguard the remainder of their property. He had kept to himself the depression that hung heavy upon him for days after her visits. The joy of seeing her held a price, indeed: the agonizing reminder of freedom, which might never be his again. And to be confined, while Johanna struggled alone, had almost been too much to bear. He had also suggested, as delicately as possible, that she should find a gentleman with whom she could share her life. Johanna had rubbished the idea, incredulous as to why any gentleman would have an interest in a penniless Royalist.

The guard ushered Daniel into the visitor's room, and an unknown gentleman rose to meet him.

"Mr. Davenport, I am Richard Leitham, a lawyer from Taunton."

"I cannot afford a lawyer, Mr. Leitham." Daniel clutched at his rags.

"Can we not be alone?" Leitham asked the guard.

The guard grunted without moving.

"I am here representing the interests of your sister, Mr. Davenport."

"What do you mean?"

"Excuse me, but…your sister is in trouble."

The constable would have informed him if there had been problems. "Explain yourself," Daniel snapped.

"A Commissioner has her—"

"Has her?"

"Arrested."

Daniel's jaw dropped. "The constable?"

"No, not him, Mr. Davenport. Manfred Hugo."

Daniel had to sit. "Hugo?" He muttered to himself. The memories, the nightmare flooded back: the shock of John facing him at Worcester, the ragged pain fossilized into his childhood friend's face as he strained to straighten his twisted back, the terror before the walls, the shot and John's lifeless body. "Manfred Hugo? I don't understand?"

Leitham leaned in closer to Daniel. "Murder and witchcraft," he whispered.

"Impossible!" Daniel leapt from his chair, and the guard tensed.

Mr. Leitham lifted his hands to calm the situation. "The constable will secure her release, but this may be temporary. I need to know more about this man and what he wants."

Daniel rubbed his neck. John had one younger brother. "Manfred Hugo? John's younger brother..."

"Yes?"

"John was an old friend. I have no idea what Hugo would want with me or Johanna?"

"Think—"

The door opened, and Lawrence Bodley thundered in with more guards. "Take the prisoner back." Bodley snarled at Leitham. "And you can get out."

"I am representing this man, and I have permission from your Captain."

"Not anymore."

"Help her, Leitham!"

"I give you my word."

They bundled Daniel out of the room. His head spun from the news. Manfred Hugo? John's brother? Vague recollections came to him as they pushed him into the cell.

"What is it, Daniel?" Robert asked

"It's Johanna—I have to get out of here."

"It's about time!"

"Where is Sam?"

"Good question. Sure as hell, I don't know."

Chapter 27 – The Eighth of March, 1655

Rochester emptied his glass. He winced as the wine's sour aftertaste stung his taste buds. He had few regrets in life, but not bringing more of his favorite vintage from the continent was fast becoming one. Massie, now changing after his journey, should have arrived the day before, and Rochester had fretted over his safety. Without Massie's spies and informants, the uprising would be doomed to fail. The Jesuit had spun the web, and only he knew how to keep everything together.

Rochester's servant knocked and ushered the priest in.

"Bring Mr. Massie a glass."

Massie bowed. "Good evening, my lord."

"I am glad to see you."

"A patrol had decided to quarter in Newark. I thought it prudent to wait." The servant filled their glasses. "The wine is satisfactory?"

Rochester swirled the wine in his glass. "It is vile. I believe it may have been poisoned." He winked.

Massie tasted the wine and nodded in agreement. "I have heard the sweet wine is most dangerous, my lord."

"Too true." Rochester set his glass down, and his face hardened. "I have heard the Tower of London and other garrisons have been strengthened. Cromwell knows."

"Cromwell knows nothing. It is precautionary. London was never an option anyway." Massie swept his hand across an imaginary map of England. "The West counties and the North will follow us, my lord."

"The King has moved to Middelburg in preparation. There are rumors Fairfax is unhappy." Rochester played with the rim of his glass. "I am certain after York and Newcastle have declared their support, Fairfax will follow." Rochester raised his glass. "To the eighth."

"And may God grant Charles the victory."

Chapter 28 – The Plot

Daniel's gaze flitted over the yard. Bodley conversed with his guards, seemingly unconcerned with the inmates around him. But one had to watch closely to detect his surreptitious glances. If he observed Daniel talking with Pierce, his suspicious nature would question it. In any case, it couldn't be helped. The yard wasn't large enough for all the prisoners to exercise together, so it would be days before he got the chance to speak with Lieutenant Pierce again.

As they circled the yard, Daniel was the first to veer off toward Pierce, matching his pace, with Robert joining them moments later. They kept on the move.

"If we can get to the armory," Daniel muttered, "it's possible."

Pierce slowed his pace. "Even if we make it there—" he glanced over at the guards "—we won't make it to the cells."

"It's happening," Robert said, though a little louder than intended, "with or without you."

Pierce's reply was interrupted by Bodley's yell.

The villain gripped Sam's throat. Sam broke free of him, but then fell in a heap after Bodley clubbed him on the side of the head.

Daniel's heart sank as the guards laid into the unconscious man. "They'll kill him."

"What about Johanna?" Robert asked.

But Daniel had already sprinted off. He rammed into Bodley, throwing him against the wall.

Robert joined the fray and tackled the other three guards. In a matter of seconds, ten guards were pummeling them with clubs. Daniel and Robert groaned from the battering, while blood trickled from Sam's head.

Bodley creaked to his feet. He pointed at Daniel. "Hold the bastard up!"

Two guards lifted him, and Cranic pulled Daniel's head up by the hair. Bodley spat in his face and then slammed his knee into his stomach.

"Hold him up!" Bodley moved closer and hissed into Daniel's ear. "Sooner or later, I'll open your throat." Bodley stepped back. "Mr. Cranic, I want them in the lower cells."

"You stood there and watched! Watched, you cowards!" Robert bellowed at the prisoners.

And these were the men who had wanted to break out of Fisherton Anger? Daniel shook his head.

Torch in hand, and with six other guards dragging the three of them, Cranic chuckled as he led the way to the lower cells. The flame rippled in the cold draft. "I'll give you a month before the rats have your innards."

They shoved Daniel into his own cell. The darkness thick about him cradled a heinous rotting smell.

Cranic brought the torch up to his face. "We like to give the most important guests their own cells." He laughed as the door slammed shut.

In the pitch black, the rats squeaked as they scattered across the cell. He sat down against the wall and massaged his bruises. Johanna needed him, and now he was powerless to help her. He shouldn't have interfered, but he couldn't let them beat a man to death.

The chatter of the guards grew fainter, and then the main door leading to the lower cells closed.

"That's done it now," Daniel groaned. "And Sam?"

"He's alive—I hear him moaning in the next cell. And I'm fine, thanks for asking."

"What are we going to do, Robert?"

"Survive. Survive as long as we can."

Chapter 29 – Doctor's Orders

A rich tapestry hung from the center wall. The comfortable four-poster bed reminded Johanna of better days when life was serene and sheltered in her parent's home—a lifetime ago. But she was also grateful beyond all measure. The constable had released her from that loathsome man, and Mr. Leitham had taken her into his home while she recovered from the ordeal. Her tears—both of joy and the deepest anxiety—reflected the pains of both body and soul after the terror of the interrogation. She needed to rest and recover, but the specter of Manfred Hugo, so ruthless and cold, stalked her nightmares.

The maid entered and announced the arrival of Dr. Banister.

"Dr. Banister?" Johanna arched her eyebrows.

The maid stepped aside, and an aged man shuffled in.

"Dr. Banister!" Johanna beamed. "So retirement doesn't suit you?"

Banister cupped his hand over his ear. "Suits me fine, Johanna, but perhaps not so, Mildred."

"I was expecting Dr. Jenner."

"Jenner refused to come, my dear, so you're stuck with this old crow." Banister laughed, banging his walking stick against the floor."

"I am happy then."

"Jenner's a coward, and I'm not going to be intimidated by this *Commissioner*."

The venerable man sat himself on the edge of the bed while the maid stood ready to assist. His wrinkled hand, almost transparent, took hers. "I can help with the physical symptoms, Johanna, but if you need someone to speak to, I'm here for that also."

"I can't sleep," Johanna sighed. "The pain has nearly gone, but I can't pull *him* out of my mind, my nightmares."

"You're among good people now, my dear. Everything fades

with time. And it won't hurt to have a glass of wine in the evening."

"I'm grateful for the constable and Mr. Leitham."

"Mr. Leitham?"

Johanna's cheeks flushed, and Bannister's face lit up with a grin.

"Now that's a better color."

"He's a fine gentleman."

"Now, let me feel your forehead. Clammy. You have a fever coming, Johanna. It is not yet serious, but you need complete rest." He turned to the maid. "Another blanket, my dear."

The maid opened a fine oak chest underneath the window, took out a blanket, and laid it over Johanna. Banister opened a leather satchel and took out a silver case. From inside, he removed a thumb lancet. "I will make an incision at the vein above your thumb."

Johanna breathed in. Bloodletting was easier when observing it being administered to a patient, rather than oneself.

He held the lancet like a quill and delicately made an incision. The spurting blood was caught and measured in a bowl.

When enough blood had been taken, the maid staunched the flow, and Johanna rested back.

Banister tied the bandage tight. "Now, confine your diet to vegetables—a little white meat is permissible, but remember complete rest."

"Perhaps I might return home tomorrow?"

"Absolutely not. Complete rest, Johanna," he scolded. "If you leave this bed before the weekend, I'll have the constable drag you back."

"Well…only for you." She winked.

"You're a good patient, Johanna Davenport. Now, a certain Mr. Leitham has recently arrived and asked if you are well enough for a visit."

Johanna nodded and tried very hard to disguise her smile. "I would like to thank him for his kindness."

"Of course you would. I told him to get some rest. Maybe he will listen to you. I will call tomorrow."

"I will get better, Dr. Banister."

"I know!"

A moment later, there came a knock on the door, and Mr. Leitham entered, dragging his feet.

The maid removed the bucket to bring fresh water.

"First Mr. Russell, and now a maid. I don't know what to say, Mr. Leitham."

"Please, regard my home as your own."

"But—"

"But nothing," Mr. Leitham said playfully, "It is better to give than to receive, Johanna Davenport. Anyway, it's doctor's orders."

"I must learn to accept each kindness with more grace. I…"

"I know, Miss Davenport. Say no more."

"Is there news from my brother?" Johanna gripped the bed sheets.

Mr. Leitham lifted the chair by the writing desk and sat down beside the bed. "I met him—"

"Yes?" Johanna beamed.

"Briefly. Daniel told me of his childhood friend, John Hugo, but remembered little of his brother. He could think nothing of why this man would hold a vendetta against your family, other than him being a Parliament man."

"And how was Daniel?"

"Worried about his sister, of course, but otherwise his health seems to be in order."

"And his release?"

"I promise I will do all I can. But first, at Daniel's own request, we must consider your safety. It has not ended, Miss Davenport."

Yes, she had seen it in Hugo's eyes. He would be relentless. "I fear you're right."

"Now, I must leave. The magistrate will arrive soon, and I must meet with the constable. I will not be home until late, but I will check with Rachel to insure everything is well."

The maid returned with the fresh water, and Mr. Leitham helped carry it to the bed. Afterward, he stopped at the door and left her with one last smile.

She lay into the soft pillow, and the maid dabbed her forehead. She'd forgotten to relay Dr. Banister's advice to rest and recover. His eyes had looked so heavy. She hadn't even thanked him for warning Daniel. She would make up for her neglect, for he was indeed a dear man.

It has not ended, Miss Davenport. She closed her eyes and tried to dream of a future that had not already been written in her own mind.

Chapter 30 – The Magistrate Arrives

Manfred left immediately when informed of the magistrate's arrival. He would not let the constable make the first move with an emotional gambit, lacking the authority of a dispassionate view of the facts.

He strode into the Great Hall, where Hart leafed through a bundle of documents at the far end of the room.

"Good morning, Magistrate."

Hart glanced up and removed the spectacles that were perched on the end of his nose.

"Magistrate, I am Manfred Hugo, Commissioner of the Peace for Taunton."

"They didn't waste time, did they?" Hart asked with a pinched expression.

"There is work to do, Magistrate."

Hart waved the handful of documents. "That I know, Mr. Hugo. Now, what do you want of me?"

"Your attention, Magistrate."

Hart glared at Manfred, but he set the documents and his spectacles down on the steps that led up to the magistrate's chair.

"To bring to your attention a case of witchcraft. The woman was in my custody but is now free. The constable threatened me with his rabble because he knows the woman."

"Would you prefer to sit in my office, Commissioner?" Hart asked.

"Very kind, Magistrate, but I won't take up much of your time."

"Ah, well now, I'm sure he had his reasons."

"Magistrate, a child is dead. It was out of courtesy for you and your office that I didn't go straight to Colonel Boteler." Manfred paused to let the words sink in. "If local authority does not cooperate with the Commission, I can promise you a thorough investigation into why."

Hart grimaced. "What is the accused's name?"

"Irrelevant."

"What is her name, Commissioner?"

"Johanna Davenport."

"Then I am not surprised the constable demanded her release."

Had everyone in Taunton been seduced by this woman? "I have told you of my suspicions. Will you examine her or not? I would rather not bother the Colonel."

Hart stood and straightened his doublet. "I will examine her tomorrow morning, but until then she is free." He stomped off, leaving his spectacles resting on the documents.

Manfred examined the spectacles. He wiped the lenses with his kerchief and set them back down. Hart would not risk his position. And now Johanna was staying with that lawyer—at least for the moment. First Lucas and now Leitham. Two weaklings seduced by a succubus. They were playing a dangerous game with her, but Manfred would not let himself be tempted by her false, rotten beauty.

* * *

Johanna had hoped against hope that her ordeal had passed. Still, the last few days at Mr. Leitham's home had fortified her, and she scolded herself when dark thoughts crowded her into depression. She must remain optimistic when her dear friends were working so hard on her behalf.

She wrapped up well for the short walk. A heavy scarf almost covered her ashen face. She passed through the market, as though in a dream, and the calls of the sellers and the beggars left no impression.

The constable walked alongside her. Since receiving the magistrate's order for her examination a few hours past, his humor had little improved. With his face still a shade of purple, he thundered beside her, sneering at everyone who dared get in his way.

"It's a formality, Johanna. The letter of the law must be applied with Hugo circling like a hawk. But a formality, and then you'll be left in peace."

Mr. Leitham had already prepared her for the magistrate's questions and had explained the procedure in detail. "The constable's correct," Mr. Leitham nodded. "The truth of your words will be enough to convince Hart of your innocence."

"Hugo will never let go of me."

"He'll have no other recourse after the magistrate establishes your innocence. It will end, Johanna."

Ushered into the empty hall, their footsteps echoed through the cathedral-like space until they reached an office at the back. Hart rose when they entered and asked them to sit opposite Hugo and Mabb.

Johanna glanced over at Hugo, but he seemed oblivious to her presence.

The magistrate cleared his throat. "I am Sir Matthew Hart. I am the Chief Magistrate for this county. I will hear both parties, and then forward your statements to the Jury. After presenting your statements, a decision will then be made as to whether the evidence warrants a trial against the accused. This is neither the time nor the place for arguments. Is that clear?" The magistrate scribbled a few notes. "Commissioner Hugo, you may proceed with your statement."

Johanna folded her arms. What lies would spew from his mouth this time?

Hugo nodded. "Thank you, Magistrate. It will be clear from the evidence presented that Johanna Davenport, being a witch, has committed murder against an innocent child."

Hart glanced up from his notes. "Go on."

"The Commission has the testimony of Mrs. Ruth Bide—" Manfred glanced at Johanna "—whose newborn was murdered by this witch. My assistants have also examined her and found witch-marks."

We always find something. The crone's mocking words thudded into Johanna's memory.

"Ludicrous!" Mr. Leitham said.

Hart glared at Leitham. "Sir, would you have me remove you?"

"That will not be necessary, Magistrate."

"Continue, Mr. Hugo."

"She used tonics with the pretense of healing, when, in fact, they were a draught of poison."

"And you have no more witnesses?" The magistrate asked as

128

he peered up from his notes.

"Yes…my assistant, Edward Mabb, has also observed her familiars."

"And you have no more witnesses?" The magistrate asked.

"I have no need of them, Magistrate. The evidence is overwhelming."

Hart raised his eyebrows at the remark before finishing his notes. "Miss Davenport, have you anything to say in your defense?"

"Magistrate, I am not, and have never confessed to being a witch." Johanna removed a handkerchief and coughed into it. "He talks of marks? Do we not all have marks? I attend my local parish, and I am well known in Taunton. I have many friends here." Johanna paused until Hart finished his notes. "I am not a witch, and I did everything possible to help Ruth Bide through her difficult labor. She asked for my help, and I never imposed myself, Magistrate."

The magistrate glanced up at Hugo, who sat as composed as ever. "And will these friends come forward?" He asked Johanna.

"Magistrate," Mr. Leitham spoke, "I believe many will come forward to speak of Miss Davenport's good character."

The constable nodded and challenged Hugo with his stare.

The magistrate continued to write, and then addressed Johanna. "You will be told of the outcome tomorrow. Until then, Miss Davenport, you will be placed under the care of the constable."

The constable, who had been perched on the edge of the chair hitherto, beamed as he leaned back.

Even Johanna dared to embrace the wave of optimism from Hart's ruling. Mr. Leitham nodded encouragingly, and Johanna clasped his hand. She had once told him to hope for nothing but her gratitude. With each passing day, her pronouncement became more perilously insubstantial.

"Magistrate." Manfred gestured toward Lucas. "The constable is a friend of Miss Davenport's."

"I am aware of that, Mr. Hugo. We are finished. Good day."

* * *

Another restless night left Johanna exhausted. Mr. Leitham had suggested she remain in bed, but she was determined to hear the magistrate's verdict on her feet. Mr. Leitham had remained with her, while the constable had left to receive Hart's verdict.

The euphoria of the previous day had also slipped away. Though she had been grateful and encouraged by Hart's decision to let her remain under the care of the constable, she could not, even with her friends' assurances, remove the nagging feeling fate's judgment had already been determined.

Mr. Leitham placed a few more logs on the fire, and the smoke drifted up the chimney. "Can I get you something to eat?" he asked.

"I cannot eat, but thank you."

"Be of good heart! It cannot be other than good news after yesterday."

"If he had tortured me until my end, Mr. Leitham, I would never have confessed to witchcraft. But…perhaps I am responsible for the child's death?"

"I do not believe that, Miss Davenport."

"I gave Ruth the tincture, and I can never know what would have happened if I had not been there."

Mr. Leitham wrapped the blanket around her and knelt down beside her. "I know you are innocent. It does not matter what you say, Miss Davenport, I feel it in my very bones."

"Why then, do I feel so forsaken and alone? Especially when I am surrounded with such goodness?"

"It is shock. It will take time." Mr. Leitham took her hand. "We…I will not forsake you."

He kissed her hand, and she pressed against him.

The constable returned in the late afternoon. He removed his overcoat and slumped down. Mr. Leitham perched on the edge of his chair, awaiting the constable's news.

The constable hesitated.

"I know what you will say," Johanna said. "Please, I am ready."

"It cannot be possible," Mr. Leitham groaned.

It has not ended. Indeed, the restless night, the nagging feeling that she had been unable to shake, had been the harbinger of the ill-gotten news. "He has influential friends." The constable fiddled with the buttons on his doublet. "But…the people will not stand for it."

The people will not stand for it...The constable was a dear friend, but his heart had not been in those words.

"We could take you away, Johanna," Mr. Leitham suggested

"We can leave tonight?" The constable almost pleaded with her.

"You are my dear friends, but I will not be responsible for your deaths. Hugo will use any excuse to hurt you. Believe me."

Mr. Leitham paced to the window, and the constable rubbed his forehead.

"To run away would be an admission of guilt. I will not do it." Johanna sat up straight in the chair. "I will not leave my home for anyone."

"Miss Davenport," Mr. Leitham said, "I would agree with you, but I am no longer certain of a fair trial."

"I cannot leave Taunton and our property behind. I will not be a fugitive. I appreciate your concern, but you also spoke of friends coming forward, of support?"

"I did, and I aim to see it through."

"Trial!" The constable spat the words out. "But you are correct, Johanna. You are innocent, and it will be proven before all."

"When?" Leitham asked.

"Four days hence, at noon."

She had almost wished it could be tomorrow. Why did Hugo hate her? She would ask him directly, but why would he tell her when he knew how the mystery tormented her so.

* * *

Richard Leitham excused himself, muttering as he left. Why acquiesce so easily? Of course, in her present condition, it would have been foolhardy to flee. It had to be her decision, but if he could have stolen her away from it all, he would have done so in a heartbeat.

In his haste, he'd forgotten to bring his overcoat, and a bracing wind stung his face. He rubbed his hands and hurried on to warm himself. The inns that dotted High Street invited him inside as the sun set. The strains of the fiddle and flute drifted from the crowded Swan Inn.

131

He pushed inside. The cacophony, together with the rich flavors of tobacco, circled the air about him. An atmosphere of inebriated revelry permeated the packed inn. A drunkard fondled a woman on the stairs, lifting her petticoat for the leering gawkers. Her inane laughter barely registered above the roars and shouts of the drinkers. Groups of men gathered around the card tables in the corner. The lively music was accompanied by the spectacle of a cripple's jig. Doubled over with laughter, the revelers proceeded to throw coppers at the man when he attempted to bow, hampered as he was with his pronounced hunchback.

Richard wove around the tables and ordered ale from a flustered barmaid. He drank the atmosphere in, and then ordered another ale, and then a third. The drink flushed his cheeks, and he glowered at the wastrels. Well oiled, he picked up a serving tray from the edge of the bar and waited until the musicians had ended their jig. He cracked the tray against the bar, spraying fragments of woods across the nearest tables. Startled patrons gaped in astonishment.

"In four days, Johanna Davenport, whom many of you know, and who is respected in this town, will be tried for witchcraft. She is innocent and needs your support."

From a card table at the back, a group of men stood. They were Hugo's men, their cold stares challenging him.

"Johanna Davenport needs you now."

Hugo's men scowled at the patrons.

"Who will defend her character?" Richard pressed on. "Who will help Johanna Davenport?"

The hunchback, with great difficulty, lifted himself onto a stool. Standing to his full height, he seemed little more than four feet tall. He cleared his throat, and the sobering patrons hushed for his words. But instead of speaking, he squeezed his misshapen hand into a pocket and scavenged out a few coppers. The hunchback proceeded to fling them at Richard, sending the drinkers into hysterics. Hugo's men returned to their cards.

Richard slapped his money onto the bar and trudged out into the cold. Let them have Hugo. They deserve nothing more.

Chapter 31 – Salisbury

In the perpetual darkness of the lower cells, sleep alone offered a window to life. While asleep, Daniel's tormenting thoughts were silenced for a time, and it was better to live in dreams or nightmares than to stare awake into the darkness.

Yes, Daniel yearned for sleep, but the rats had other ideas.

In the lower cells, one lived in a fitful slumber. They waited until he fell asleep before feasting on him. That's how it had been hitherto, but now the bolder rats took their chance even when he was awake. But he thanked them as he scratched his scabs. For they kept him alive, kept him moving and alert. Only when he gave up the fight, only then would be over for him.

The other cells were just as quiet. Each man trapped in his own nightmares. Even the explosion from outside was initially ignored. Daniel laughed as another deep rumble reverberated through lower cells, for reality had already faded in the underworld of darkness.

"Explosion?" Robert croaked.

Daniel crawled over to the wall and lifted himself to his feet. "Shots?" Had Pierce finally grown a pair?

Then the heavy door to the lower cells creaked open and footsteps could be heard descending the steps. He steadied himself, catching every sound beyond the cell. A flame flickered through the grill, and keys rattled in the lock. The door opened, and Daniel squinted into the light. Bodley's sneering face emerged. In his other hand, he trained a pistol on Daniel.

"Back against the wall!"

Daniel shuffled back. The barking of orders and musket shots rang from above. "I heard an explosion."

"Royalists." Bodley's laugh sounded like a threat. "But nobody's rescuing you."

"Let us go, and I'll make sure you're treated fair."

"Aye, strung up. I don't think so."

"Why me?" Daniel spat back.

"Money." Bodley sneered. "But the truth is I'd murder you for free." He squeezed the trigger and sparked the frizzen, but there was no explosion, no shot.

"Damp powder!"

Bodley reached for his dagger, but Daniel lunged at him and wrestled him to the ground. The torch skidded across the cell. Daniel rammed his head into Bodley's face, and the jailer yelped in pain. Daniel pinned Bodley's right arm, and clawed at his face with his free hand. With his weaker arm, Bodley jabbed Daniel and threw him off. He lunged his dagger at Daniel's gut.

Still lying prone, Daniel grabbed the blade and screamed as the edge sliced his hand. He let go, and Bodley fell forward with his momentum. Both men panted as they lifted themselves up.

Daniel retreated a step. The still burning torch lay at his feet. Bodley bundled forward, and Daniel kicked the torch at him. Bodley swatted it away and lunged again with his dagger. Daniel's eyes were better adjusted to the gloom, and he pivoted to avoid Bodley's thrust. The dagger punctured the wall.

Daniel's uppercut lifted Bodley off the ground, and he hit the floor. Bodley groped for the dagger, but Daniel stomped on his hand, and the weapon dropped. Bodley's curses were drowned out by the noise of the fighting above them.

Daniel kicked at Bodley's head, but Bodley rolled away, and the blow glanced off him. As Bodley attempted to rise, Daniel's kick connected to the back of his skull. Bodley slumped and then turned onto his back gasping. Before he could raise his hands in defense, Daniel stomped down on his chest. With a sickening crack, Bodley's ribs gave way beneath the violence of the blow. Bodley's back arched, but Daniel stomped down again.

Bodley's wheezing quieted, and then his life ended with a drawn out rattle.

Gasping, Daniel fell back against the wall. He wanted to lie down, but the shouts of Robert and Sam pushed him to his feet again. He checked Bodley's body and pocketed a few coins. If Bodley would have killed him for free, Daniel wasn't going to return the favor. He stumbled to the door and removed the keys.

After releasing Robert and Sam, Daniel glanced back to the steps, half expecting Shaw's men to charge down after them.

Obviously, they still had their hands full. But then light flooded into the darkness as the door opened. Hurried footsteps slapped down the steps. "Mr. Bodley?"

"The rats are already picking at the scrawny bastard," Robert said, emerging from the shadows of his cell.

Daniel and Sam followed.

Cranic glanced back the way he'd come.

"Royalists," Daniel said, "I'll make sure you get what you deserve."

With a yell, Cranic sprinted forward. Robert matched him for speed and size, and the two collided. They locked in a furious tangle, and Robert drove Cranic back. Cranic clawed at him, but Robert grabbed between his legs, and the guard howled. Cranic punched and kicked. Robert took the punishment and grappled him to the floor. Cranic tried to throw Robert off, but Robert pressed his weight down on the tiring man. He smashed his forearm into his face.

Robert slid his forearm under Cranic's chin and pressed down on his throat. He arched his head back to avoid Cranic's gouges. He crushed down on Cranic's windpipe. Cranic's eyes bulged as his face turned blue. He flopped back, and Robert released his pressure. Cranic was dead. He stood over his enemy and let out a guttural roar.

"Thank the Lord you're on our side," Daniel said to Robert, who was still shaking from the fight.

The firing continued as they crept up the steps. It was just the three of them and Michael Brown—the two left behind were too weak to leave their cells. Daniel's hand throbbed and was slick with blood. He wiped it on the rough grey stone, leaving a red streak. The stone wall was cleaner than his rags. With the door ajar, they peeked over the last step. Ten guards, about twenty paces in front of them, took cover behind a wall. Two men were busy priming matchlock muskets. They frantically worked their scouring sticks and then passed on the loaded weapons. Their rate of fire was enough to keep the Royalists pinned down.

"We can rush them," Robert whispered.

Daniel held up Bodley's dagger. "We need weapons."

"To hell with weapons," Robert snarled.

Before Daniel could voice his protests, Robert charged into

the fray. There was no time for fear; they just followed the big man.

Taking them by surprise, Robert crushed two guards against the wall. Hampered by the close range fighting a guard shot himself in the leg as he engaged the prisoners. Two panicked and ran. One got a shot off, and Brown hit the ground clutching his thigh. Daniel headed straight for Shaw, who was still on his knees. Using his musket as a club, Shaw swung it around. The strike on Daniel's left hip wasn't enough to break his stride, and his blade dug deep into Shaw's shoulder. Shaw, his teeth grated in agony, grabbed for the dagger, but Daniel already held it to his throat.

"Enough, Captain!"

"Stop! Throw your weapons down," Shaw ordered.

The guards threw up their arms, and the Royalists surrounded them.

It wasn't long before the prisoners had been released. They changed their rags for new uniforms. The guards, who had been stripped of everything useful, huddled together in the yard. Weapons were laid out on the ground and checked. Four bodies, not yet covered, were laid out at the far end of the yard. The Royalist officer in command—a tall man with fair shoulder-length hair in the Cavalier fashion—approached his sergeant. The colonel pointed to the damaged entrance of the Gaol, and the sergeant bellowed orders for his men to take defensive positions at the entrance. The Royalists jumped to action. This was no rag tag militia but determined, well-trained cavalry. Could it be true that England was in revolt? Had Cromwell lost his grip on Parliament?

Sam carried over a pail of water and set it down in front of Daniel. He poured a trickle over the gash. Daniel winced as the cold nipped at the wound.

"You'll need this seen to," Sam said after examining the injury.

"First, I need to talk to that officer," Daniel said.

The colonel gestured toward the approaching men. "Sergeant, did you release these men?"

"No, Colonel."

The colonel regarded Daniel. "Explain yourself?"

Daniel was about to open his mouth when Robert reacted to the implication. "If it wasn't for us, your men would still be

136

cowering for cover."

The sergeant nodded. "They came from behind." He pointed at Robert. "This one had no weapons."

"Colonel, I am Captain Davenport of the King's Lifeguard, captured at Worcester and—"

"I will need good men like you, Captain."

Before Daniel could reply, a scout wrested the Colonel's attention. Both horse and man were close to collapse. The scout handed a letter over. "Urgent, from the Earl of Rochester, Colonel Penruddock."

Penruddock broke the seal, and his face sagged.

"Colonel, I cannot march with you. I have a grave personal matter to attend to."

Penruddock rifled through the letter. He met Daniel's gaze and shook his head. "We need every man we can get. I'm sorry, Captain."

"Not good enough!" Daniel snapped.

"I cannot force you to fight, but if you refuse, you will remain here behind bars."

"I was there as the king escaped the city. I stayed behind and nearly lost my life. Four years I've rotted in this place. And now my sister needs me."

"Captain, you have me in a quandary. If I let every man go who needs to save a sister, then I will have no army, but…" Penruddock glanced at Sam. "I have no need for a Quaker." He addressed Robert. "I will let them leave, if you fight for your king?"

Daniel remained impassive as Robert shook his head. He knew Robert was torn, but he would not influence his decision.

"Agreed," Robert said, casting his eyes down.

"Sergeant, get this man something to eat."

Robert followed the sergeant.

"Captain, walk with me."

Daniel followed the colonel to a quieter part of the yard.

"The rebellion has stalled in the North. If I let you leave, you must do something for me. Carry this letter to the Earl of Rochester after you have finished with your own business. I will tell you where his safe house is, but you must reach him before the twentieth. Tell him of our success here. Tell the earl we march west. After you have fulfilled your obligations to me, you are free to follow the earl or go on your own way. Give me your word, Captain."

The twentieth wouldn't give him much time. But it would be stupid not to take the opportunity of safe passage. "I give you my word. I will deliver the letter to the earl after I've helped my sister. I promise."

Penruddock eyed Daniel's hand. "Go to the surgeon first, and then get what you need from the Quartermaster. Then return for the letter—I will add my seal to it."

Penruddock ambled over to his officers, and Robert returned with a fist of Dyett bread. They hadn't eaten in days, and they tore into the bread.

Robert winked at Sam, who had barely come up for air. "I hear they have Cockle bread, Sam." He playfully punched Sam on the arm. "If you're interested?"

"Nev—" Sam managed to swallow the lump wedged in his throat. "Never."

Daniel patted Sam on the back. "You'll never corrupt our Quaker, Robert White."

"Not with privy bread." Sam frowned.

"Sam." Daniel regarded the Quaker thoughtfully. "This is my fight. From my heart, I hold you to nothing."

"I'm with you. Even if you hadn't saved my life, I'd still help you."

Robert grasped Sam's hand. "Look after him, Quaker. You might have to pull a sword."

"I'll not let him out of my sight. And you stay away from the wine and women."

Daniel clasped Robert. "Thank you. It's only because of you I'm able to leave."

"Be quiet. You'll make me tear up."

"Until next time."

"I hope to meet her one day," Robert said.

"You will. If Penruddock changes his mind, there's the water mill in Nimmer we stayed in, just outside Chard. We aim to be there by the fifteenth, God willing. If I find the earl, we'll have passage to Holland. Think about it, Robert, you'd finally be able to meet those Dutch women you've always been yapping about."

Robert jabbed him with his elbow and winked.

"The water mill!" Daniel called as Robert bounced away.

Daniel sent Sam off for supplies while he sought out a surgeon. He flexed his hand, and blood oozed from the wound. If he couldn't hold a blade, then all the luck in the world wouldn't be enough to reach Taunton and his sister.

Chapter 32 – The Pikeman Cavalier

It was a brute of a horse, nearly seventeen hands. Horse riding required a certain level of skill, finesse, and dexterity, none of which Robert was renowned for. He enjoyed keeping both feet on terra firma, and his nickname 'Root' illustrated his talent for rooting himself into the earth like some massive oak. This particular talent, combined with his sheer size and power, had allowed him the distinction of never falling during a push of the pike. However, if any man had the courage to ask about its meaning, he told them it had more to do with his prowess in the bedroom. But all these particular talents counted for very little on the back of a galloping horse.

They'd explained that the placid gelding was perfectly suitable for him. Robert had gazed into the creature's eyes and questioned if they had insulted him or the horse. They also brought him a sword that must have seen service in the Hundred Years War and a carbine, which he fitted into his belt along with a flask and cartridge case. The biggest prize of all was a decent buff coat, but it was far too small, and it took nearly an hour of work just to be able to put the damn thing on. After an hour of rudimentary instruction on horsemanship, they had finished with the helpful advice of "don't fall off" and "don't fire the carbine while in the saddle."

Soon after, the Royalist force followed Penruddock to the market square. It was still morning, and Sir Joseph Wagstaffe had lined up the magistrates and the High Sheriff in the square. Bound and still in their nightdresses, they were sorry to behold.

Rumors had spread that the king had landed, and Robert yawned as the curious gathered in the square to catch a glimpse of King Charles II. Others gawked at the hastily erected gallows, waiting for their morning entertainment.

Penruddock joined Wagstaffe in a heated discussion before Penruddock addressed the crowd. "These traitors have been arrested in the name of the king, but today there will be no hangings. Hangings will not bring us victory. We have four hundred men and more will follow. We ride west to gather support. Join us, and you will have your king back."

The people were sympathetic, but the fires of rebellion had all but been extinguished within them. Still, along with other volunteers, Robert persuaded a few locals to join them, but in the end, the number of commandeered horses far outnumbered the men who joined to fight for Charles.

The farther they rode west, the more Robert itched for a fight. However, as they entered Blandford, the garrison had already fled, and the only things to assail them were a few hags, who dared to leave their hovels to view the Royalists. The mayor had also emerged to sing the king's praises while trying to sell Penruddock supplies at twice the market rate.

In the end, they passed through Blandford after a short rest, having obtained only a few more volunteers. The men muttered that their Colonel's hopes for a general uprising were misplaced. Discontent spread around the campfires, but the conspicuous absence of the New Model Army gave them hope. Robert would have done anything to help Daniel, and so he had left with Penruddock, but this fight was not his fight. He was already planning how to reach Nimmer by the fifteenth.

On the fourteenth, they reached South Molton. A Parliamentarian troop of horse from Exeter had been shadowing them from the previous day.

Penruddock coordinated their defensive positions around the town square. Carts and wagons were barricaded across each road except the main road leading to the market square. With one route available, all firepower would be brought to bear against the Roundheads as they were funneled down the main thoroughfare.

The row of houses overlooking the town square was occupied after their owners were escorted at gunpoint to the nearest parish church. From the upstairs bedroom, they prepared their muskets.

Robert had learned long ago to listen to his feelings before a battle. Those unearthly signs swirling about the battlefield told him more than the mutterings of the men or the proclamations and orders of the officers. And as he crouched by the window, an unnerving pressure weighed upon him. "A foolish enterprise," he muttered to himself.

An hour later, the rumble of cavalry announced the approach of the enemy.

"They've taken the bait. Be ready."

Robert stuffed some cloth into his ears to protect them from the blast of the shot. Their muskets rested on the transoms of the open windows.

"A few straight shots can be the difference between defeat and victory," Robert instructed. "Don't fire until I tell you."

The youngest of the men, no more than twenty, with the mere wisp of a beard, wedged his musket against the window frame to stop it from shaking.

"And don't fire on our own cavalry when they counter attack. Try to bring down their officers."

The volunteers were too nervous to reply, but they hung onto his advice.

A moment later and at full gallop, the Roundheads flew past the window.

"Fire!" Robert shouted.

Their cavalry moved fast but were also well spaced. Only one horse fell, and between fifty and seventy Roundheads galloped straight for the colonel's position. The defenders fled before the Roundhead charge. Some riders jumped the barriers, while others skirted them, probing for weaknesses in their defenses.

"Fire!" Robert shouted again and discharged his weapon. He missed the Roundhead officer, but the soldier beside the decorated man clutched his side and slid off his horse.

The Roundhead officer pointed his sword toward the gunpowder smoke bellowing from the window. The sunlight reflected off their breastplates as the horses gathered pace toward Robert's group of men.

Robert grabbed the last loaded musket and fired. The shot missed, falling short. His cowardly companions had already fled. He threw the musket down and drew his carbine. He ran to the stairs, and musket fire cracked below. The struggle of hand-to-hand fighting came from the hallway. He bounded down the stairs and men crashed against each other. The weight of the Roundheads pushed the Royalists back.

Robert fired at the tallest Roundhead. The headshot threw him down; the ringing noise from the blast reverberated around the enclosed space, drowning out the cries of the men. There were too many. He could take down two or three, but double that would take their place. Robert sprinted the opposite way and crashed through the back door.

He found himself in a tight lane with a heavy faced hedgerow running along it. A horse ambled up from a side street. Groaning, a Roundhead slumped forward in the saddle. Robert threw off the injured man. Shouts came from behind, but he drove the horse forward into a gallop. Shots flew past him, and he crouched low. Were they coming? No clatter of hooves trailed after him, so he dared to look back. Clear.

Soon the lane came to a crossing, and he took the west road and then doubled back, taking the quiet country roads toward Chard.

By late afternoon, he had reached Bampton. He would have preferred to skirt around the town, but his horse, like himself, needed to be fed and watered.

His previous visit to Bampton had been an unhappy one that had stalked his memory these past eleven years. As raw recruits in General Goring's army, they'd been tasked with suppressing The Clubmen. The exuberance of victory had led to wild pillage and murder. The town burned for six days. There were few experiences that had shamed him more. The sack of Bampton had stained every defeat and victory since then, and the prospect of returning weighed him down.

With the timeworn memories came the remembrance of the evening spent at the Old Exeter Inn just outside the town. The inn had been one of the few places to escape the flames.

The mediocre moonlight was barely enough to reveal the path that led along the river Exe. The bulrushes bent toward the river in the evening breeze. Robert straightened himself in the saddle, wincing as his back cramped. He patted the exhausted mare. Her sweat glistened when it caught in the light and foamy saliva dripped from her mouth. He removed his cap and smoothed back his tangled hair, letting the cool breeze clear his head.

In the twilight, with the looming hills arching over the roof, the sinister outline of the inn came into view. A few streaks of light came through shuttered windows. Robert dismounted and led his horse to the empty stables at the back. There was no sign of a stable boy, so he tethered the horse himself.

The soft light inside was more welcoming than the cold stares of the patrons. Robert scrutinized their faces. Ten folk—mostly old men and a few women. The barkeep, a man in his fifties, wiped his bald forehead with a handkerchief.

"Evenin', sir. What can I get you?"

The locals started up their conversations again.

Robert nodded to the innkeeper. "Where's your stable hand? I have a horse out back that needs tending quickly."

The barkeep motioned for a lad to come over and scooted him out. "A room? Food?"

"Only food."

"Very good, sir. My wife makes the best mutton pie in Devon."

"I'm glad I happened by then." Robert took out a pouch and emptied it on the bar.

The barkeep sorted through the halfpennies and coppers.

"That's all I have."

"Well…eh…" He glanced up at Robert. "Should be coverin' it."

Robert shunted to an empty table at the back of the inn, which afforded a good view of the door. It wasn't long before his food was placed in front of him. His stomach tightened as the fine aroma wafted about him. He lifted a spoonful to his salivating mouth. But before he shoveled it in, the door swung open, and three Roundheads appeared. Robert's heart sank when they spotted him in the corner.

Two of them pointed their pistols at him. "On your feet."

Robert set the spoon down and rubbed his tired eyes. As their prisoner, he would be transported or hanged. More likely, they would string him up in a barn or from the nearest tree as soon as they got him outside.

"Can I finish my pie?" Robert spooned a bite into his mouth and nodded his approval to the barkeep.

The Roundhead on the far left moved a step closer. "Stand up! I will not ask a third time!"

Robert exploded from the stool, holding the table in front of him like a shield. Immediate gunfire sent shots spraying through

144

the wood. One ricocheted away, and the other hit him in the middle. The shot never penetrated his buff coat.

Still holding the table, he bulled forward, tearing a path toward the Roundheads. Two spun away in time, but the Roundhead on the right, closest to the door, was knocked back, doubled over onto the floor. The other two drew and shifted toward Robert.

He grabbed a stool and swung across their path. The injured Roundhead moaned, and without taking his eye off the other two, Robert stomped down on the man's neck. Fury blazed in their eyes. They were going to make sure he died slowly, but their anger might lead to mistakes.

Their advance was quick but measured. He turned aside their rapier thrusts with the stool. Robert swung his sword low, but they avoided the attack, and overextended, he wobbled to find his balance. They saw their chance and attacked together.

Robert lifted the stool and blocked a head strike. Almost at the same time, the second man thrust at Robert's abdomen. He swiveled, and the edge of the blade nicked his side. There was no pain. He battered into them with his sword flailing. They bowled over, but Robert also lost his footing. They fell in a tangled mess, and his sword skidded from his grasp. He crashed his fist into the nearest man's face. The soldier's head cracked against the floor, taking his helmet off.

The other Roundhead stabbed at Robert, but in the cramped space, his rapier was too unwieldy. Instead, he raked his hilt across Robert's face, ripping through his cheek. Stunned, Robert received another blow to his temple, knocking him back. Dazed, he groped for his sword as the blur of the Roundhead stumbling to his feet shook him into action. Only the Roundhead's lobster pot helmet came to hand, but the soldier's arm blocked Robert's blow. The soldier made to slash him with his rapier, but Robert, half a second quicker, brained him with a vicious blow. After the fourth blow, the Roundhead lay dead. Robert tossed the battered and bloodstained helmet to the ground.

Robert lifted his sword. The other soldier lay unconscious. Robert held onto the table to steady himself and then stumbled over to the Roundhead, using the soldier's dagger to cut his throat.

The patrons gasped in horror as he turned around.

His face a bloodied mess, he stumbled to the bar, holding up the meat of his cheek. "I need a fucking bandage!"

The barkeep winced when Robert removed his hand from the wound.

"Help me, or I'll hurt you," Robert growled.

The barkeep nodded and set down the half-filled tankard that had been glued to his hand for the past few minutes. He ran upstairs as fast as his bulk could carry him and returned with a woman who held linen cloth. Robert downed the ale. A few locals tried to slip out, but skulked back to their stools when he threatened to castrate them.

Breathless, the woman squinted at Robert's face. The blood had nearly stopped, and after examining the gash, she cut a length of linen and washed it into a glass of whiskey. He gritted his teeth as she gingerly wiped the wound.

"I will have to stitch it," she said.

"Do it." He banged the tankard onto the bar, and the barkeep refilled it. "What is your name?" Robert asked the woman.

She opened a small wooden box and took out a long darning needle. "Catherine." She prepared the thread and then stitched the wound.

"You have a steady hand, Catherine."

"I have had enough practice." She dabbed the wound again and checked the stitches. "You'll need someone to take them out."

Robert took another drink and lifted off his buff coat. Blood stained his shirt. He lifted his shirt, and Catherine examined the wound on his side.

"A nick. A bandage will be enough." After she had cleaned the wound, she cut another length of linen and tied it round his waist. She gaped at his old scars, which ran across his body like rivers painted on a map. "You should rest," she muttered.

"Aye, I should, but I can't." If he wanted to reach Nimmer, he would have to ride through the night. Robert raised himself up and sneered at the patrons. "If you want my advice, get rid of their bodies and tell no one what happened. The soldiers who come looking for them will kill you for not helping them." Robert ignored their quarrels and called the barkeep over. "I have nothing to give you for the damage—" he turned to Catherine "—or for your help. I will take my horse and one of theirs. Take the rest for yourself."

The barkeep's eyes widened at the suggestion.

"Whatever you decide," Robert continued, "on your life, get rid of the bodies." He finished the ale and fixed his shirt before squeezing the buff coat on with a groan. He searched the nearest Roundhead and took a pistol and some cartridges.

A shout came from behind. "You!" An elderly man with a patchy grey beard banged his walking stick on the floor. "That one's still breathing." He pointed his stick at the Roundhead lying by the door.

Robert examined the man, and sure enough he clung to life. He shook his head and walked out. Let them do their own dirty work. There had been enough killing for one night. Anyway, he had an appointment to keep.

Chapter 33 – Homeward Bound

With the numerous patrols using the main roads, Daniel and Sam skirted the villages and towns, sticking to paths, tracks, and packhorse trails. The only soul they came across was a farmer driving geese to the village market.

Daniel had asked Penruddock's Farrier for horses, but all he could give them was an ancient, bad-tempered hack. With just the one horse, and one better bound for the knacker at that, they had taken turns to ride, and only occasionally rode double.

After four hours on the road, Sam led Daniel to a stream he had come across during his numerous travels spreading the message of the Lord. The yew trees lining the path were glorious, and the hedgerows were beginning to thicken with the promise of spring. Sam dismounted, leaving the horse to graze, and walked to the river bank. A small waterfall gurgled farther downstream.

Daniel lay down on the grassy river bank and closed his eyes. He tried to clear his head of the problems that lay ahead. If the constable had released Johanna, so much the better, but Daniel would still have to deal with Hugo. His thoughts had been revolving around the battle of Worcester. Had Manfred Hugo fought there? Very likely. He tried to picture what the man would look like. But his memories of John's younger brother were hazy. He could only remember that Manfred's hair was darker than John's. He had followed John like a lapdog, and they had played further afield to get rid of the boy. Well, he would soon enough see what he looked like.

"I've come back a few times. The trick is to lift the rocks slowly," Sam said.

Sam reminded him of a huge black heron waiting for its lunch to appear as he lifted the rocks. "Rocks?" Daniel squinted through the sunlight.

Sam splashed through the water. "Aye, crayfish."

Daniel sat up and rubbed his feet as Sam waded through the

water. The quartermaster had given him latchet shoes, but they were a little big, and his feet were already blistered. He bathed his feet in the cool water to keep the swelling down.

After thirty minutes of fishing, Sam had caught eight crayfish, each no bigger than his fist. Without cooking them, Sam retrieved the best meat from the tail and claws. A small meal, but the sweet meat tasted wonderful. Satisfied, Daniel stretched himself out to digest the food.

"I come from the north, a small village called Maghaberry." A vague smile crept across Sam's face. "There aren't many crawfish there."

Since that time in the yard, Daniel had avoided speaking of Sam's family. He had seen the pain in Sam's eyes. It had been clear that he had suffered some terrible tragedy.

"I was a Church of Ireland minister," Sam continued. "A small church with a smaller congregation. When a storm came, the locals often came to shelter. It didn't matter who they belonged to. We had our rooms upstairs. My wife, Heather, and our daughters, Rachel and Miriam were sleeping…They came at night. Broke in through the back of the church and torched it. By the time we noticed, it was too late to reach them. I still believe it was the local landowner. He wanted the land. The Bishop had refused."

"I'm sorry."

"Nothing left in Ireland for me. I gave up all thought of love and goodness. I blamed God…but God hadn't started the fire. It was the darkness inside of men. The darkness drove them to it. So now I'm here—a bog-lander skulking through England."

"At least you're not skulking alone. I'm fortunate you came, Sam. I'll never be able to repay your kindness."

"I know what it's like to lose your family, Daniel. It's something I need to do."

Here was a man who understood him. Robert was Daniel's greatest friend, but he had never lost his family. Robert was a fighter and an adventurer. Life on the road had been his choice. But now, Daniel yearned to leave the war and the fighting behind—to settle to a life of peace, if only life would let him. Sam understood his longing, because Sam wanted the same.

Daniel lifted himself up and put his shoes back on. Sam collected the remains of the crayfish and threw them into the stream. They watched the remnants of their lunch sink under the water before setting off again.

Chapter 34 – The Trial

Johanna clasped her hands as Taunton castle came into view through the drizzle. A heavy mist had settled upon the town, and with a light breeze, it seemed content to visit for the day. The mood of her companions mirrored the dreary overcast weather. The constable hadn't spoken in hours, and Mr. Leitham, grave and pensive, trudged along at her side. No one was in the mood for talk—each quietly reflecting upon the moment and the coming trial. Daniel would have told her that he'd let nothing happen to her. She was a gifted healer, who had always given her best to her friends and neighbors. That he believed in her, and even if the whole world set itself against her, it couldn't change his conviction of her innocence. Daniel would have told her all these things. But Daniel wasn't here, and so she struggled to convince herself of these truths as she walked with her dearest friends.

The constable escorted them through the inner gates, and now it was clear why the markets had been empty. All of Taunton had decided to watch the trial. The inner courtyard was already bursting with people who had been shut out of the Great Hall. The Town Watch had accompanied them, but Hugo's men had already cordoned off the walkway, and they were able to reach the entrance unmolested.

The warm, stale air engulfed the newcomers. The mob hushed with Johanna's arrival. Every head turned. Johanna caught glimpses of cold, hard stares. Their cackling and their whispers mocked her as she hurried past. The babble of noise returned again after their curiosity had been satisfied. Most of the spectators had to stand at the back, with the better sort able to sit on benches at the front.

"Hugo has filled the hall with his rabble!" Mr. Leitham thundered. "Base insipids, one and all."

Hugo had not yet arrived. They settled down on the bench at the front. Hawkish spectators stared from the second floor balcony.

The judgment seat loomed ahead. Soon Hart would take his place there. The jury would follow and take their places to his left, and all would be ready to decide her future.

From Johanna's left, the farthest side door opened, and Hugo strutted into the hall. He surveyed the spectators without making eye contact with Johanna. His clothes were new, but still the same somber brown color. He sat down on the other side with the loathsome Mabb sweating beside him. Hugo removed his felt hat and dabbed his forehead with his kerchief. He fidgeted with his cuffs. Could the unflappable Hugo actually be nervous?

A few moments later, Hart lumbered into the hall from a door behind the judgment seat. Accompanied by his clerks and guards, he strode imperiously to his seat. He wore an abundance of clothing with his heavy white mantle and flowing robes weighing him down. Hart adjusted the ceremonial trappings of his office while the spectators rose to their feet. He spoke to his guard, and the man hurried off. He returned a few moments later with the gentlemen of the jury. Twelve in all, they took their seats on the far side of the hall under the large window.

The chatter died to a whisper, the audience eager to hear Hart begin the proceedings of the trial. Hart adjusted his robes again, nodded to the clerks, and cleared his throat.

"This session of the Assizes has been brought to determine the guilt or innocence of Miss Johanna Davenport, who has been charged with the crime of witchcraft and murder, under the Witchcraft Act of 1604."

A section of spectators scuffled at the back of the hall. And the uproar swelled about the hall. When they didn't cease their agitation, the trouble makers were removed by soldiers. The hall fell silent again.

"After hearing evidence brought by the prosecution, Miss Davenport will be given the opportunity to speak for herself. If it is her wish, she may also bring forward witnesses to speak on her behalf. Thereafter, the jury will consult, and return their verdict at noon tomorrow." Hart raised his eyes from his notes and slid his spectacles back in place. "Johanna Davenport, come forward."

Johanna stood and walked before Hart.

"Johanna Davenport, do you understand this process of law?"

Yes, Johanna well understood she was guilty until proven

innocent. "Yes, Your Honor."

"Then take your place."

Johanna returned to the bench.

Hart gestured at Hugo. "Commissioner, you may begin with your evidence."

Hugo stood and walked over to the stand. "Thank you, Your Honor. My first witness is Mr. Edward Mabb."

Mabb, who wore the same listless expression as always, straightened out his doublet. His beard had been trimmed, but there were still sniggers as he waddled over to the stand. Hugo glared at the hags, who took little notice, and carried on with their cackling.

Hart stood from his seat. "This is no bawdy inn!" he thundered. "I'll have any indecorum punished."

The spectators, including those who had mocked Mabb, quieted.

Hart nodded at Mabb. "Do you swear before the court you will tell the truth before Almighty God?" Hart asked.

"I do—I mean, I swear, Your Honor," Mabb said.

Hugo faced the jury. "One of the infallible signs of a witch is the presence of a familiar. This is the sign of a covenant between the witch and the Devil. Mr. Mabb, did you ever witness strange occurrences while guarding Johanna Davenport?"

"I did, sir."

"Report to the jury what you witnessed."

Mabb removed his hat and smoothed his hair down. "I saw a toad."

A few sniggers interrupted him but were quickly silenced with Hart's glare.

"I know not whence it came from, but it was large—the size of my fist. It came to her and stood before her while she slept. It stood its ground for a long time—as if it was conversing with her."

Johanna ignored the murmurs from the spectators. Mabb really seemed to believe his own lies. His furrowed brow and steepled hands suggested ringing sincerity. Could a person lie so convincingly that they lied even to themselves?

Hugo waited for the noise to subside before continuing. "Did you witness anything else that night?"

"I'll admit I was fearful. They say demons take the form of animals. I considered leaving the room. I walked to the door but then caught my wits. I told myself God would protect me. When I turned back, the toad had disappeared."

"Disappeared," Hugo repeated to the jury.

"There was one more experience. I believe another familiar came to her later that night. She was sleeping, and I observed a mouse go to her."

"And what does this prove, Mr. Mabb?" Hart asked.

Johanna sat forward, and both the constable and Mr. Leitham nodded at Hart's question.

"It's what it did, Your Honor. It came before her and stood its ground. Then climbed up the table." Mabb pointed to the floor as if the mouse had returned. "After a while it went to her bare leg and appeared to suckle on it."

Johanna shook her head. Suppressed laughter mingled with hushed muttering rippled through the Hall.

"Your Honor," Hugo said, "I would like to remind the jury of the common knowledge familiars must feed on the witch through a witch mark—also called the Devil's mark—so that a connection may be maintained between them. The connection is maintained through the blood."

Hart scribbled down some notes. "Noted, Mr. Hugo.

"And then what happened, Mr. Mabb?"

Mabb blew the air from his cheeks. "I crept toward it. It pulled away from her and looked straight at me…There was a red glint in its eyes." Mabb took in a breath. "Then it crept away."

"And that is all, Mr. Mabb?" Hugo asked.

"There was a little blood on her leg where the mouse had been."

Mr. Leitham shot up. "And you saw this all in the dark?" he called out.

A wave of arguments and chatter broke out. Mabb frowned at Hugo. Hart banged his hammer until the noise subsided.

"Mr. Leitham, if you disrupt these proceedings again I will have you removed. Is that clear?"

Leitham snorted and sat down again. Johanna clasped his arm.

Mabb turned to Leitham. "I had a torch with me. I saw blood."

"Any further questions for this witness?" Hart asked.

"No, Your Honor."

Mabb plodded back to his seat, and a flood of whispers swept forward from the spectators.

"He will call his two women," Johanna said to the constable and Mr. Leitham.

The constable shook his head. "I've heard Maidstone will be called. The other has disappeared."

"I call Maggie Maidstone to the stand, Your Honor."

From the same side door, Maidstone strode in. Johanna noted the same scowl that permanently darkened her features. The thin slit of her lips curved when she glanced at Johanna.

She repeated the oath and then nodded to Hugo. "Miss Maidstone, how many years have you searched for witch signs?"

Maidstone stood straight and held her head high. "For nearly three years, sir."

"And what signs do you search for?"

"A witch mark, sir. A spot on the body—most often a reddish color."

"Explain to the jury why this witch mark appears."

"I'd say it's like a...teat, sir." She bristled at the snickering from the back of the hall. "For the feeding of the familiar."

"Miss Maidstone, most people in this room will have some mark or other on their person," Hart said.

Maidstone solemnly addressed Hart. "It's not just the mark, Your Honor, but if you prick the spot and there's no blood, then you have a witch mark." She snorted at the spectators. "It's well enough known."

"Did you search Johanna Davenport for witch signs?" Manfred continued.

"I did, along with my assistant, Martha Wood."

"When you examined her, did you observe anything that resembled a witch mark?"

Maidstone's thin lips curled up when she glanced at Johanna. "We did, sir. We found a spot below her knee and near her belly button."

"Did you prick the marks?"

"Yes, and there was no blood."

"That is a lie!" Johanna shouted and a rumble of noise broke through the hall.

Hart rose again from his chair. "Miss Davenport, you will have your opportunity to speak. Until then, you *will* be silent."

Johanna's chest tightened as Mr. Leitham helped her back onto her seat. The scuffle at the back of the hall was broken up, and two women were dragged out by soldiers.

"Miss Maidstone," Hugo continued, "can you describe the size and color of the witch marks?"

Maidstone nodded her head vigorously. "They were nearly the size of my fingernail, sir. And red in color."

"And when you later examined her?"

Maidstone faced the jury. "They were gone."

Hugo drifted over to the jury. "In a matter of hours?"

"Yes—disappeared."

Hugo paused for the gallery to quiet. "Have you experienced this before?"

"Only once, sir." Maidstone lifted her chin and gazed into the past. "We caught a witch who had been killing cattle with the evil eye. Her spots were similar to hers." Maidstone gestured toward Johanna. "They also gave forth no blood and disappeared the next day."

Hugo bowed his head and walked back to his seat. He dismissed Maidstone, who strode back the way she had come.

"Are you not calling Martha Wood?" Hart asked Hugo.

"No, Your Honor. Her mother is gravely ill, and she has traveled to Wells."

The mumbling in the audience grew louder.

Hart turned to the jury. "Any reference to Martha Wood may not be considered in your verdict."

"Your Honor, may we have a short recess?" Hugo asked Hart.

The frown that gripped Hart's face lengthened.

"My next witness has been feeling unwell, and I would like to know if she can continue today."

"One hour, Mr. Hugo." Hart slammed the hammer and retreated to his room with his clerks and guards in tow.

The men of the jury stretched their legs but did not leave the room. And amid the noise of the revelers leaving the Great Hall, Hugo and Mabb disappeared into the side room.

"He has played his part well—a theatricality that deserves a stage," Johanna said to her companions.

"Which," Mr. Leitham said, "if one believes the rumors, will also soon be outlawed."

156

The constable sidled closer to Johanna. "The jury must see how ludicrous this is."

"Have you ever read King James' treatise on witches?" Johanna asked.

They shook their heads.

"I have. Everything I have been accused of is written in those pages. Hugo accuses me; a king condemns me."

Mr. Leitham clasped her shoulder. "We no longer have a king, Miss. Davenport."

* * *

Manfred shut out the noise from the hall. Strain colored Ruth's features as she fingered the small silver pendant in her hand.

Her husband—agitated and tense—paced. "She's been blubbering all morning."

Manfred laid a hand on his shoulder. "It is to be expected. It's—"

"It's not difficult. Witches are witches," he whined.

"I need to speak with Ruth alone."

Bide screwed his face. "She needs me here."

"I know." Manfred stopped Bide's pacing. "But it's a matter of law, of procedure."

Bide glared at Ruth. "It's too close in here anyways. I need air."

Mabb escorted Bide out, and Manfred pulled the chair closer to Ruth. He handed her a handkerchief, and she dabbed her eyes. Her clothes, as she had been instructed, were presentable but hung loosely on her frame. He had to help her through this final and most trying test. "Have you been feeling unwell?"

"Can't keep nothin' down, Mr. Hugo."

"The doctor will come by this evening."

"Thank you." She blew her nose.

"I am proud of you. God's blessing is with you at this time. Soon it will be your turn to do the Lord's work. Are you ready for this?"

She caressed her pendant. "It's...it's difficult."

"I know. You trusted this woman with the life of your child. She pretended to be your friend. Her smiles, her helpfulness—all from a cold, diseased heart."

The tears began again.

"Nothing is more despicable. But I believe in you, Ruth. Are you ready to do God's work?"

"Yes."

He gazed deep into her eyes. "You are an instrument of God's justice, Ruth."

"Yes." She straightened herself, "I am.

* * *

Ruth, bent forward, hobbled to the stand.

Mr. Bide marched behind her and then halted in front of Johanna.

Johanna shuddered. Pure hatred filled his eyes, and Johanna had never seen Ruth in such a state. The poor woman seemed to have shrunk and withered since she had last seen her. Her eyes were distant—vacant. Hugo had put her up to this. Ruth would never have believed she had murdered her child. A drunkard and a power hungry zealot had brought her to this.

Hugo appeared next, as composed as ever. After the stragglers had taken their places and Mrs. Bide had sworn the oath, Hugo faced her. "Mrs. Bide, will you tell the jury of the evening you lost your child."

"Yes...my sister was on a visit. She was helping me with the chores, me being with child...then I felt a terrible pain." Ruth placed her hand over her stomach. "She laid me down to rest. She said it was the baby, but I didn't believe her at first 'cause I thought it too early." Ruth used the handkerchief to dab her eyes. "I was in labor for a long time. The pain was getting worse. My sister told me she was getting Johanna Davenport...'she will help,' she said."

"Why did your sister assume Johanna Davenport could help?"

"She'd helped Marie Polson one other time. She said she knew things from her mother."

"Knew things?"

"Using the herbs and the like."

Manfred again waited for the chatter to cease. "Continue, please."

"I was in pain. She gave me herbs for the pain. She pushed down on my belly."

"After she gave you herbs, how did you feel?"

158

"Still in pain, sir."

"Please continue when you are ready, Mrs. Bide," Manfred said.

Johanna sat forward, wringing her hands. Mr. Leitham clasped her arm.

Ruth's hand trembled as she brought it to her mouth. "She tried to move the baby...told me to push. When he was born...no crying...no breathing...because of what she gave me!" Ruth jabbed her finger at Johanna. Ruth trembled as she stood, her neck corded, wringing her hands.

Hart nodded to Hugo, and he moved to Ruth's side, clasping her shoulder. He whispered something to her. "No further questions, Your Honor." Hugo led Ruth away from the stand, but she broke free from him and tore toward Johanna. Richard put himself between them, but Ruth pushed past him.

"My boy would be alive!" Ruth spat, her face twisting in rage. "You're a devil! I trusted you! You said you were my friend!"

"I have always been your friend!" Johanna said.

"She needs a doctor!" Hart thundered above the clamor.

"I'll watch you hang! Justice is coming for you!" Ruth screamed.

Why had she tried to help? Johanna shifted uncomfortably as she held her head; she rubbed her strained and heavy eyes as the soldiers led Ruth and Mr. Bide away. It hadn't been the first baby she had delivered. Many babies had survived delivery, but she hadn't used the dwaul. It had been her mother's. The cord had been wrapped around the child's throat. But the child had also been moving before she had given the dwaul. She had followed her mother's instructions. But it had to have been the cord. *It was the cord.*

Hart rose and called Hugo forward. They disappeared into Hart's office behind the judgment seat.

The constable nodded encouragingly. "This bodes well. Now he'll dismiss the case."

"I told you, Johanna, justice will be served," Mr. Leitham said, clasping his hands together.

Even Johanna felt a glimmer of hope as Hugo traipsed behind Hart. But it soon left her as the monstrous expression on Ruth's face filled her mind, haunting her.

* * *

Hart waved his notes toward Manfred. "As matters stand, I will ask the jury to acquit Johanna Davenport."

Manfred scowled. "I still have to question her."

"Let's be honest, Commissioner, you can't prove she murdered Mrs. Bide's baby, and the Jury will not convict her of witchcraft based on your acquaintances' testimonies."

"Magistrate, I have been charged with the task of cleansing England of evil and our Government's enemies. Let me be clear: only those who cooperate with the commission are needed in our New England. Do you understand? I demand the jury be given the opportunity to return their verdict."

Hart reddened. "I...I understand you perfectly. Now tell me what you really want, Mr. Hugo?"

"Justice. And I will have it, Magistrate."

"God help us all then, Commissioner." Hart stumbled out of the room, leaving Manfred alone.

* * *

The Magistrate shuffled to his chair, a pained expression seemingly weighing him down. While Hugo, in contrast, hurried behind him. Hart fixed his papers and waited until the jury had seated themselves again. After the spectators had quieted, he cleared his throat.

Johanna sat forward in her chair.

"Commissioner, you may begin with your questions."

"I call Johanna Davenport to the stand," Hugo announced.

A heavy sigh escaped from all three. Johanna struggled to rise, and Mr. Leitham gave her his arm. Together they padded to the stand. She glanced back at Mr. Leitham's pained stare. Her gaze flitted over the packed hall. Many gawked at her like she was already dead, but there were also faces where she perceived silent prayers rising for her deliverance. She let it all sweep over her.

Hugo moved closer to her, his countenance as inscrutable as ever.

Hart addressed Johanna. "After this cross-examination, you or anyone else will have the opportunity to speak on your behalf. As the accused, you may not swear the oath."

160

"How long did Ruth Bide work in your service?" Hugo asked her.

"She worked for my family for nearly ten years."

"Why did she leave the service of your family?"

Mr. Leitham's feverish eyes locked onto Hugo.

"I repeat, why did she leave the service of your family?"

"After my father died, we could no longer afford to pay her."

"I don't understand—" Hugo gesticulated to the spectators "—your father was a wealthy landowner. Your brother inherited the land. How could you not afford to pay her?"

Johanna met Hugo's stare head on. "We lost nearly everything after the war."

"Oh yes, your brother fought in the war. A Royalist!"

Some spectators standing at the back heckled Johanna, and arguments broke out.

Mr. Leitham sprang to his feet. "Who is on trial?" He pleaded to the jury. "He speaks of the war, for he has nothing else to say!"

Hart banged the hammer. "I will have order in this court!"

The soldiers threw out the agitators at the back.

"And remove this man from my courtroom!" He thrust a finger at Mr. Leitham.

The constable tried to calm Mr. Leitham, but it was useless.

"You can't silence me! She is not her brother! Where is justice? Where is justice to be found here?" Mr. Leitham yelled even as three soldiers dragged him away.

Johanna fought to hold back her tears as everything collapsed around her. Hugo spun around. His features softened for a moment, but his mouth tightened and the cold severity returned to his dark eyes once more. "Did you know Ruth's brother was killed at Newbury?"

"Yes."

"Did you know that he fought for Parliament against the tyranny of the Crown?"

Johanna ignored the question.

"Answer the question," Hart said.

"I knew he fought for Parliament."

"What did you give Ruth Bide that night?"

"I gave her harmless herbs—dwaul for her pain."

Hugo snorted. "Harmless? Dwaul is also known as Belladonna

161

or Deadly Nightshade. It's a poison and is also used by witches in their Satanic rituals."

"My mother taught me herb lore," Johanna defended herself. "She helped many people and passed the knowledge to me."

Hugo walked to the jury. "The Devil will employ his servants to do good in order to trick us. His servants appear as good shepherds," he preached, "but they are always waiting for the moment to serve their true master: Lucifer. Johanna Davenport—" Hugo angled his eyes toward her "—poisoned Ruth's child that night. She took the opportunity to do her master's work and gain revenge for her family's downfall."

"It's not true." Johanna's voice trembled. "I have always been a friend to Ruth. I wanted to help her. She wanted my help. The cord was wrapped around the baby's throat!" Johanna entreated the jury.

"Yes, you tricked her well. You hid the burning hate within you. You lost everything, and you couldn't bear it. The mistress became the servant. Your brother fought for the crown, and now he rots in prison for his crimes. You used witchcraft for revenge. You sold your soul for revenge."

As suddenly as it came, the fight left her again. Hugo would have an answer for every reply. No one could help her: not the constable, nor Mr. Leitham, or Daniel. She slumped forward. "You lie," she stammered.

"And your master is the father of lies. For the good of your eternal soul, admit the truth before everyone to save yourself."

Johanna said nothing.

"Speak for yourself. Why will you not save your soul?"

Johanna maintained her silence. A ripple of laughter echoed through the hall after a wretch shouted for her to answer the question.

"Answer the question, Miss Davenport," Hart interjected, losing his patience with the whole proceedings.

Johanna stared off into the distance.

"No further questions, Your Honor."

The constable helped Johanna back to her seat.

Hart spoke to his clerks, and then wrote down more notes. Yells of "hang her" were shouted and sides were being taken.

Hart wiped the sweat from his brow. "Miss Davenport, you

may speak to the jury if you wish."

"Your Honor," the constable spoke up, "you said others may also talk on behalf of Miss Davenport. I know Richard Leitham will speak on her behalf."

"Your Honor," Hugo interjected, "Richard Leitham is in contempt of this court. He should not be permitted to speak."

"I agree. Constable, I will allow you to speak, if you so wish."

"I wish it, Your Honor." The constable laid his hand on Johanna's shoulder and strode to the stand. His eyes didn't leave the Jury after swearing the oath. "Perhaps I'll make myself a few more enemies this day. But I also live in this town, and I'll say my mind, and I will speak my conscience." He glanced over at Hugo before continuing. "I have known the Davenport family for many years. I knew her father and mother, and I called them my friends. Even though I supported Parliament in the war, even though my son lost his life in that cursed war, I have always known them to be honorable people. I can also say the same for Johanna Davenport, whom I've known since she was a child." He paused to acknowledge Johanna. "She did not murder that baby. She is a Godly woman and no witch, and to treat her as such is a crime before God."

A few spectators clapped at the constable's speech.

Johanna clasped his hand as he returned to his seat.

"Miss Davenport, you may now speak if you wish to."

Johanna lifted her head. "Yes, I will, Your Honor."

"They will believe you, Johanna. Or to hell with them!" the constable said.

Johanna stood and ignored the whispers circulating amongst the gallery. *I am no witch.* Her steps were measured, and she held her head high as she reached the stand. "This is my town—where I've always lived, and my family before me. Taunton and the people who live here are a part of my life. You—" she cast her eyes over the spectators "—are the people who know me. I believe, in your hearts, you know I am no witch. That is the *truth*. I never hurt that child. I only wished to help—just to help. As God is my witness that is the truth."

Johanna pushed through the wave of murmurs, whispers, the shouts of encouragement, the curses and the hatred. She sat down and gripped the constable's hand. "I am no witch," she whispered to him. "But I pray every night for the certainty that the poor child did not die at my hands. God help me."

The constable embraced her. "You are innocent. Always remember, Johanna."

Hart cleared his throat, and called Hugo to conclude his case against Johanna.

Hugo arranged himself, and then walked forward to meet the Jury. "Exodus 22:18: Thou shalt not suffer a witch to live. Leviticus 20:27: A man or a woman that hath a familiar spirit, they shall stone them with stones: their blood shall be upon them.

"Our lord Cromwell urges us toward Godly reformation, for are we not approaching the end times? When will the Lamb of God bring us to Judgment? I believe sooner than all dare to imagine. It is then incumbent upon me, and all, to fight the evil within our midst."

Hugo gestured toward Johanna. "Witnesses have sworn that strange and mystical happenings occurred in the presence of this witch, Johanna Davenport. In addition, we have the death of a child after the mother was administered some herbal poison, given by Johanna Davenport. You must do your duty and fight the evil that has taken possession of Johanna Davenport. For…it is the only way to save her eternal soul."

Hart dismissed the Jury.

Hugo had already called his men forward. "Magistrate, the constable, as a witness for Miss Davenport, must not be allowed to harbor her before the verdict is given."

The constable leveled a withering gaze at Hugo. "Your honor, I give you my word, Johanna Davenport will be led safely back to my own home and brought to hear the Jury's verdict, tomorrow."

"I believe you, Constable," Hart snapped, "but in this instance, it would be inappropriate for Miss Davenport to be placed under your care."

Hugo's men surrounded her, and the constable's protests were shouted down.

"The verdict will be returned at noon tomorrow," Hart bellowed before disappearing through the back door to his chambers.

They shoved Johanna away, and the constable tried to get through the cordon of soldiers to reach her. "I am a fool, Johanna.

A fool to believe you would find justice here!" He shouted after her. The constable slumped down onto a bench, his face buried in his hands.

The crowds pushed toward her, but the ring of soldiers held firm. She closed her eyes to the baseness and hatred enclosing in upon her. She strained to block out the screams and recriminations. Hugo had her in his power again. And now he had her to himself.

Chapter 35 – To Nimmer

They spared the horse as much as possible, but after fifteen hours, with only a few breaks in between, Daniel could barely walk. With his swollen, blistered feet, he hobbled forward, grimacing with every step. But his knees gave him more trouble. More than once they had buckled under him, and only with Sam's help was he able to mount the horse.

At one point they had been spotted by a patrol, but were fortunate enough to reach the woods, and the patrol soon gave up the chase. Thereafter, they followed the rivers as much as possible. At other times, they had no choice but to stray closer to civilization if they were to reach Nimmer by the fifteenth. But as necessary as it was, it was also a grave risk. Patrols searched the roads, towns, and villages for Royalists. Locals were weary of strangers and were avoided—it would only take one passerby to alert a patrol, and they would be done for.

Nimmer was not too far now. The undulating hills overlooking the river Lsle encircled the valley. The river stretched below them, flowing fast through the meadows and fields. Daniel flopped down onto the wet grass. The wagtails swooped and wheeled amongst the rocks, while a few jackdaws squabbled in the tall grass. He stretched out and closed his eyes. He ran his hands through the damp grass and rubbed the moisture over his face. He picked up the faint floral notes of the wild flowers growing along the hillside. Rabbit burrows dotted the hillside, and the young rabbits sat as still as statues until they sensed danger. The wily creatures bolted inside their burrows as Sam approached, and he soon gave up the hunt. Sam wandered back defeated and sat down beside Daniel.

"Quicker than crayfish, eh?" Daniel said.

Sam snorted. "Might be easier if you helped."

Daniel laughed bitterly and rubbed his knees. "I'll be lucky if I can stand up again, Sam."

"Look." Sam pointed to the crest of the hill at a thicket with clusters of white flowers. "Over yonder."

"Beautiful."

"Them's Whitebeams. A pity it's not Autumn—their berries are good eating."

"Don't remind me." Daniel sunk back down into the grass. "Will we save her, Sam?"

Sam lowered his eyes and ran his hand through the grass. "It's probably been a misunderstanding. She'll be safe and sound, and worried about you."

"Will you come with us?"

"I don't think so." A weary grin shaded across his face. "I think I've had my fill of England. Time to go home."

After an hour of rest and a meager meal consisting of the last of the bread, they climbed the rest of the hill to get their bearings. Leading the horse, they climbed through the dense wood that hugged the hill. The trees were bent toward the slope from the strong north-easterly wind, which ran across the valley. Daniel sucked in a lungful when he reached the summit and peered across the valley. Above the tree line, they had a clear view for miles in every direction.

"I knew they wouldn't follow us here," Daniel muttered.

Sam shielded his eyes from the sunlight and squinted toward the northeast. "You spoke too soon."

Distant figures made toward them. Four or five riders—probably a Roundhead patrol—approached, sure and steady.

"I told you to skirt the village," Sam said.

"Have they spotted us?"

"Let's not wait to find out."

"Time to get our feet wet then." Daniel grimaced as they bounced down the hill. "Robert's probably having the time of his life: a girl on his knee and ale in his hand."

"Isn't it time we used this bloody horse?" Sam blustered.

Daniel clambered up onto the nag and then gave his hand to Sam.

"After the river, we can head for the tree line. We'll lose them then, Sam."

"I just hope horses can swim better than me."

Chapter 36 – The Verdict

Hugo's men led Johanna to the same cellar room. A mattress had been placed on the floor, and she sagged down and closed her sore eyes. She fought to stay awake, but eventually exhaustion claimed her, and she fell into the recurring nightmare of her execution.

The hooded executioner placed the noose around her neck. Daniel was there, but he was frozen in the likeness of a pale granite statue, with only a trickle of tears suggesting life. Richard rushed the gallows, but he was hacked down before he reached her. Johanna screamed as they butchered him in a frenzied attack. She struggled to free her bound wrists. The soldiers stepped away to reveal Richard's bloody corpse, and she yearned to be able to hold him. Only then did the rope bite into her neck. She dangled, fighting for life as the rope crushed her throat. Hugo's haunting stare pursued her. She closed her eyes and let death come for her. She was ready, but she couldn't lose consciousness, and even when she twisted on the rope to avoid his gaze, he was always there, his cold, calculating stare devoid of life.

Johanna sat bolt upright in the darkness. She struggled for a breath as she fought to remove the noose. No, she was alive, but where was she? Hugo. The cell. Johanna sucked in another breath and her heart rate slowed. She caught the faint haze of candlelight seeping under the door. Heavy footsteps paced outside. Hugo had placed at least two guards in the hall.

"What does he expect?" She lay back on the mattress. *No one is coming for me.*

The rattle of keys woke her. She turned on her side, pretending to sleep. The door closed softly, and the radiance of the candlelight crept up the wall ahead of her. The light steps of one person approached.

She shivered as the man came closer. It had to be a man—his rapid, heavy breathing. Her body stiffened when he stood over her. Should she scream? No, she clamped her mouth shut. Not even

Hugo would let her be violated.

A candleholder scraped the stone floor. Johanna clasped her hands. She trembled as he inched closer. He caressed her leg, and her brain screamed to run, but every muscle gripped tight like iron and paralyzed her. Fingers explored the length of her body toward her breasts. He lifted her shift and lips feathered her lower back.

"Please, God, no," she whimpered. The words barely escaped her mouth so soft they were.

He panted as his fingers moved down to her navel and then lower still.

Johanna wept. *Lord, forsake me not!*

His hand stopped...and it seemed that his fingers only gradually lifted from her skin—how a man's touch lingers on a most exquisite object before it will forever be lost, never to be touched again.

He stood, darted to the door, and slammed it shut.

Hugo!

She placed her hands over her mouth to suppress her cries, terrified that he might return. His chilled touch ghosted down her spine, and she retched at the memory. In his haste, he had left the candle, and its flickering light beckoned her. She had never seen anything so beautiful—she drank in its orange-yellow brilliance. She knelt beside it, so that its halo surrounded her from the dark of the room. A prayer coursed through her: "Lord, thank thee for the light of deliverance!"

* * *

After Mabb joined the other two guards, the carriage trundled off to Taunton Castle. Johanna's mouth quivered, but she raised her eyes to the heavens when Hugo did not join him.

Mabb never spoke to her, only opening his mouth when he instructed the guards to keep the people back when they arrived. And sure enough, crowds lined Corporation Street, and then farther ahead until they reached the outer courtyard of Taunton Castle. The anticipation of a hanging had whipped the rabble into a frenzy. And it appeared every lay preacher in the county had either come out to condemn her or to pray for her salvation.

With her head bowed and Mabb by her side, she walked through the corridor of soldiers, over the drawbridge, and into the relative quiet of the inner courtyard. They entered the hall, and Mabb escorted her to a seat at the front. Hugo was already present. He glared at her in disgust, but Johanna met his gaze with liberating contempt. At least now she knew him, and he knew it as well. She would take with her at least one victory.

Now she felt a little lighter and even managed to smile when Mr. Leitham and the constable arrived. She caught Mr. Leitham's gaze and placed her hands over her heart. Traces of anxiety and fear shrouded his eyes, but also love and devotion lit up his features. She bowed her head, and an overwhelming feeling of loss pervaded her. She would never share her life with this beloved man.

A moment later, the clerks appeared from the back of the hall. One of them held the door for Hart, who stood behind his judgment seat and waited for the court to rise. After the ceremonies were completed, the jury also appeared. Their expressions were as inscrutable as before, but not one of those fine gentlemen looked her in the eye as they sat down to their places.

Hart rose and addressed the line of men to his left. "Members of the jury, have you reached a verdict?"

The jury member at the far end stood. "We have, Your Honor...we find Johanna Davenport guilty—" an eruption of noise filled the hall, and he had to raise his voice, "—*guilty of witchcraft and murder.*"

Johanna slumped down amid the tumult; she didn't hear the accusations and recriminations, but was suddenly all alone in that great hall. She felt sick and hollowed out inside. She had known what the verdict would be, but still she wasn't prepared for the utter loneliness of the judgment.

Hart banged his hammer until his arm was tired. He fumbled a back cap on his head. "Johanna Davenport, the sentence for witchcraft and murder is death by hanging. The sentence will be carried forth at sundown tomorrow."

She shook her head. She didn't want to wait any more.

Mr. Leitham and the constable were shocked into dumb silence. Then Leitham shook free of the inertia. "Your Honor—"

"The verdict has been reached and stands!" Hart shouted, already scurrying away as he spoke.

Johanna was surrounded by a ring of Hugo's men.

Mr. Leitham ran to her. "Johanna! Johanna, God help me, I will not be without you!"

"I pray for it, Richard!" She reached out for him, but they dragged her away before she could hold him.

Chapter 37 – The Watermill

It took Daniel and Sam another six hours to reach the outskirts of Chard. It had been ten years since Daniel and Robert had passed through when their company had stopped to resupply. With a few hours to spare, they had explored the area and had come across a watermill about a mile from the town in Nimmer. The mill had been badly damaged by fire, but the far end of the roof had survived the blaze. After the long march, it had been a relief to find a dry floor to rest on.

The patrol had gained on them and was barely thirty minutes behind. They took a route through the forest, skirting Chard, hoping to lose the Roundheads before the sun went down. After a few wrong turns, Daniel managed to locate the watermill. The forest had claimed it as its own, but the structure remained largely intact.

Sam led the nag into the watermill while Daniel covered their tracks. He then scouted around the mill to get a lie of the land.

The mill was sheltered on two sides by trees. The wheel had collapsed and lay on its side in the stream. He enjoyed the gurgle of the trickling water as it snaked past the wheel. He drank in the beauty of the picture before him: the damp forest smells, the calling birds, and rich earth colors of nature revived him. And all at once he knew he could never go back to Fisherton Anger.

Lost in the moment, he felt a gun dig into his back. Daniel cursed his stupidity and lifted his arms in the air.

The assailant stepped back a yard.

Daniel turned slowly—his arms still raised. "You big bastard!"

Robert's grin was big enough to stable a horse. "Davenport, you are a cuckold! I've been waiting here all bloody day."

They embraced.

"You're getting old, my friend. You should be ashamed." Robert slapped him on the shoulder.

"That I've been bested by a block-headed blunderbuss?" Daniel countered. "I knew you were behind me." Daniel winked, "And Sam?"

"Aye, I was waiting in the mill. I told him I was never so happy to see a Bog-lander."

Daniel peeked under Robert's bandage. "Nothing but a gnat's bite."

"I had a disagreement with three Roundheads." Robert lifted the edge of the bandage a little more, and Daniel winced. "They came off the worse for it."

"Sure as hell, you didn't stitch it," Daniel joked, "but it's clean."

"Dammit, Daniel, I've had a few gigglers give me bigger scratches."

"I knew you'd make it."

"Wouldn't miss it. Now what are we waiting for? I've got a damsel to rescue."

"A patrol—four or five men. I can't lead them to Taunton."

Robert caressed his pistol. "So we have work to do, Betsy."

* * *

From cover, Daniel eyed the Roundhead patrol drift toward the watermill. The Roundheads rode two by two, with a straggler further back, watching after the rear. They traveled light, with only the front two wearing buff coats, while the others had the appearance of hedge-creepers rather than soldiers of the New Model Army. No doubt the rewards offered for the capture of rebels tempted every common rogue from Devon to Surrey to try their luck for a slice of the bounty. Daniel held up five fingers to Robert then crept back to his hiding place.

About ten yards from the mill, the front two dismounted and removed carbines from their side holsters. The double doors of the mill had not survived the fire, but the mill was long enough and scattered with all and sundry to take cover behind. The other two dismounted, but waited until the straggler had caught up to hold the horses.

Opposite Daniel, Sam kneeled behind a broken cart, while Robert took cover behind a large cross beam on the upper level. The late afternoon sunlight streamed past the soldiers and into the mill. They halted at the entrance when they spotted the horses tethered together at the far end.

The Roundheads peered into the mill; their eyes flitted over the charred beams, barrels, and an old cart missing its wheels. The buff-coated soldier at the fore walked forward to the entrance. "If you make me come in there," he growled, "I'll shoot you dead. If you come peacefully, you'll be treated well enough."

"A chivalrous offer," Daniel said, crouching behind a barrel. "Mind yourself, stranger, and ride back from whence you came." They may have had the advantage in numbers, but it would be blind stupidity to attack a well defended position.

"Another step and you'll meet your maker!" Robert growled.

They followed the voice, but Robert remained hidden in the gloom of the loft.

"There'll be easier money to make," Sam chirped in.

"You're blind. Now ride away and keep going!" Daniel shouted.

They conferred, shrugged and backed away.

Moments later, the horses galloped off. Daniel crept out with the others. They waited at the entrance, eyeing the trees around them. Was their retreat merely a strategy?

"They thought we were only two, but they could be waiting for us," Daniel said.

"We should head for Ilminster, then make for Taunton," Sam said.

Daniel considered Sam's suggestion. "No more detours, Sam. Let's ride. If they're stupid enough to follow, then we'll deal with them."

Robert sneered. "Those curs will follow no one."

"Well, time and tide waits for no man," Sam said as he skipped to the horses.

"True enough," Daniel said. "We're coming, Johanna."

Chapter 38 – Taunton

Even late in the evening, the streets of Taunton were lively as the market sellers packed away their wares. Little had changed. The broad streets were still well pitched, but many of the timber-framed houses in the center of town had been replaced with brick and stone. Daniel and Robert kept their heads down as they passed the boisterous taverns and inns. It may have been six years, but Daniel wasn't taking any chances.

After passing through the market square, they came to a quieter road lined with a row of houses. They walked to the end house and knocked on the door a few times before they heard footsteps. The door opened, and Mr. Leitham, carrying a candle, squinted at them.

"I need to speak with you," Daniel said.

Leitham's mouth dropped. "Daniel?" He immediately stepped aside for the two men and locked the door once they were inside.

"Where is she, Mr. Leitham?" Daniel asked.

"They are going to hang her, Daniel!"

Daniel sat down on the stairs. "When?"

"Noon tomorrow in the main square."

"The constable," Daniel gritted his teeth, "has let me down."

"Daniel…" Leitham hesitated. "Hugo has thirty men and the power of the new government behind him. When the magistrate ruled against us, there was nothing we could do."

"The question is…what are we going to do now?" Daniel asked.

"She'll be heavily guarded," Robert said.

"Yes, in Taunton keep," Richard said.

Robert folded his big arms. "They'll have to bring her out tomorrow."

Daniel and Mr. Leitham nodded in agreement.

"What we need is a distraction," Daniel said.

* * *

Robert had left an hour ago to collect Sam and to stable the horses. After handing Robert the money, Mr. Leitham had suggested a quiet inn south of the market square.

Daniel sat alone running plans through his head. They wouldn't have a hope in hell unless they drew off the bulk of Hugo's men. They would need horses as well and would have to steal them—five if Leitham came, plus one more for backup. What about the constable and his men? Daniel shook his head. The task seemed impossible.

Soon after, Robert returned with Sam, and Daniel helped them set aside their weapons and knapsacks before sitting down again beside the fire. He stoked it into life, and the flames beckoned the others closer.

Leitham brought in bread and milk for the famished travelers. "A distraction," Daniel said, wiping away crumbs that had settled in his beard.

"What about a fire?" Sam suggested as he warmed his hands.

"Certainly draw men away in a hurry," Robert mused.

Leitham broke off some bread. "Then what?"

"Then we get Johanna before he hangs her. We've been lucky so far, and we'll need a lot more tomorrow. But at least it's not complicated: we rescue her, or we all die trying."

They nodded as the stark reality of his words confronted them.

"Listen," Daniel continued, "I mean it, this is my—"

"Don't you dare, Davenport!" Robert growled. "You say it, and I'll slap you from one end of this room to the other, and then rescue your pretty sister myself."

Daniel held up his hands and said no more on the matter.

Sam flicked the breadcrumbs off his breeches. "Mr. Leitham, will the constable help us?"

"I don't think so. He'll not risk his men against Hugo, but I don't believe he'll hinder us either."

"Heaven help us." Robert yawned. "But I need to sleep in a proper bed if I'm going to break some heads tomorrow." He glanced up the stairs. "I take it you have a spare bed in this hovel?"

"Actually, I was going to offer it to Daniel."

"Well, he's welcome to join me." Robert winked.

"Very generous, but I'd rather have my eyes plucked out than share a bed with you." Daniel winked back.

"After damp hedges, the floor will be most welcome," Sam said.

Robert was already thudding up the stairs when Daniel walked with Leitham into the hallway. "I never got a chance to thank you for helping Johanna."

Leitham raised his hands to deflect any credit. "You can thank me when we are all safe."

"I just need to know why?"

Leitham arched his eyebrows.

"Why are you helping her?"

Leitham stiffened. "A fair question, and one that needs to be answered."

Daniel nodded encouragingly.

"I love her, Daniel. Even from the first moment I met her outside Worcester."

"At Worcester?"

"Yes—sectioned under Lambert's Horse. We were patrolling, searching for Royalists east of Worcester, when I happened upon her." He shook his head, and his jaw tightened. "A band of militia had captured her...Thank the Lord I came across her when I did."

"She never told me."

"They never got the chance to...hurt her. With all she suffered, she still had fight enough to scold me like a child." Leitham chuckled briefly before his features clouded over. "I let them go. I should have strung them up there and then, but..." He caught Daniel's eye. "You know how it was there."

"Yes, I remember."

"From that time, my memory of her took hold of me and never let go. She was dressed modestly but had the bearing of a queen. I would never ask for her hand without your permission," Leitham said earnestly.

"I know, and if we somehow survive, you shall have it, Richard."

Daniel walked back into the drawing room where Sam was already snoring. He rubbed his eyes and yawned before stretching out on the floor. Tomorrow's plan circled in his head. A *Fire. A ruse. Hugo, Manfred Hugo.*

* * *

Sam opened his eyes. He lay still, giving his vision time to adjust to the darkness. There were still a few hours until dawn. Daniel, facing the dying fire, slept soundly. His riding coat was draped across a stool by the table. Sam lifted himself up and tested each floorboard as he made for Daniel's coat. He stepped over Daniel's legs and then lifted the coat off the stool. He pried open the inside pocket and slipped out the earl's letter. He stopped for a heartbeat, then turned on his heels and tiptoed back, again testing each floorboard as he went.

He reached the front door and stopped dead. Robert's snoring resonated from upstairs. The door was locked, but he'd noted where Leitham had placed the key. He slotted the key into the lock and winced as it clicked open. He waited, but no one stirred. He grasped the handle, yet hesitated, though only for a moment, before stepping out into the cold night and made for the market square. The streets were quiet, and even the beggars and drunks who huddled together in the back streets didn't stir when he walked past. After reaching Corporation Street, Taunton Keep stood grey against the black sky. He quickened his pace and continued the climb toward Taunton Castle.

Sam woke the two guards into action when he approached the western gatehouse. They held their pikes ready, but Sam skipped toward them unconcerned.

"I will see the commissioner immediately," Sam said.

The taller guard with the tattered coat snorted at the Quaker. "You'll turn 'round and piss off."

Sam wrapped his cloak tighter still to fend off a sudden breeze. "I am Samuel Tripton, and if Manfred Hugo does not receive my news, he will have you both flogged."

The other guard ignored his friend's objections and led Sam into the outer courtyard and hence to the main gate of the inner ward. They passed through the gate into the inner ward, and then climbed steps to rooms that ran along the inner walls. They stopped at a door, and the guard ordered Sam to wait.

Some minutes later, Sam followed the guard into a large room to the right of the gatehouse. Hugo sat behind a desk, drumming his fingers. Sam retrieved the letter from his coat.

Hugo's eyes widened. "Give it to me."

"Where is my family?"

"They are safe, Samuel. You know that. Give it to me."

Sam's heart sank as he placed the letter on the desk. He had betrayed himself and Daniel for the smirking horror in front of him.

Hugo lifted a candle closer. A tight smile spread across his face as he read the contents. "Where is he?"

"You gave me your word."

"Nothing has changed. Now tell me?"

"The lawyer's house." Each word choked him. "He is with the lawyer, Leitham."

Chapter 39 – Betrayal

Pain drifted into his dreams, and Daniel gasped as he awoke. He shielded his ribs, but the shock of swords and carbines trained on him was far worse than the agony of the kick. He was surrounded. They had to be Hugo's men. Even before the despair of failure could take hold of him, a kick to the temple flattened him out.

They mocked and chided Daniel, believing him for a coward. The others? Sam was not in the room. A shout from upstairs and a short sharp struggle was enough to tell him Robert and Richard were captured. Then Robert's heavy footsteps plodded down the stairs until he appeared at the door with three soldiers in tow. With a carbine shoved into his back, they ushered him into the drawing room.

A tall, heavy-set Roundhead with small rat eyes entered the room and gawked at the prisoners.

Perhaps Sam had made it out? The soldiers weren't searching for another man.

"He'll be comin' for you bastards soon enough," the rat-eyed Roundhead barked. "So keep your holes shut until then."

Robert sneered at the Roundhead and straightened himself to his full height.

Daniel shook his head, for he knew what was coming next.

"Maybe if you shut your cake-hole more often, pig-man," Robert said, "you wouldn't be panting every time you took a shit!"

The soldier's face changed from red to purple. He snatched a carbine from the nearest soldier and pressed it against Robert's head.

"Enough of this!" Leitham said.

The guard nearest to Leitham rapped his legs, and he crumpled to the floor.

The tall Roundhead took his finger away from the trigger. "You're goin' to stand still while I club your ugly face," he said. "If you move an inch, I'll shoot you dead." The Roundhead jabbed the musket butt into Robert's face. The blood poured from his broken nose.

"You are one ugly bastard," Robert said, flicking his blood in his assailant's face.

"Stand that bastard against the wall!"

Robert sauntered over himself and glared at the Roundhead.

"You'll do nothing unless Hugo tells you!" Daniel shouted.

The big Roundhead wiped the blood from his face and aimed the carbine at Daniel's head. "I'll have that dotard's brains paint the wall, and then I'll have your sister's witch-maidenhood. That slut's far too succulent!"

Before Daniel could react, the door opened. Two men strolled in. A stocky, bearded man and the other, a dark-haired, clean-shaven man of similar height to Daniel.

"Hugo?" Daniel hissed.

"Commissioner Hugo."

Sam followed them in, and Daniel's shoulders slumped. They had captured Sam, as well.

The fat Roundhead stood back and kept his mouth shut.

Hugo sneered at the sweating bulk in front of him. "Garsten, check them again for weapons, and then take the splitter-of-causes and that blockhead to the keep."

Hugo pulled up a chair and waited for the room to clear, leaving only his bearded lackey, Sam, and a few soldiers. Hugo glared at Daniel. "Blood for blood, Daniel."

"John was my friend."

"He was my brother!" Hugo screamed. "Blood for blood—the blood of my son, my brother, and the woman I loved. That is what you owe me, Daniel."

"It was a war," Daniel pleaded. "I killed many people at Worcester, but I did not kill John, and certainly not your son or the woman you speak of."

"You are responsible," Manfred spat. "And for that, I claim according to the law of justice: an eye for an eye."

"What about forgive thy enemy?"

Hugo was silent for a moment. "I know the scriptures, but for too long I have dreamt only of...justice."

"You mean revenge."

"To watch you suffer in every possible way." Hugo lifted his head to the heavens as if he were receiving a Divine message. "Of late, I have seen clearer, and for the greater good, I am willing to spare the life of your sister and you—if you do what I want."

Daniel leant closer. "Tell me?"

"Blood for blood, Daniel. I want Rochester—"

Daniel involuntarily glanced at his coat.

"Ah." Hugo smirked. "The letter was there, Samuel?"

Sam lowered his head.

Then it struck Daniel like the blast of a thunderclap. It was written on Sam's face. Daniel's mouth fell open. "Sam?"

Hugo rolled his eyes. "You are a trusting fool, aren't you? You've done nothing without me knowing."

"Why, Sam?" Daniel asked.

"He belongs to me. His wife and daughters are in my care." Hugo crossed his arms. "I could have had you murdered in Salisbury Gaol, but when we heard about the rebels, well…They helped me immensely. We knew Rochester was in England, and because of your service in the army and at Worcester, we knew they would trust you. I was persuaded to consider the greater good, Daniel."

"The rebellion has nothing to do with me."

Hugo produced the letter and held it up to Daniel. "It has now." He pointed at a signature. "Penruddock's seal of rebellion in your possession. I want Rochester and Charles. When they are mine, I will gift you and your sister's life back."

Daniel shook his head.

"If you refuse, you will all swing from the gallows before nightfall."

"I am no traitor!" Daniel glared at Sam

A closed-lipped smile gripped Hugo's face. "It matters not. For I will happily see that justice is administered. But know this, your witch sister will die slowly. I will make sure she dies in the most unimaginable agony. And you will watch, knowing you could have stopped it."

Daniel dropped his face into his hands. "So revenge has given way to ambition."

"Call it what you will, but I work for the greater good. Now give me your word."

"I want to see my sister."

"Give me your word."

The weight of the treachery hammered through his brain, and he hesitated.

Hugo grabbed Daniel's throat. "I will wait no longer! Agree, or you'll see her quartered!"

Daniel gasped for air as Hugo crushed his windpipe. He nodded, and Hugo released his grip. Daniel spluttered and coughed as he sucked in air.

Hugo motioned for Sam to sit down in front of him. "Samuel, you will be free before the day ends. I will ask one more thing of you before your wife and daughters are brought to you."

Sam nodded.

"With Charles and the earl," Hugo said to Daniel, "you have given me two, but blood for blood, Daniel, you owe me three."

"A king is not enough for your bloodlust?" Daniel croaked.

"I would have given you a choice, but with the lawyer it wouldn't be so easy. He did fight for Parliament after all," Hugo said, ignoring Daniel's question. "And Johanna has taken such a shine to him."

Daniel felt sick each time Hugo uttered his sister's name.

"So, I will have to take your traitorous friend."

"No!" Daniel screamed.

"The multitudes have come for a hanging. And better a Royalist traitor than dear, sweet Johanna?"

Daniel gesticulated. "Please...please, I will do as you ask! He is innocent in this!"

Hugo flicked away the words. "Mr. Mabb, take him to his sister, and I want the scaffold ready for three." He pointed at Davenport and Samuel. "And they will watch."

"I won't do it!" Daniel cried out.

Hugo sneered. "We shall see."

* * *

Daniel trudged toward the north tower door, avoiding the soldiers' mattresses strewn across the floor. He gripped the wall as he shambled up the steps, scraping his hand across the rough stone. With each step, he cursed Hugo until he reached Johanna's cell.

The soldier escorted him in. Johanna lay with her back to him. She didn't even bother to turn.

"It is I!"

She slowly turned around. Her eyes narrowed. "Daniel?"

Pale and drawn, Johanna sat up on a mattress. With only a single blanket to protect her from the cold drafts, she trembled.

"Yes!" He skipped over to Johanna.

Her eyes blazed, and she gripped him tight. "It cannot be?"

"Flesh and blood, Johanna. I came for you!"

She kissed his cheek and then buried her head into his arms. "My prayers are answered."

For one brief moment, the guilt and shame fell away from him. Her tears were for him the garnering of the rain clouds, spilling over the parched earth of his soul.

"You've looked better!" Daniel kissed her forehead.

"As you have." She beamed through her tears. "Daniel...he will hang me today."

He embraced her again and whispered. "He has agreed to release us both. Soon you will be free."

She pulled away, astonishment and disbelief plastered across her face. "How?" she stammered.

"Believe it, for it is the truth. It matters not how or why, only that you will be free." Daniel broke away from her gaze. The hollowness of his words formed only a glaring accusation.

"And the price?"

"What price?" The lie stuck in his throat.

"I will never leave this room alive if you do not tell me!"

Daniel walked over to the window. She mustn't know about Robert. "He wants the leaders of the rebellion. He wants the king."

"It cannot be!" Johanna clutched her breast.

Daniel grasped the cold wall to hold himself up.

"It would be better for us to die together."

He grasped her hand. "I will never do it," he whispered, "I need time."

"Yes, promise me?"

"I promise...It is pretense. I will play along then we will flee to safety."

Johanna sank back again exhausted. She sobbed as he stroked her fair hair.

The door opened, and the guards rattled in.

Johanna kissed his cheek. "I have always believed in you

184

Daniel. I always will."

"I will come back soon. One day, this will feel like nothing more than a bad dream."

He walked out and fell against the wall. The picture of Sam following Hugo into Leitham's sitting room mocked him. He wasn't a traitor like Sam. He would play along for the moment. So much could happen between now and then.

The soldiers pulled Daniel down the steps.

"God help me," he muttered.

* * *

Daniel's request to visit Robert had been rejected. He paced the length of his cell, trying to stay one step ahead of the approaching madness. Wild schemes of their miraculous escape flitted through his mind. They would all escape together. Daniel gripped his hair. It wasn't betrayal—Robert had wanted to help Johanna. It was Sam who had betrayed them. His was the guilt. Robert's sacrifice would not be in vain. Daniel had to save Johanna. After everything she had gone through—he banged his fists against the wall. What was pain compared to this inner desolation? What else could he have done for Robert?

Hugo's guards came. He refused to leave, so they softened him up with a beating before dragging him out. They bundled him into the coach opposite Sam. The guards jumped in beside him, and the coach made off.

The wheels rattled over the cobbled street, but as they trundled into market square, the coach halted before the crowds. Hugo had talked about the multitudes, and he had not exaggerated. The flow of people, all in the same direction, sickened Daniel.

"They have all come to see my sister murdered, Sam." Daniel clenched his teeth. "And now they will laugh and joke as Robert is murdered in her stead."

Sam bowed his head.

"Speak to me, you bastard!"

The guard elbowed Daniel. Blood spattered from his nose onto his breeches.

"Now keep your mouth shut." The guard snapped.

"Will you tell your wife and children about this day? You should have told me. We would have helped you."

185

The soldier lifted the butt of his weapon.

"Enough!" Sam said, raising his hands.

"Then you tell him to shut his mouth, Quaker."

"Please, let him speak."

Daniel jabbed his finger at Sam. "Make sure you watch today, *Samuel.*"

The carriage pulled up at the far end of the square, and the guards pulled them out. Daniel cursed Hugo as the insane spectacle presented itself across the square. The gallows stood before him like some monstrous tree. A line of soldiers kept the spectators back as they jostled forward.

People from all walks of life and every imaginable station descended upon the square. They were in a festive mood. Mothers cradled babies, while old men and cripples were helped to the front to get a better view of the entertainment. Merchants and vendors sold their wares, and publicans sold drink.

"*Samuel,*" Daniel said, seizing Sam's arm, "see how they take odds! How long will it take Robert to die?" His tears melted away in the fire of his indignation. If he could have butchered the onlookers there and then, he would have done it with exquisite relish.

Sam's mouth sagged as the group of men exchanged money amid their curses and recriminations. And then the cart trundled forward, carrying the bound and hooded Robert. Hugo and his entourage rode beside. The crowd strained to glimpse what was happening. Father's hoisted children into the air. The crowd grew restless when the stranger appeared kneeling upon the cart. Shouts of "where's the witch?" chorused across the square.

The cart rattled closer to the gallows, and then halted underneath the rope. Boos and hisses surged ominously, and the soldiers readied themselves for trouble. Hugo stepped onto the cart and held up his hands. "Friends, so great is God's mercy and power even a witch can find repentance and forgiveness through recognition!"

The jeers increased, and Hugo waited.

"Johanna Davenport acknowledged her guilt to me last evening and prayed to God for forgiveness."

Curses and mockery filled the square.

"And the Almighty took her in her sleep!"

The crowd surged forward, but the line of soldiers checked their advance.

"I know how this town suffered at the hands of the Royalists: siege upon siege, death and privation! Today, I give you some small measure of justice. Behold the escaped rebel and traitor! You will see justice this day with his execution!"

The crowd roared with approval.

Shame of the spectacle branded Daniel. Justice was dead, and madmen murdered at a whim.

Hugo removed Robert's hood, and the crowd cheered again. Robert squinted into the sunlight as they lifted him to his feet. He towered over Hugo and his soldiers. The crowd delighted in mocking the big man, who searched around him for a friendly face. The mongrels bated and cursed him, but his forlorn smile still reached Daniel.

Daniel clasped his hands together in prayer and Robert nodded.

Hugo raised his hands again. "Have you any last words?"

Robert scowled over the crowd. "No!"

The crowd jeered him, upset by his insouciance. They expected more entertainment.

"Will you not ask God for forgiveness?" Hugo asked, playing up to the crowd.

"God knows my sins and all that lies in my heart! That's enough for me!"

"Very well!"

Hugo stepped off the cart, and the masked executioner stepped up. Robert acknowledged him. The noose was fixed about his neck. The hangman spoke a few words, and Robert nodded. The hangman was about to fix the hood, but Robert shook his head. He raised his head toward the clear sky.

A whirlwind of Robert's stories battered into Daniel's memory. Robert's anecdotes and recollections that kept them sane over the long, cold afternoons in Fisherton Anger seared his heart. Robert's father, the hard-drinking stonemason, who had spent his time breaking stone and men's jaws. He had taught Robert to be a man. He had told Daniel about his mother, who died when he was a lad, and who had the sweetest smile a man ever did see. When he had spoken about her, it was the first and last time Robert had cried in Daniel's presence. He spoke of his dear sister, who had doted on him, but whom he hadn't seen these past ten years.

The stories flooded through Daniel, and he swayed on his feet when Robert mouthed a few words to himself. Daniel knew the sense of those words. For after Worcester, they knew not if the rope awaited them. Robert's words trumpeted through Daniel's brain: "I'm not afraid to die, Daniel. But sweet Jesus, I'm afraid to foul myself!"

Daniel had to watch and remember. For one day, the picture of Hugo's corpse would obliterate the memory.

The great figure of his friend slipped from the cart, turned off, and then lurched up as the rope snapped straight. Robert's eyes bulged in the agony of constriction. His agony assaulted Daniel and crushed down on his soul.

Robert struggled, and then he struggled more. Would the rope snap, with the fight in him? But no, the rope held firm. The crowd enjoyed it. They cheered as the big man fought. They cheered as he turned ashen and then blue of face. But still his legs twitched, and still Robert fought, and then, even the jeers and clapping ceased after the eternity of those minutes.

Daniel's greatest friend stilled. Robert was dead. Dead strangled eyes, dimmed black forever. Or would those eyes open again in the light of God's glory? "I swear we will meet again, my friend!"

Sam stood apart like a statue. His arms folded and eyes fixed on the figure of Robert.

With a grunt, a guard led them to Hugo, who addressed Sam. "Your family is in the Swan Inn. If you cross my path again, Samuel, I'll assume you mean me ill, and then I'll kill you."

Daniel fixed his gaze on the Quaker as he made his way across the market square until he was lost in the departing crowds. Heaven help the Quaker if they ever met again.

"When you have been successful, Johanna will also be freed. I keep my word, Daniel."

"What about Robert?"

"That's not your concern. You need to think about the living."

Daniel caught his eye. If he could have killed with a look, Hugo would have crumpled lifelessly to the ground.

Chapter 40 – The Earl's Letter

Everything had been prepared for their journey. Mabb and the loathsome Garsten were chosen to accompany Daniel to the earl's safe house. Hugo and the rest would leave a day later and catch up. New mounts were given, along with civilian clothing to give the impression of travelling merchants on their way to London. Only their tucks were visible to dissuade hedge robbers, while their carbines were concealed in their blanket rolls.

It had been quiet on the roads, and the company quieter still. That suited Daniel well enough. The patrols, which scoured the land for rebels, had kept folk off the roads. The few others they met, whether farmers driving their beasts along the drovers' ways or through the pack-horse trials, or simply wanderers using the other tracks and ridgeways, were shy of the three strangers passing through, rarely speaking more than a few words. They also had time, for according to the earl's letter, the Black Swan, a small Dutch trading vessel, would leave with the tide on the twentieth. They were in no hurry and could afford to sleep overnight in any inn they happened to pass.

Late evening, they came to Samson's Inn on the outskirts of Bristol. It was quiet, so they were able to share the same room. The innkeeper had brought them chicken broth, which had gone down a treat. And he had had the sense not to question the sour fellows, instead, wishing them a comfortable night.

There were two straw mattresses—enough space for four men to lie upon—but Garsten had already claimed one for himself, laying his considerable mass spread-eagled across it. Mabb was welcome to the other; for Daniel couldn't stomach the idea of sharing with a bed with either of them. Even with new clothes, a stench lingered about them.

With Garsten already snoring, Mabb retrieved a Bible from his knapsack. He thumbed each line, squinting through the candlelight.

"King James?" Daniel asked.

Mabb raised an eyebrow. "Geneva."

"Rare indeed."

"Aye, so I've been told," Mabb said, without taking his eyes from the page.

"Plunder?"

"It was a gift," Mabb snarled.

"A fine gift, but can you read it?"

"Some."

Daniel had expected the bearded man to thump him, but his reply was tinged with pride. "Yes, it's a fine edition."

"The Captain received it from some colonel, and then he gave it to me."

"The Captain?"

"Captain Hugo."

"Do you enjoy being his slave, Mabb?"

"Put your head down, Davenport. There's near a day's travel until Aylesbury."

Daniel lay down and shifted himself until he felt a semblance of comfort. He closed his eyes and, as in previous nights, the past wormed its way back to him: The blast of the musket and the hole in John's head, the king fleeing from the Roundheads, the crack of Bodley's ribs, the horror of Robert's bulging eyes.

Daniel sat up in the darkness. His ragged gasps mingled with the chorus of snoring. He wiped the sweat from his brow and neck. He banged his chest with his fist and his breathing slowed. He lay down again, and after hours of listening to their snoring, finally fell into a listless sleep.

Mabb woke him an hour before dawn.

Garsten groaned. "It's this mattress," he said, clutching his head.

"Nothing to do with the ale?" Mabb said.

"The bastard also served me bad ale. I'm goin' to force my fist down his throat."

Mabb set his knapsack down. "You're going to get ready and keep your mouth shut. You hear?"

Garsten heaved to his feet, and took himself over to Mabb. He bent down, bringing his beady eyes level with Mabb's. "You watch yourself with me, tramp!"

"Get ready. That's an order."

Garsten stepped back and smiled. That 'smile' was Garsten's final warning and the most sinister expression of his cruelty.

As the sun came up and they ambled along the road to Aylesbury, Garsten related, with a lick of his lips, the tale of when Hugo caught a pickpocket in some hole of a village on their way to Taunton. "Hugo told the thief to beg God for forgiveness," he snorted. "For thieves are despised by all righteous men, Hugo told the runt. And you know what the Dripper did to Hugo?"

Daniel rolled his eyes, and Mabb didn't bother to reply.

"He spat on him! He had balls. I'll say that for him. Balls." Garsten snorted again. "Hugo ordered the men to form a circle, and the thief was thrown in the middle. Hugo said he's only needin' to escape the circle and he would be free. The maggot was a whippet-like youth, light on his feet, and he grinned at his good fortune, thinkin' it be easy to jump past us." Garsten laughed. "Problem was, Hugo pulled a pistol on him and put a hole in his leg. We battered that prick for five minutes—in the end, Woolstone broke his neck, when the prig tried to crawl under him."

Mabb shook his head.

Daniel kept his gaze on the meadows, drinking in the beauty around him.

"Anyway," Garsten continued, "there's nothin' like givin' a beatin' to a blower."

A kestrel hovered above a small hill in the meadow. A perfect place for rabbits.

"I like the ugly ones 'cause they're grateful and they're used to a few cracks. It was near midnight, and I picked up this whore in Exeter. I took her to my room and inspected her in the candlelight. Shit!" Garsten shook his head. "An ugly, pug faced whore if ever—"

"Silence! Or I'll cut your tongue out!" Mabb shrieked, removing a vicious curved dagger from his doublet.

The horses stopped, and Garsten licked his lips. "You're a fine fellow—a fucking sodomite if ever I saw one! I ought to gut you both and be on my way." He glanced behind him, checking that the road was clear.

Mabb readied himself as Garsten drew his sword. Instead, obviously thinking better of it, Garsten wheeled around and, kicking his heels into his mount, galloped away. Mabb was about to give chase, but Daniel grabbed the reins.

"Leave it. We have work to do."

The reins quivered in Mabb's grip. His tension faded, and he relaxed in the saddle, patting his nervous cob.

"Will he come back?"

"I doubt it. We're safer without him anyway. His type will get us lynched."

"If the bastard comes back," Daniel said "I'll help you kill him myself. But I tell you now, that pig's not one to forgive or forget."

Chapter 41 – Reborn

Sam knocked on the constable's door, and then again before the key turned in the lock. The constable's withering sneer greeted him.

"Wait! I need to speak to you," Sam said before the constable could slam the door in his face.

"Well, I don't need to speak with you."

Reviled as a Quaker, Sam had experienced how persistence had opened nearly every door for him. "I can't help Daniel, but we can help Johanna. She's going to need our help before long."

"Do you really believe I could trust you?"

"It matters not. You need not place any trust in me to help her."

The constable peered up and down the street before standing aside for Sam. An old woman with a bent back hobbled out of the kitchen. "Will ye be havin' a drink, Mr. Lucas?" She asked, cupping her ear.

"Yes, Ms. Eddy, thank you!"

She nodded and wandered back to the kitchen.

Apart from a fine oaken table standing against the wall, it was a rather spartan drawing room. Obviously, the constable was a man unaccustomed to visitors.

The constable set down a stool for Sam, and then planted himself down opposite. "Was it worth it?" He spoke through gritted teeth.

"I'm not here to talk about that."

"Well, you better, otherwise you can leave now."

"I don't know what you want me to say."

"The truth, you bastard!"

"I'm sorry it happened." Sam lowered his gaze. "But I would do it again. I'm guilty, and I accept that, but Hugo has the lion's share of it. He took them away from me. He would have murdered them—murdered my wife, Marie, and my daughters—two young girls, just as innocent as Johanna and Daniel. When we were reunited, I felt almost reborn. Their relief flooded over me, and their tears were my balm." Sam rubbed his eyes. "I made my choice, and now I have to live with it. Maybe it was the wrong choice. But I'd still make it again."

"Because you're a coward."

"You're right. I am a coward. I'll never be as courageous as Robert. I'll never be as strong as Johanna. I'll never be as generous or as good as Daniel. I am who I am, but that's all my girls have, Constable. Perhaps that's why Hugo chose me."

The constable sat with his arms folded. "I'm listening."

"Hugo spared Johanna's life on one condition—to bring him the Earl of Rochester and…"

"And?"

"Assassinate Charles."

"Huh!" The constable rolled back in the chair. "I knew he was a Bedlam Tom!"

"That's why we have to help, Johanna." Sam said. "For sure as hell, when Daniel fails, he'll murder her."

The constable gesticulated his annoyance and helplessness with a sweep of his hand. "The Magistrate has left already. He left Taunton last night like a thief in the night."

"Let us then entreat John Disbrowe."

"Don't you think I've explored these possibilities?"

"The rule of law had been set aside in Taunton. Robert was hanged without a trial. Don't you suppose Disbrowe will want to know? Leitham is a lawyer."

"Cromwell's Major-Generals are here. They will use their commissioners to suppress all unlawful assemblies. And Hugo," the constable continued, "in his warped mind, believes in everything he does. I don't believe he would attempt such an enterprise without the knowledge of a higher authority."

Carrying a tray with a pitcher of ale and tankards, Ms. Eddy swayed through the door. Lucas jumped up to help her before it all came crashing down.

"You need me to pour it?" she asked.

"I can do it, Ms. Eddy. Thank you." Lucas poured for them both before gulping down a draught. "She's been brewing ale for nearly fifty years."

Sam sipped some down and wiped his chin.

"Why Daniel?" The constable asked.

"If anyone could get close to Charles, it would be Daniel. Daniel fought at Worcester. He told me of the king's escape at Worcester. And...he has the letter of passage from the Earl of Rochester."

"Lord, help us. You have a lot to answer for," the constable said, slamming down his tankard. "I will draft a letter and hand it personally to Disbrowe. With our list of grievances, perhaps we can convince him to free her."

"And if that fails?"

"Then...then we fight."

* * *

Armed with letters from the constable and Johanna's doctor, and a hastily drawn up legal draft without legal validity, Richard demanded an audience with the underling Hugo had placed in charge.

He was taken to a young man in his twenties, who rather haughtily pronounced himself as Corporal Wells. He had bookish look about him, but he described how he had achieved rank in Lord Grey's regiment of foot before he saw twenty years. Richard passed him the letters, and Wells skimmed through them.

Well's handed the letters back to Richard. "Seems to be in order, but my *orders*, from the commissioner himself, are no visitors."

"Of course, but he put you in command for a reason. Obviously he wanted a man with initiative."

Wells nodded in agreement.

"But the last time I saw Johanna Davenport she was dangerously ill. And if she dies, he will hold you accountable."

He hemmed and hawed, then requested the letters again. As before, he skimmed over the contents. "The letters will remain in my keeping."

"Of course, I wouldn't expect otherwise."

"All subsequent visits must be approved by myself beforehand."

"Yes, I agree."

With everything settled, Wells escorted Richard to the North

Tower. He half expected to be denied access, but now with that particular hurdle overcome, his nerves were beginning to get the better of him. What should he tell her if she asked about Daniel? He pushed his concerns away. After they had freed her, they could begin worrying about Daniel and Hugo.

Richard was searched before the guard opened the door for him. Johanna set down her Bible, stood and nodded to both Richard and Wells.

"You see how pale Miss Davenport is?" Richard said. "It's important her physician hears about this today. I can tell him if you wish."

"As you wish, Mr. Leitham. You have two minutes." Wells inclined his head to Johanna before leaving them alone.

Richard escorted Johanna back to her chair and then planted down beside her. "Don't ask. But you are pale, Johanna."

"My brother?"

"He left with Mabb—"

"He told me he would never do it, Richard," she said, whispering. "It's part of his plan. He will come back for us."

"Yes." Richard lowered his head. "I'm sure you're right."

"Then why do I dread what is coming, Richard?"

"Trust him." He took her hand. "He's a good man."

"It's the helplessness."

"The constable has left to petition Major-General John Disbrowe. We hope he can help you. Hugo's abused his power—hangings without a trial can't—"

"What hanging?"

Too late Richard recognized his mistake. "He hanged Robert White."

"It cannot be?" Johanna clutched her Bible against her chest. "Daniel never told me."

"It's all too much for him, Johanna. He's trying to protect you." Richard poured some water for her, but she ignored it. He had to protect her from such news. Her constitution had always been strong, but now her fragile form seemed almost ethereal.

The door opened, and the guard called time.

"Don't give up. Promise me that?" Richard asked.

"I swear it."

"I...need you also, Johanna."

She kissed his cheek and gazed into his eyes. "We need each other."

Heat flushed his cheeks, and he lowered his head. She raised his chin, and their eyes locked. "I will come tomorrow, my dearest, Johanna."

"As God is my witness, I will honor you both."

Chapter 42 – Aylesbury

Each step brought Daniel closer to treason. The earl had been with the king at Worcester, and Daniel knew him to be a capable and loyal general. *Loyalty.* Six years Daniel had fought for Charles. He had lost his father, lost his freedom, and now his sister. Those years of loyalty would count for nothing if he went through with it.

Treason.

He shuddered each time the word thudded into his brain. How many times had he told his men that a traitor was the most despicable of all creatures?

Each step brought him closer to Rochester's safe house. He should have stayed on the continent. It was Rochester's choice to come back to England on a foolish enterprise. And Aylesbury? An odd choice after the town declared for Parliament during the war. Still, perhaps the best place to hide was under the lion's nose. As it was, they found themselves half a mile north of Aylesbury.

"It's over yonder, past those trees," Daniel said.

"What are you waiting for?"

"It doesn't need to end like this. Is there not another way, Mabb?"

Mabb scowled. "Not if you want your sister to live."

"And what's in it for you? Has he threatened to kill someone you love?"

"He's my Captain. And I understand the meaning of loyalty. It's men like him, willing to sacrifice everything to fight evil, who'll bring us the new Kingdom."

Even Mabb looked down upon him with scorn. Mabb lived and breathed loyalty. "Why am I here anyway? Hugo knows where the earl is. Another game? A test? Moving his victims around the chessboard—cold-blooded sacrifice for his cold-blooded ambition."

Mabb shrugged and walked on toward the tree line. For him, loyalty meant following orders. Mabb didn't need to know his master's plan.

When they reached the tree line, a modest country house sat off an overgrown path. Two men sat in the shade by the door. Their plain garb couldn't disguise their martial bearing.

Mabb stepped back into cover. "What now?"

"We introduce ourselves."

As they emerged from the trees, the two men leapt to their feet. They drew pistols.

Daniel held up his hands. "I am Captain Davenport of the King's Lifeguard, and I am here to see the Earl of Rochester."

The soldier on the left with a clipped goatee stepped forward. "An Earl here?" He snorted. "Be on your way, stranger."

"I have come from Colonel Penruddock." Daniel produced the letter. "Charged to return the earl's letter with Colonel Penruddock's message."

"Bring it forward," the other soldier spoke up, while his partner kept his pistol trained on Daniel.

Daniel handed him the letter, and the man disappeared through the door.

It only took a few minutes before he came back. "So you fought with Penruddock at Salisbury?"

"No, the Colonel liberated Fisherton Anger Gaol in Salisbury. He asked me to deliver the letter in person."

"And him?" he said, pointing his pistol Mabb.

"This is Sam Tripton—also, until recently, a prisoner at Fisherton Anger."

The soldier waved them in. They lowered their pistols, but they were still jittery. Daniel and Mabb followed them into the drawing room. The Earl of Rochester stood by a table. It had been four years since Worcester, and apart from a few more grey strands threading through his hair, Rochester looked much the same. Four years before, he'd had cut a dashing figure as he'd entered Worcester Cathedral with the king's generals trailing behind. The man standing before Daniel looked the same but cut a rather less spirited figure. An aristocratic lady sat at the table, eyeing him easily. Daniel acknowledged her before giving the earl his full attention.

Rochester scrutinized Daniel. "Where is Penruddock?"

"I know not, my lord, but I heard he was captured at South

199

Molton."

"I am wondering how you came by this intelligence when you had already left Salisbury for Aylesbury?"

"It is a long and tragic story, but the briefer version being that my friend fought with the Colonel in my stead, so I could help my sister."

Rochester seated himself without taking his eyes off Daniel.

"He escaped South Molton when Penruddock was defeated by a troop of horse."

"A deserter?"

"No. And Never. He was the bravest man I've ever known, and he fought for the king from Naseby to Worcester."

"Was?"

"We met at Nimmer before travelling to Taunton for my sister. He was captured…and hanged."

Rochester's expression didn't change. "And your sister?"

"Safe." Daniel bristled. "Do you not remember me at Worcester? I remember you, my lord Wilmot, who escaped the cauldron with the king. And who is now made an earl."

The guards raised their weapons, but the earl calmed them with a wave of his hand. "Should I?"

"I was there in New Street when the dragoons charged the king. I warned His Majesty, and we guarded the door as the king— and others—made their escape. After I had recovered from my injuries, I was jailed in Fisherton Anger."

"Please sit—" Rochester gestured "—both of you." He poured the wine himself, offering each a glass. "This is Lady Anne Farmer."

Both Daniel and Mabb inclined towards her.

"She has been a great friend to our cause. It's fortunate you came when you did, for I was also recently informed of the Colonel's misfortune."

"A brave man, my lord," Daniel said.

Mabb gulped down the wine, and his cheeks flushed.

"Your quiet friend has a thirst."

Mabb nodded and knocked more wine back.

"Help yourself, Mr. Tripton." Rochester dismissed the guards. "We would have already left but for the patrols."

"We were fortunate to get here at all, my lord."

"Yes, we have people spread over all England. God willing, they'll find safety."

"Your letter mentioned safe passage?"

"We have many friends in London. The ship is inconspicuous enough—a small Dutch merchant ship called The Black Swan. The captain knows his business, and we will follow his lead in this."

Rochester finished his wine.

The small talk made Daniel want to vomit. *Traitor.* Hugo was only minutes behind. It was now or never.

"Allow me, my lord." Daniel refilled the earl's glass. Before Rochester raised it, Daniel held his dagger against the earl's throat.

Rochester froze. Lady Farmer called out for the guards.

Mabb pulled his pistol on Farmer. Her eyes latched onto the door. The guards rushed in with pistols drawn.

"Drop your weapons!" Daniel pressed the dagger tighter still.

They lowered their pistols. "My lord, Roundheads are minutes away—"

The guard lifted his pistol to fire, but Mabb fired first, and the guard dropped, clutching his chest.

"Control your man! You will need him to help this woman!"

"Throw your pistol down," Rochester ordered the soldier.

The soldier let the pistol slide from his hand, and he raised his arms.

Daniel motioned for the soldier to back off, and Mabb snatched up the pistol. "We have only a short time before they arrive."

"Please, take her to safety," Rochester entreated the guard.

"Go north," Daniel instructed Lady Anne. "And on your life, do not turn back or travel to the Black Swan."

Daniel lowered his eyes before her withering gaze. She clasped the earl's hand and kissed his cheek.

"I hear Scotland is nice this time of year?" Rochester said.

Rochester's guard grabbed her arm, and they fled from the room.

Mabb moved over to the window.

"Your sword, my lord," Daniel said.

Rochester pulled the weapon from its scabbard and threw it on the table. "May I?" he asked, pointing at the glass of wine. "I find myself rather thirsty all of a sudden."

Daniel refilled the glass. "I would apologize, but what difference would it make?"

Rochester took another gulp. "Sometimes it can make all the difference, Captain."

"Is there more wine?" Mabb said, drumming his fingers on the window.

"I'm afraid not," Rochester said.

"If I said I had no choice, would it make a difference?"

"We always have a choice, Captain."

"You are right, of course." Daniel smirked. "It was my choice to follow the king. It was his choice to flee Worcester and leave us behind. It was my choice to save my innocent sister. It was your choice to return to England, my lord. You are correct, we always have a choice."

The earl took a moment to consider the words. "Am I innocent? The king?"

"It matters not. I've made my choice."

Rochester nodded. "Well, Captain, I hope you and your sister can live with it."

"To live? I want my sister to live. Nothing more than that."

* * *

In the meantime, the earl had remembered there was another bottle of wine in his room. After Daniel had fetched it, Rochester poured himself another glass. He took a moment to regard its rich color before Hugo's arrival disturbed him from his reflections. After taking a sip, Rochester set the glass down and glided ceremoniously toward the door.

Daniel blocked his path.

"At least let me welcome my guests."

Daniel led him out, with Mabb following. Hugo shouted some orders and his men dismounted.

"I didn't get a chance to finish my wine. I think you must be early?"

"I believe you'll find you're late," Hugo said with a pinched expression. "But do not worry, I'll make sure you're not late for your execution."

"How considerate of you."

"As a Commissioner of the Peace," Hugo continued, "I am

here to arrest you for treason. You will be taken to London for trial. Are you alone?"

"I am."

"He was alone, sir," Mabb said in reply to Hugo's questioning look.

Daniel rolled his eyes in relief.

Hugo barked out more orders, and the earl's hands were bound. With a leg up, Rochester mounted the horse.

Hugo passed the lead rider the bottle of wine. "For your nerves, my lord?" He smirked when Rochester ignored the jibe.

Daniel counted ten soldiers escorting Rochester, leaving eight, including Hugo and Mabb. He followed Hugo into the house. Hugo slid his hand over the tall chair which Rochester had sat on moments earlier.

"I believe the property belongs to his wife," Hugo said matter-of-factly. He sat down and made himself comfortable. "I wonder how many of the Sealed Knot sat at this very table."

The question was rhetorical, but Mabb mumbled ten.

"Daniel, Edward, please sit." Hugo waited until they were comfortable. "Where is Garsten?"

Mabb fell into a coughing fit.

"He left us," Daniel answered, "I don't suppose he enjoyed our company."

"He's a gutter rat and a raper," Mabb said with unexpected venom.

"Yes, his uses were limited. A vulgar man, but no matter, he's no great loss. I think we've come to an understanding, Daniel."

Daniel winced at the assertion. Hugo lounged back in the chair without a care in the world. *Does he believe he is untouchable? His men are outside. It would take only seconds to kill him.*

"You saved me time and effort. Now I have the information I need without having to having to resort to more unsavory methods of persuasion. You could have acted unwisely, but you acted in your sister's interests."

"Just tell me what I need to do next."

"As far as we know, Charles is still in Zeeland, but we have no idea where in Middelburg. When he returns to Cologne, then that will be your time, Davenport. When you kill Charles Stuart, our debt will be settled."

"Swear it to me."

Hugo's face tightened. "When you complete the task, I swear, I will free her."

"And the earl?"

"Thanks to you, Rochester will rest comfortably in Aylesbury. The nearest Justice will be informed, and he will be taken to London tomorrow."

Daniel walked away from the table. Hugo and Mabb left him alone with his thoughts. The house was ransacked for provisions and anything of value taken and shared among the men. Daniel rolled out his blanket under the window. He lay down and closed his eyes. He was spent, but no sleep came to release him and the hours crept by.

I hope you and your sister can live with your choice. Rochester's words drummed in his head again and again. His eyes snapped open, and he let out a low groan as he fell into the black void.

Chapter 43 – Last Flight of the Earl

Tom Gilvy ascended the stairs with a plate of stew. The two soldiers guarding Rochester's door glared at him. Their empty bellies chorused together when they got a whiff of the food. Downstairs in the bar, the regulars were celebrating with the soldiers after news of the quashed rebellion had reached the town. The revelry downstairs made it all the more difficult for the two soldiers. The soldier snorted when Tom waited before the locked door.

"Now don't be worryin' you'll miss all the fun." Tom winked. "My wife is fixin' you something to eat, and I'll even try sneakin' past some ale for the *real* soldiers upstairs." Their faces sparked with a smile, and Tom entered the room with a pat on the back.

He closed the door and nodded to the prisoner. The commanding officer hadn't mentioned the prisoner's name, but had warned him not to speak with him. "Evenin', sir. Fixed some supper for you."

"I'd rather be at the celebration. I imagine it will be a long evening?"

"I'm thinkin' that, as well."

Gilvy nodded awkwardly to leave, but Rochester motioned him over before he reached the door. Rochester laid his greatcoat out on the bed. He produced a sliver of wood and ripped at the material close to the rear vents. He squeezed in his hand and wrangled out a fine gold chain and a handful of Jacobus gold coins. "I am the Earl of Rochester, and if you get me out of here, this is yours," he said, whispering.

Gilvy's eyes lit up at the fortune.

"Yes, the chain alone is worth more than a hundred."

Gilvy sat down on the bed, shaking his head. "I'm thinkin' what will happen to me and my wife, my lord?"

"It's going to be a long night, Mr. Gilvy. Plenty of time to toast Cromwell's victory over the king."

Gilvy hemmed and hawed and scratched his head.

"My Cavalier luck has not yet run dry, my friend. Consider my offer."

Gilvy mumbled to himself as he left the room. He nodded to the guards as he walked past, and they smiled back, obviously anticipating his return. He made his way through the throng of men, who had now been joined by a gaggle of prostitutes, descending upon the inn as the smell of money filled the air. With the new arrivals and Pete the Fiddler striking up some tunes, the evening was now in full swing.

Tom hurried to his wife, Elsie, who was dishing out more stew for the hungry soldiers. "Elsie, the Earl of Rochester is upstairs." It was so loud next door he didn't bother to whisper.

"And?" Elsie said, continuing to dish out the stew.

"And? He has money," he gibbered, "and he's willin' to part with a gold chain and a handful of gold shillings if we help him."

Elsie stopped her work. "Yes, but it's of no use to us if we hang for it."

"Yes, exactly what I said to his lordshipfulness. But then he said it's a fine time to toast the Lord Protector with his victory."

Elsie's eyes sparkled as a wry smile spread over her face. "So we'll be needing another barrel, then."

A few moments later, Tom rolled out an ale barrel. He lifted it onto the table and hollered for silence. The music stopped, and Tom banged in the tap before pouring himself a flagon of ale. "Gentlemen, I would like to raise a toast to Cromwell, our free Commonwealth and the New Model Army, who crushed another rebellion!"

The cheers were deafening, and it took a few minutes for them to quiet before Tom spoke again. "If you please, I will say one more thing: *the drinks are on the house!*"

The cheers far exceeded the toast, and Tom pushed through to the commanding officer, while Elsie had her work cut out serving the ale. The officer, already bleary eyed, thanked Sam.

"Sir, those two upstairs be lookin' sour. You be mindin' if I brought them up one?" Tom asked.

"Aye, but only one. They'll get their chance another time."

He filled the tankards and placed them on a tray with the stew. He negotiated the stairs with his tray and dished out the food and drink to the beaming guards. "Don't be worrin' now, your officer said you deserved it. I'll see you right."

It had been the longest three hours of Tom's life. The party had only ended when the fiddler lost consciousness halfway through a song. Inebriated customers sprawled across tables or lay passed out on the floor. Elsie shook her head at the devastation.

Tom, carrying another flagon, made another trip up the stairs. One of the guards lay unconscious, while the other mumbled incoherently. Tom knelt down and filled the soldier's empty tankard. "One for the road, my friend." He helped the soldier to find his mouth and most of the ale found the guard's gaping maw. Tom stepped back and waited. One mouthful later, the young soldier keeled over with a thud. Tom rubbed his hands before fishing out the soldier's key.

The earl waited at the door, grinning. Rochester peered outside the room and patted Tom on the shoulder.

"The devil couldn't wake them, my lordship."

Rochester presented Tom with the chain and coins. "What is your name?"

"Tom Gilvy, my lordship."

"I thank you, Master Gilvy. I will tell the king of your courage this day."

Gilvy locked the door again and placed the key back into the soldier's pocket.

As the earl vanished into the night, Tom said to himself, "There flies another bird."

Chapter 44 –The Constable Returns

Worn out, the constable laid himself out on his bed. He was getting too old and soft for such long journeys. He sank into the soft embrace of his feathered mattress. Ready to drift off, he grumbled as loud knocks at the door interrupted his slumber. He groaned and pulled the blankets over his head, but the banging continued, and he hobbled down the stairs, cursing the sleep-wrecker.

He flung open the door, ready to give hell, but…it was Mr. Leitham.

"Couldn't it wait until the morning, man?" Lucas growled.

"I promise I won't stay long."

Muttering to himself, the constable labored into the drawing room. "I drank the last of the ale when I arrived home, so I've nothing to offer you."

"Just tell me what happened."

The constable rubbed his eyes in between a mighty yawn. "It took me three days to be admitted—three days. One excuse after another, hoping I'd leave."

"But he met you?"

The constable yawned again. "As I said, when he realized I wasn't leaving until I saw him, much to my surprise, his secretary found me out and advised me to come that very day."

"And?"

"I related to Disbrowe all the past events regarding Hugo and his many abuses of power." A tired grin spread across his face. "He tried to mask his surprise, but I saw through it well enough."

"What about Johanna?"

"If you give me a chance, I will tell you," Lucas snapped. "I told him Hugo has been missing for nearly two weeks, and an innocent woman had been pardoned by the said man, but she was still in custody."

Mr. Leitham shifted in his seat while the constable sifted through his memory.

"In addition, a Royalist prisoner had been hanged without a trial, and all in the name of the new Government. Is that how Cromwell's Major-Generals want to begin their task, sparking resentment and fear, I asked?"

"Good, but what has come of it all, Constable?"

"Disbrowe mentioned an investigation is warranted, especially with the commissioner missing presently. He promised a new commissioner would arrive to investigate Hugo's activities in Taunton."

"So, we can release Johanna?"

"No, not yet. We must wait for the new commissioner."

Leitham frowned. "Well, let us hope Hugo never finds his way back. In the meantime, I will tell Johanna the good news."

"Quite right, excellent idea."

Mr. Leitham was already backing toward the door.

"And I don't want to see you before tomorrow!"

He wasn't sure if Leitham had heard him, but it didn't matter, for he was certain it would be the last time Mr. Leitham would bother him this day. Perhaps a corner had been turned? Disbrowe had actually seemed a reasonable man. Even if Hugo returned, he'd be most likely moved from Taunton.

The constable smiled as he realized all of Hugo's grand pronouncements had turned out to be nonsense. Taunton would receive a new commissioner and life would return to normal— nothing wrong with quiet and predictable. He grimaced as he loosened his boots and kicked them off. He sat back in the chair and thought about going back to bed. "In a few minutes," he said to himself, before drifting off to sleep.

Chapter 45– Dover

Even at the late hour, the harbor was busy with ships preparing for early morning departures. Returning from leave, sailors stumbled back to their ships. The salt air and the low moan of the sea cleared Daniel's head after the ride. With luck, he would soon meet Charles. Or perhaps, fate would come to his rescue and whip up a storm like she had against the Spanish. They would sink into the depths, and he would die knowing he'd done everything he could to save Johanna.

They rode further into the docks. Hugo called his men to a halt. Sailors argued on the deck of a brig called *The Marianne*. The Watch had been called after cargo had disappeared. Evidently, the captain had stopped his thirsty crew from leaving the ship, leading to a mass brawl. In the end, The Watch managed to calm the sailors, and Hugo's offer of assistance was politely declined.

They rode on, searching for *The Black Swan*. A Captain Farelly had been chartered to take the earl back, and with Hugo's armed men, Daniel didn't envisage any problems from Farelly.

On the far side of the harbor, they found their caravel moored between two, three-hundred-ton Fluyts. Although dwarfed by the larger Dutch trading ships, their fifty-ton caravel would be adequate for their needs. Two sailors, who had been moving cargo, stopped their work when the soldiers dismounted beside the ship. Hugo and Daniel, with the rest following, boarded using the ship's gangway.

The sailors bristled at the strangers.

"Is Captain Farelly on board?" Hugo asked.

The sailor nodded.

"Bring your Captain to me immediately," Hugo said with a wave of his hand.

The sailor folded his arms and stood his ground. Hugo removed his firelock pistol from its holster. The sailor's jaw tightened as Hugo inched toward him. He struck him with the pistol butt, and the sailor crumpled to the deck. Hugo raised his pistol to the other sailor's head. "Bring me your Captain."

The man slunk off and returned with a bald-headed reed of a man. With his elbows flailing and a face like thunder, he strode over to Hugo. "Speak!"

"You are Captain Farelly?"

"No, I'm bloody Queen Lizzie! Who's asking?"

"Captain, the Earl of Rochester won't be joining you."

Farelly's gaze darted to the gangway, but Hugo's men blocked the way. He ran for the ship's edge and the murky depths of the sea, only to be wrestled to the deck. Spitting and cursing the Roundhead dogs, he struggled against his assailants. It took four men to drag him back to Hugo.

"Until now, I wasn't certain you knew the earl!"

Farelly continued to struggle.

"Hold him still."

The soldiers dragged him down to his knees.

"You will take us to Flanders as planned—"

"Give me a night with your whore wife, and I'll think about it!" Farelly cackled.

Hugo snorted at the insult. "Bring me your cat," he said to the closest sailor.

"Sir?"

"Bring it, or you'll join your Captain."

Farelly was stripped and tied to the main mast. Hugo passed the whip to Mabb. "Mr. Mabb, Captain Farelly needs to be reminded how an officer and gentleman should behave."

"If you don't have a wife, I'll take your mother instead, you bastard!" Farelly spat.

The crew—fifteen men in all—were ordered to watch, and Sam's punishment in the yard came back to him. Daniel feasted on the brutality as he imagined his own hand wielding the whip, each lash stripping the flesh from Sam's naked back. What a fool he had been to trust the Quaker.

After thirty lashes Farelly's cursing had stopped.

"You will take us to Flanders, or I'll hang you now," Hugo demanded.

Slumped on his knees with rivulets of blood seeping down his lacerated back, Farelly could barely nod in agreement.

It took nearly an hour to winch the terrified horses into the hold. Farelly's crew helped to settle the poor animals into their slings. After the remaining equipment and supplies were squeezed into the hold, there was barely enough room for Hugo's men. Each man found a place and waited for the tide to turn.

The gulls circled *The Black Swan* as it glided out of the harbor. Choppy and fathomless, the sea rippled out ahead. Daniel was leaving England. Johanna, left behind alone, would be shivering in Taunton Keep. As a boy, the adventures of Drake and Raleigh had captivated him. He'd dreamt of a life exploring the oceans. And now, for the first time in his life, he was sailing away from England's shores. He felt sick. The men had talked about seasickness, but it wasn't just that. It was the sickness of his soul. He'd killed men before, but he'd never murdered them in cold blood. *Regicide. Regicide.* The words drummed through his skull as he swayed down into the hold.

Daniel kept to himself and rarely entered into any conversations with Hugo's men. They weren't shy with voicing their distrust, and Daniel ignored their jibes. They were a rag-tag bunch of veterans and youngsters, who were too old or too young to be fighting in the wilds of Scotland or Ireland. From their whispers, they had little idea of why they were sailing to Flanders, but they had guessed the 'Cavalier' had some role to play. They chastised a veteran for not asking Hugo for more information, but he joked it would be impossible to separate him from Mabb long enough to get an answer. Anyway, the veteran snorted, he didn't want to be responsible for breaking up such a sweet marriage. They sniggered, and then curled themselves up on the floor.

Daniel turned for hours, but eventually, the rhythmical swaying of the ship put him under for a time. No nightmares plagued him, and for the first time in weeks, he felt rested when he woke. He ambled over to the bucket that served for their latrine. He pinched his nose as he relieved himself then made his way up to the deck. Dark clouds threatened overhead, but a light gale had helped them make time.

"Davenport." Hugo emerged from the captain's quarters on the rear deck. "We have business inside."

Daniel followed him in and sat down on a stool beside Farelly's writing desk. With a small bed running the length of the wall, there was little enough space in the cabin for the four men.

"Thank you, Captain. And close the door behind you on your way out," Hugo said.

Farelly bit his tongue and managed to exit his cabin without saying anything.

Mabb spread a map over the desk.

"Farelly has been very cooperative. This is a map of Cologne, and we know Charles has his residence here in this street. I assume this was destined for Rochester." Hugo smirked.

"And you expect me to saunter in, asking for an audience with the king?"

"That's up to you, Daniel. I've gotten you this far, and now you have to make it work."

Daniel's jaw tightened.

"Remember why you are doing this. You have one chance to save her—don't waste it. Besides, you have Mr. Mabb, and Cromwell isn't entirely without ears in the Royal Court."

"You ask for the impossible. But...if I should fail, you must release her."

Hugo snorted at Daniel's suggestion.

"Damn you! You know I will die in the attempt. And if I survive they will execute me anyway. Promise me you'll release her."

"No, Daniel. You're weak, and you would be happy to end your miserable life if it meant saving her and Charles," Hugo said, leaning back in the captain's chair. "Blood for blood—Charles's blood for your sister's life. That was our agreement."

Daniel's neck corded. "I should kill you now, instead."

Hugo snorted. "You could try, but it wouldn't save her."

Daniel trailed the door open and gasped in some air. Land appeared on the horizon. He staggered to the side of the caravel. The dull grey color of the sea called to him. The swell slapped against the ship's side. He leaned over the edge, and the grey oblivion reached out for him. The waves became grasping arms, and out of the grey swell emerged his father's face, screwed up in contempt and hatred. Just as he had appeared when he had cursed and disowned his rebel son. Johanna's arms enclosed him as he teetered on the edge, as they had the night his world collapsed.

"I must yet live awhile," Daniel whispered.

"They're in a hurry," Mabb said.

At least five riders, and with the dust cloud trailing behind them, they were indeed in a hurry. There was no cover—only bleak flatlands peppered with dangerous marches stretched toward the coast. "We don't panic," Daniel said.

"Speak for yourself."

The lead rider slowed the horse to a trot. They were Cavaliers. The officer, a tall, fair-haired man, lifted his hand to halt the cavalcade. A plume sagged from his felt hat. He studied the two men.

"Name yourself?" The young man's horse started pulling on him, and it took considerable strength and skill to control the stallion.

"Captain Davenport of the King's Lifeguard."

"Where is the Earl of Rochester?"

"The earl was to rendezvous with us at Dover. He never arrived."

"Oh?"

"I have his letter," Daniel continued, "and urgent news for the king."

The cavalier's mouth drooped as he studied Mabb. "I am Lieutenant Ayres, and I will escort you both to Cologne for questioning. We have a long journey, but I see you are well provisioned?" Ayres questioned, raising his eyebrows.

"Indeed, Lieutenant." Daniel bristled. "You'd be surprised how many friends a Royalist might find back home."

Questioning was precautionary and expected, despite Ayres' scowl and obvious mistrust. Charles would be anticipating news from England, especially from a man who had been liberated from Fisherton Anger Gaol. In the past, the prospect of interrogation would have shaken Daniel to the core. But now the threat washed over him with hardly a second thought. Let life takes its course, for fate could do nothing more to him.

* * *

They placed Daniel under house arrest. He hadn't seen Mabb in two days, but then again, it would be easier getting a horse to talk than Mabb. Daniel had been well treated, but the days were slipping by. Hugo had given him seven. Every day confined made the almost impossible task more difficult.

The knock on the door shook Daniel free from the entertainment of the street bustle. Ayres stood aside for a gentleman who was unknown to Daniel. With a dark rings under his eyes and a rather studious appearance, he was probably a man of the letters. This was in stark contrast, however, to the extravagance of his rich blue satin doublet and matching cape.

The gentleman paced. "You have been treated well?" he asked without making eye contact.

The man's piercing voice grated Daniel. "I've been treated very well, sir. The room is very comfortable, so much so it's easy to forget I'm under house arrest."

The gentleman raised an eyebrow then continued to pace with hands clasped behind his back. "Hmm, well I'm glad you're comfortable. The Chancellor sent me to enquire after you, and he is much interested in your service to His Majesty and your escape from Salisbury."

"And your name, sir?"

"Henry Manning. Not long arrived from England, Captain."

"Well met, sir." Daniel shook Manning's hand. "As I told Lieutenant Ayres, I was wounded and captured at Worcester. We stood our ground as their dragoons charged His Majesty down close to St.Martin's Gate."

"I'm certain the king remembers your courage, Captain. He has a wonderful memory for faces."

"I survived but spent the next years in Fisherton Anger in Salisbury. I would still be there but for Colonel Penruddock."

"Interesting, but I don't understand your connection with the Earl of Rochester?"

"Call it fate or luck, but fortune smiled down on Sam and me that day. Colonel Penruddock received a letter from the earl— which he would later entrust to me—relating to him the rebellion's failure in the north. Instead of leaving his men, Colonel Penruddock ordered Sam and I to rendezvous with the earl. We were to pass on news of his victory at Salisbury, and his plan to gather support for the king in the West."

The Lieutenant, a sentinel straddling the door, scrutinized

them. Was it Manning or Ayres giving the interrogation?

Manning for the first time stood still. "Unfortunately, fate did not smile so kindly on Colonel Penruddock. And His Majesty and Court are deeply saddened the earl is missing. His Majesty is most anxious to hear about our beloved Earl, but I believe he would prefer to hear it from you, Captain."

It sounded more like a question, and Manning, for the first time, met Daniel's gaze.

"I would be deeply honored to relate my experiences to the king."

"Good, I will arrange it. In the meantime, I trust you are happy to remain here until I receive the king's permission."

"Of course, sir."

"Ah." Manning plucked a remembrance from the air. "Mr. *Tripton* is quite well. No need to worry."

So, Daniel would have his audience with Charles. It seemed far too easy. Daniel couldn't put his finger on it, but there was something queer about Manning. The way he had intonated *Tripton*. Perhaps Daniel should have enquired after '*Mr. Tripton.*' He had made a mistake there. But Manning had known more than he'd admitted. And now Charles would question him about the rebellion—perhaps about Worcester. Maybe even thank him for his sacrifice. Daniel would have to weave his lies around the truth of his experiences. And as he did so, Johanna would be wasting away, confined within Taunton Keep, praying for his soul, praying he would keep his promise to her.

Chapter 46 – Out with the Old

"Uncle!" Alistair hollered as he skipped down the road.

The constable was happy to wait for the lad and checked for a second time that the door was locked.

"Uncle, soldiers are here." The boy stooped over, hands on his knees, and sucked in another lungful of air. "I think it's the commissioner."

"Hugo?"

"No, no, the new commissioner."

"Well, I'll be damned."

"But, you told me he was coming?" the boy asked.

"Aye, true enough, but that doesn't mean I believed it."

"I saw him, Uncle. I think he's coming to see you."

And sure enough, just as Alistair related, the commissioner rode into view, accompanied by two riders on either side of him. "And the rest?"

Alistair shrugged.

"Has he not more men, boy?"

"Yes, there must be half a company. Is that good, Uncle?"

"Well." Lucas massaged his beard. "It depends on the new commissioner. Now run along. Tell your father, I'll call by later."

Pouting, Alistair trudged off.

The constable strode over to the commissioner. A gentleman in his forties, who, by the cut of him, was accustomed to hard graft. The commissioner dismounted and held out his hand.

"Vincent Lucas. I welcome you to Taunton, Commissioner."

"Peter Hardy."

He gave the constable a firm handshake. "Are you local, Commissioner?"

"Not far from Bristol, Constable. Has Commissioner Hugo returned to Taunton?"

Here was a man who got straight down to business. The constable nodded his approval. "No. Nor have I heard any news of the man."

"Who did he leave in charge?"

"A Corporal Wells. Hugo took near half his men with him."

"I will freshen up, and then meet the corporal in an hour. I would appreciate it if you would accompany me."

The constable nodded. "I hope you will be able help us here, Mr. Hardy."

Hardy shrugged. "One hour, then."

Hardy rode off. The constable rubbed his hands together. Here was a grafter he could relate to. If only he had gone to Disbrowe sooner, then Hugo's mad schemes could have been stopped.

* * *

"I'll have to give the boy more credit," the constable muttered to himself. He'd counted thirty-five foot marching for Taunton Castle.

The news of their arrival had brought folk onto the streets. Many watched with curiosity, some with resentment, while others exuded a palpable sense of relief since news of the quashed rebellion had filtered down. Rumors had circulated of the West rising in support for the king. Apparently Fairfax had turned traitor and pledged allegiance to Charles Stuart. A wild story of an Irish invasion helped by the Spanish was another popular tale. It had made little difference how often he had told them the truth of the Protectorate's easy victory, and that the Irish were still in Ireland minding their own business. The scaremongering continued right up to the new commissioner's arrival.

"Another headache lifted," he had told his brother.

As the invasion rumors faded, so they were replaced with gossip of Hugo's disappearance. On good authority, Royalists had murdered him in revenge for the hanging. Johanna Davenport was also still alive, and she had been responsible for Hugo's disappearance. The constable had vehemently denied the rumors as ludicrous.

As predicted, Wells was already waiting on Hardy. The lip stickle gave his hand to Hardy as he dismounted, but Hardy waved it away, leaving Wells to prance back, smiling to hide his embarrassment. "If I'd known you were coming Commissioner—"

"If you'd have known?" Hardy said, interrupting him.

218

"We...I... would have given you a proper welcome, Commissioner."

"Take me somewhere quiet, Corporal."

The constable ignored Well's sneer when the corporal realized he had been invited. Wells led them to his office, and pulled a chair for Hardy, leaving the constable to stand. The corporal sat down and cleared his throat a few times.

"Do you know why I am here, Corporal?" Hardy asked stone-faced.

"I cannot rightly say, Commissioner."

"I've been sent by Major-General Disbrowe to investigate a number of grievances charged against Commissioner Manfred Hugo."

Incredulous, Wells spread his arms. "Grievances? There must be a mistake."

"Perhaps, however, the matter must be cleared up one way or another. Now, tell me where Commissioner Hugo is?"

Wells lounged back in his chair and clasped his hands behind his head. "The Commissioner, after leaving me with command, informed me he had important business connected with the security of the Protectorate."

"Where is he?"

"I assumed it had to do with the uprising—"

"*Where is he?*" The tone of Hardy's question made it clear this would be Wells' final opportunity to answer.

Well's face reddened. It was good to see the arrogant ninny squirm.

"Truly, I don't know, Commissioner."

"Tell me about Robert White?"

Wells shrugged.

"The *Royalist* who was hanged, Corporal."

"What is there to tell? He was hanged for treason."

"The man was not given a trial, Corporal."

"The people didn't seem to mind. They were there for a hanging—"

"The hanging of an innocent woman, who is still in your custody," the constable broke in.

"She was tried by Magistrate Hart and found guilty," Wells snapped back. "They came for a hanging, and they got it."

The constable cut in. "Commissioner, hand on heart, I promise you Johanna Davenport is not a witch."

"The woman," Well's said pompously, "will remain in my custody until Commissioner Hugo orders otherwise."

"Commissioner," the constable said, "I will be her guarantor. Release her into my custody."

Hardy stood from his chair, towering over the sitting Wells. "You and your men are now under my command."

The constable held back his smile. Wells squirmed in his chair like he sat on a bed of nettles.

"I have my orders from Commissioner Hugo," Wells snapped.

"And now countermanded. Now get out of my sight before I charge you with insubordination."

Well's skulked out the door, leaving the two men alone.

"She's yours, Constable. I will hold you responsible if anything happens."

"I understand."

"As for Commissioner Hugo, I assume Major-General Disbrowe will be anxious to interview him and uncover the mystery of this *secret* mission."

Chapter 47 – Freedom

Johanna's heart lifted as the cottage came into view. She floated along the narrow path leading to her home. And yet, only a few hours earlier, when the constable had told her she was free, she had not dared to hope. There had been too many false dawns, and Hugo had always found a way to claw her back. But now Hugo had disappeared, the constable had reminded her, and the new commissioner had given the order himself.

Mr. Russell was waiting at the front door. Beaming, he removed his cap. "Our prayers have been answered, Miss."

"I thank you for them, Mr. Russell," she said, shaking his hand. She cast a glance over the small field running beside her property. "The crop comes on beautifully."

"Aye, Mr. Leitham asked me to stay on, if it's all right?"

"You've been such a help, Mr. Russell. I have finally come around to the idea of being indebted to Mr. Leitham," she said, lowering her gaze as heat flushed her cheeks.

Mr. Russell said his goodbyes, promising to stop by in the morning.

Johanna opened the door and waved away the musty air. "Please come in, Constable."

"I thank you for the offer, but I must get back. I believe Mr. Leitham will call by later to check all is in order."

"You have done so much already, but…" Johanna hesitated. "I'm almost too afraid to ask, but have you heard from Daniel?"

The constable shook his head. "I'm sorry, Johanna."

"When I pray for him, it comforts me. But I don't know if it helps him."

The constable's warm smile lit up his face. "Perhaps you should speak to Mr. Russell. His prayers work very well. In the meantime, my men will call by from time to time."

"If you hear—"

"I will come straight to you."

Johanna beamed as she moved through her cottage. Each small kindness delighted and moved her as much as the great ones: the firewood left for her in the kitchen, the fresh straw laid out for her homecoming, and even the cracked window pane at the back of the cottage that had been replaced. She ran her hand over each precious possession, which now radiated with new life. Possessions saved from the fire once more had a story to tell. All the small things she had worked so hard for in the difficult years comforted her more than ever.

Johanna threw on another log and used the bellow to stoke the fire. She pulled the stool closer and warmed her hands.

A knock at the door startled her, and she forced herself to break free from the mesmerizing flames. She peered out of the window. Richard waited with a wicker basket. She scampered to the door and fumbled with the key until the lock clicked open. Before he uttered a word, she flung her arms around him.

He beamed and tapped the basket. "I thought this might help."

"Yes it will. That was very thoughtful, Richard. Please come in."

Richard carried the basket into the living room. He moved the eggs to one side.

"Trout!"

"I thought we could prepare it together?"

She skipped into the kitchen and brought out the spit then attached it to the crane standing over the fire.

"I didn't know if you'd been to the well," Richard said, "so I also brought this." He set a jug of ale onto the floor.

"You read my mind," She said. "And they called me a witch?"

"And I would ask you to inform no one of my secret identity."

"I will think about it, Mr. Leitham."

"I have one more request." Leitham hesitated.

"Please?"

"Stay with the constable or with me until Hugo shows himself."

"Oh…"

"I've spoken to Hardy and the constable. They agree with me. It's just the cottage is so isolated."

"It's just…difficult."

"I know. You have just arrived home, but…I don't trust him,

Johanna." He clasped her hand. "I would never ask unless I believed it necessary."

His conviction. She loved that about him. He was crystal clear, and his inner stirrings flooded out of him unchecked and alive. "Yes...I will, Richard."

Soon, the fish was cooking on a spit and the mouth-watering aroma awakened their hunger. They washed the bread and cheese down with the ale. She savored each mouthful.

"I spoke to the constable about Daniel, but still he's heard nothing," Johanna said.

"I hope he is safe, Johanna, but...you must prepare yourself."

"I know." She cast her eyes down. "I've tried."

"When I first visited, you said I must never hope for anything other than your friendship," Richard's voice cracked. "I am grateful for your trust, and, from my heart, I thank you."

She leaned closer to him.

"But I love you more with each passing day, and I cannot imagine my life without you by my side."

Her palms pressed lightly against her cheeks. Only weeks ago, his words would have withered away in her parched heart, but now, of late, her dreams had overflowed in moments like these. Her soul's spring renewal exulted in his loving words.

He took her hand. "Johanna, I want to marry you—to shield you from all the terrible things happening in this world and...even if you do not love me in this way...I still offer you my love and all that I am. I cannot accept you should face the Hugo's of this world alone."

"Then—then let us face this life together."

A searing warmth gripped Johanna and flowed through her. She stroked his cheek and caught a glimpse of his grey eyes. She embraced him and whispered, "I love you...I give you all that I am."

He lifted her chin and haltingly brought his lips to hers. He kissed her, and the release of tension rippled through her body. She gripped his hair, and her lips feathered down his cheek until they reached his lips.

He caressed her neck, and her head fell back as his hand moved down her body. She trembled with his touch, and the warmth from his body united with hers in the spirit of their love.

223

Chapter 48 – The Poorest King in Christendom

Hours of pondering circled back to the same stark conclusion: *It can't be done.* Even if Daniel gained admittance, he would be searched. If he were lucky, he would die in the attempt. Otherwise, he could look forward to torture and execution as a traitor. But that was as nothing compared to the horror of murdering the king in cold blood. That was his living nightmare. Blood for blood: the king's blood in exchange for the life of his sister. "It will kill her anyway!" Daniel groaned. The infamy of his traitorous name would live on forever. *Regicide and treason.*

The door opened, and the peacock Manning interrupted the maddening cycle of his brooding.

Daniel held his head in his hands. "I will not do it!"

Manning gaped at Daniel.

"I will not do it."

Manning froze still and put his ear to the door. He sprang to Daniel's side. "Do what?" he whispered.

"I...I confess...I am a traitor...here to murder the king."

Manning gawked at the man.

"I was sent to murder Charles...for the life of my sister."

Manning moved very close to Daniel, who was now sitting on the floor, rocking back and forth. "She will die slowly, Daniel," Manning hissed.

Daniel lifted his head—his eyes narrowed.

"He can keep Johanna alive for days—unmentionable torture, Daniel."

Hugo's words shot through his memory. *Cromwell isn't entirely without ears at court.*

"Yes...A beggar-king is no king. Shamelessly, the mummer picks the scraps from Europe's table. Cap in hand, he begs from prince to prince, merchant to merchant."

"The guards," Daniel said, "had mocked him as the poorest King in Christendom."

"Thousands killed at Worcester for a fool's enterprise. He took four years from you while you rotted in prison. And now you're going to betray your sister?"

"No...To kill him is also to betray her."

"No! Allowing her to be cut into pieces is betrayal."

Daniel's eyes flitted around the room. He wiped the glistening sweat from his forehead. "No, it can't be done."

"At the king's table, you will be shown to your chair. A blade has been planted underneath your chair. For your sister's sake, do not weaken in your resolve at the last."

"He'll kill her anyway."

"So you say." Quick as lightening Manning pulled free his dagger and held to Daniel's throat. A trickle of blood rolled down his neck. "Charles Stuart or Johanna? Make your choice, for I grow tired of your cowardice."

Quartered—cut into pieces. "Charles Stuart."

"Good. Ayres will escort you this evening. You need to pull yourself together before he arrives. Johanna's life depends on two people: You and I. If Hugo does not receive word from me, she dies."

"And Mabb?"

"Charles will not admit him, so you're on your own."

After Manning left, Daniel repeated the two choices over and over again. He stopped pacing and fixed on a small looking glass resting on the dressing table. He tilted the glass toward his neck. It was a nick, and the blood had already dried. He licked his finger and wiped it clean. He held up the looking glass again and examined the man staring back at him. Was that him? Daniel's inane laughter descended into a pitiless rage. "At last, Father will be proud of me!" He spat back at the reflection.

* * *

"It is a short walk from the Innenstadt," Ayres said. He held Daniel back as a coach sped past. "The coaches will not stop here, Captain."

"They told me an overturned cart protected the king's escape through Sidbury Gate."

225

Ayres had not fought at Worcester. What would he know of that disaster? "Many sacrificed themselves for the king at Worcester."

Ayres raised an eyebrow. "They did their duty."

And now Daniel must do his. Ayres looked the part. The quintessence of Prince Rupert's dashing cavaliers. What had Ayres sacrificed? "Look at my clothes." Daniel lifted his soiled coat. "I am ashamed to walk before His Majesty."

Ayres smiled—his first since meeting the lieutenant on the road. "At least you bathed. His Majesty appreciates the hardships of the road as much as anyone. After Worcester, he spent six weeks on the run disguised as a woodcutter."

They turned onto the old market square, which was dominated by a grand Cathedral rising behind the market. At mid-afternoon it was quiet, and if it not for the grey sky and suffocating anxiety crushing Daniel's spirits it might have made a pleasant walk. But as it was, each step brought him closer to death.

Ayres described some of the grand houses on their way. Soldiers marched from a side street. "They are known as the Rote Funken."

Daniel nodded and feigned interest. First the red-uniformed troops disappeared from view, and then the rhythmical slapping of their marching faded.

They reached another square. "They enjoy their markets here. This is *Der Heumarkt*—the Haymarket."

Daniel grunted.

"And His Majesty's residence," Ayres said, pointing to a rather unremarkable house.

Daniel was shown in and searched for weapons. He cast an eye over the grand hallway. Along with rich tapestries, probably donated by the generous burghers, an array of precious objects and *objet d'art* adorned the walls.

Manning was not amongst the horde of guards and servants milling about. The guards escorted them until they were stopped by the king's steward. He screwed his nose at Daniel's appearance. "You will address the king as His Majesty." As he spoke, the man's finger tapped the palm of his left hand. "Do not speak until spoken to. And try not to eat like a pig."

Daniel's jaw tightened as he followed the steward into the

room. A table had been prepared, but no food had been laid out as yet. Daniel was ushered to his chair about five feet from the top of the table. Ayres sat beside him, but closer to the head of the table. Six more places had been set, but were as yet unoccupied.

The steward breezed back to Daniel. "When His Majesty enters, you must stand until His Majesty has seated himself."

Daniel nodded dumbly to the waspish servant.

"I felt the same way when I first met the king," Ayres said.

Daniel sat down. He surreptitiously moved his hand to his chair. His fingers explored its underside. His heart skipped a beat when he touched only wood. Daniel wiped his forehead with a kerchief. He slid his other hand underneath, and his finger touched cold metal. Ayres drummed his fingers. Daniel's heart raced, beating so loud he felt certain the guards could hear it. He wiped his brow again then held his right arm to stop it shaking. Daniel felt that he would split apart from the inside. His gaze clung to the door. Was it too late? He closed his eyes and drew in a lungful of the stale air. His frame stiffened and then even the drumming of his heart slowed to a stutter. "Johanna...forgive me," he stammered under his breath.

Just then the door opened, and a gentleman entered. He was short of stature with short dark hair that did nothing to hide his prominent forehead. His gaze rested on Daniel. "I am Henry Massie. His Majesty has taken ill and will not be coming, Captain." He motioned, and soldiers entered. "Will you accompany me, please?"

It had been taken out of his hands. Daniel tilted his head toward the ceiling. *Johanna!* "Yes." He pushed himself up from the chair, and the soldiers took him by the arms and led him out.

Massie followed him into a waiting carriage. "He has my sister."

"Who?"

"You can save her."

"The Earl of Rochester escaped, Captain. He sent word from London."

"He's in Middleburg on *The Black Swan*. Please, the guilt is not hers! He would be valuable to you!"

"Valuable? An important man?" Massie asked.

"Yes—yes, a Commissioner of the new Government."

227

"Ah." Massie couldn't hide the hint of disappointment. "A Commissioner is of no interest, Captain."

"But...he must have connections," Daniel stammered.

"The king knows nothing of the assassination plot. His Majesty has had his fill of bad news. I would have executed you immediately, but for the earl's request for clemency."

"I don't want your clemency! Shoot me, hang me, or quarter me, if it pleases you! I confess everything! I'm a traitor...but please...save her!"

Massie's gaze rested steady on Daniel. "You will be taken to a local gaol—"

"What will it take?"

Massie's eyes widened. "You're a traitor, Captain. There's nothing you can give me."

Despondency choked Daniel. He slumped forward. He was emptied of pride and hatred, of the desire to kill his enemy or to struggle for his life, and defenseless, gave his self, his very soul, into the power of Massie.

"I killed my father...when I told him...when told him I would fight for the king. I was dead to him—an outcast. It killed him. I betrayed my flesh and blood for Charles. He told Johanna he would disown her too if she ever talked to me again. So that's what he did. She lost everything because of me. To spite us—" Daniel sniffed "—he sold nearly everything and gave the money to Parliament. In the end, he killed himself in that house. Burnt it to the ground. You cannot know how she's suffered for my sake...please...you can help her."

"I am sorry for you and her. But sometimes you have to stop fighting, Captain. Sometimes there's nothing you can do but to accept your fate. One insignificant life for the life of a king?" Massie shook his head. "No, Captain, for tens of thousands of lives are dependent on the life of His Majesty."

"You have a traitor at Court! I will tell you who it is if you help her!"

Massie's eyes narrowed. "I know we have a traitor—since the rebellion that much is clear."

"You don't know who it is."

"Even if I wanted to help her, I couldn't. It's too late."

"But—"

228

"Nothing," Massie interrupted. "We will find him without you. But you can still do what is right by telling us."

"Then you're a fool, Massie. Take me away. It's at an end for me."

Chapter 49 – I Will Repay

The tower of St Mary Magdalene Church peaked in the distance. Manfred exhaled, and the tension left his weary muscles. He pulled the brim of his hat forward to cover his face as he rode into the teeth of the wind and rain. His bucket top boots were sodden down, and he dreamt of a fire. "Soon," he said.

It had been a somber journey. The roads were quiet, and the excitement that the rebellion had brought had long faded in the monotony of daily life. The men were tired and their grumbling had robbed Manfred of the scraps of peace he had still retained since news of Davenport's failure and Rochester's escape had reached him. Only the anticipation of justice had kept him in the saddle. Once he had dealt with Johanna, then he would begin anew with his task. Other plans would inspire him, and this time, he would not fail to consult Disbrowe. They would forgive him for they must know of his gifts and commitment to the Protectorate.

He lifted his head when a call from ahead reached him. A rider straddled the road about a hundred yards away. The rider trotted toward them, and Manfred called the group to a halt. He squinted through the slattern rain as the bulky figure approached closer. Recognition came to him a second later, as a cruel grin spread across the man's face. "Garsten."

"Captain, a word alone, if you will?" Garsten smirked. "I don't think you want to ride on, Captain."

"What are you talking about, man?" Manfred asked as sidled closer.

"Well." Garsten leered through his smug maw. "A new commissioner arrived, and he's meanin' to arrest you."

Manfred grimaced. Disbrowe had been told—betrayal. He turned pale. "If you help me," Manfred whispered, "I will make you a rich man."

"I'm listening."

Manfred called Beaden over. "Take a few days leave—you

and the men deserve it." Manfred handed the man money, and Beaden's eyes lit up. "Now, if anyone asks after me, tell them I'm away on business and will return in a few days."

"Aye, sir." And the hardships of their journey were forgotten with the prospect of a warm fire and ale.

"Five shillings. Don't be spending it all in one night."

"I hope you'll be givin' me more, Captain?" Garsten asked, when the others had left them alone.

"I keep my promises, Garsten. I want the witch."

Garsten smirked. "Won't be so easy now. They moved the whore to the lawyer's house. The bitch even has Hardy's men sniffin' around her."

"Hardy?" Manfred scoffed. "I have almost one hundred pounds. It's yours, if you help me."

Garsten's smug sneer disappeared. "I don't believe you."

"Fifteen now, and the rest when we reach the safety of my estate."

Garsten hemmed and hawed.

"You won't earn that in five years."

"No use to me, if I'm dead."

"Time is running out. I need your answer now."

Garsten's smirk came back. "I'm a deserter anyways. But if you double cross me—"

"I keep my promises."

Manfred rummaged inside his coat and tossed Garsten a leather string pouch. Garsten weighed the pouch, listening to the clink of the coins. He examined the contents and nodded.

"Tonight," Manfred hissed, "we pay the witch a visit."

They found a small inn outside of town. It was practically derelict, but it had a fire, and it was quiet. Garsten had already finished his business with a local prostitute when he planted himself down beside Manfred.

"Nasty, but cheap." Garsten snorted and slobbered down a swig of ale.

Manfred folded up the letter he had been reading and placed it inside his coat pocket.

"So, why is Hardy lookin' to arrest you?" Garsten asked as he wiped the dripping ale from his mouth.

"The fool's not going to get the chance. He'll destroy

231

everything I've worked for. And now he consorts with traitors and evildoers."

"Lucky bastard!" Garsten licked his lips, and Manfred's jaw tightened in disgust.

"I'm surrounded by fools," Manfred muttered, "but I keep my promises, Garsten. Before the end, she will pray to God for forgiveness and for salvation from the Devil she worshiped instead of the righteous Lord. And when she had been purged and made clean and has begged me for death, I will anoint her as the sacrificial lamb."

Garsten grunted and walked over to bar, shaking his head.

"Then I will weed out the delinquents who oppose the Godly reformation: the gamblers, the idle and the wastrels, the whoremongers, and the drunks. Disbrowe, in the end, will thank me for my diligence and industry," Manfred muttered, without taking his eyes from the blazing fire.

And if they betray me? The prickling heat of the fire brought color to his face. *Hardy!* He cursed the name. He cursed Cromwell and his Major-Generals. *Betrayed! Cowards. Unworthy to serve in the new Kingdom.*

"Soon the circle will be completed," he whispered.

The whore who had been with Garsten earlier joined him at the bar. The picture of Johanna sprawled on the table assaulted Hugo. She had tormented him. *She had enjoyed it.* Her charms had tormented him. Her temptations had ground away his strength. He had nearly faltered in the face of such tainted, ungodly beauty. But he had come through the fire and had resisted her enchantments. He cursed the Darkness which always found a way to destroy his plans. But the Darkness had only delayed the inevitable. Soon, Johanna would taste the purifying fire. He would keep his promise and save her.

* * *

Taunton slept and all was quiet except for the gurgling of the rivulet that flowed down the middle of the street after the heavy rains. The striking picture was augmented by a shard of moonlight catching the water flow.

"How many guards?" Manfred asked.

"Two men—both Hardy's, Captain. Are we going to stand

232

here all night? What's the plan?"

"One must knock, Garsten. It's only polite," Manfred replied. He walked across the road with Garsten muttering behind him. "Be ready."

Manfred knocked on the door, but there was no answer. He rattled it again and a shuffling came from inside. Someone pressed against the door.

"Who is it?"

"Commissioner Hugo—open the door."

A whispering came from within, and then the door opened a crack to reveal a soldier holding a candle. "Commissioner Hugo?" The soldier held the candle up, squinting at the stranger.

"As I said, now let me in."

"I'm sorry, Commissioner..." The soldier hesitated. "But I have my orders not to let anyone in."

"I'm not asking, now stand aside."

The soldier stood his ground. "You'd best speak with Commissioner Hardy. No one is coming in."

Manfred kicked the door, and the soldier fell back with the force of the blow. The other soldier stepped back and withdrew his sword. Manfred challenged him with a forward thrust which was parried. Garsten bounded through the door behind him and swiped at the other soldier who had yet to recover from his tumble. The soldier fell back again to avoid the blade, and Garsten's thrust skewered the air.

Yells came from upstairs as Manfred rained down a torrent of blows, which the soldier desperately blocked. The final thrust caught the soldier's arm after the blade slid off his hilt guard. His cry of pain distracted the other soldier for just a second, and Garsten's blade slid under the man's defense, piercing through his buff coat, deep into his chest.

Groaning, the other soldier backed up the stairs. Manfred swung down and slashed his thigh. The man shrieked and threw his arms up.

"Throw down your sword!" Manfred said.

The soldier threw the weapon down, and it thudded down the stairs.

Manfred bounded past him. When he reached the top, he stopped to listen, but he only heard Garsten's laughter as he stuck his sword into the injured soldier's belly.

"Quiet!" Manfred snapped.

Garsten grunted as he continued to climb the stairs. Just then, a heavy crash came from inside the far right room. He ran over and put his weight against the door, but it held firm.

Garsten lumbered over, and they charged the door together. The door splintered under their combined weight, but without fully opening. A window broke from inside, and Johanna's screams pierced the night.

"Again!"

The door crashed open, and Manfred poked his head through. It was instinct that made him pull back, for the shot slammed into the wall behind him. Now they both charged through.

Johanna cowered behind Leitham.

"Come no closer!" Leitham said.

"Ah, chivalry lives on," Manfred mocked.

"Hardy's men are coming!"

"Not quick enough for you, lawyer."

Garsten raised his sword.

Johanna sank down into the corner.

Leitham jumped forward and swung his blade in a downward arc toward Garsten's neck. The big man blocked the attack, and Hugo pressed forward, probing for an opening in Leitham's defense. Leitham's blade glanced off Garsten's sword and caught Manfred by surprise. The blade clipped the top of his boots before biting into his leg above the knee. Manfred groaned and limped back.

Garsten jabbed his sword forward at Leitham's exposed side, and the blade found his ribs. Leitham collapsed, and blood seeped through his nightshirt. Leitham moaned, and Garsten readied his blade to finish him off.

"Wait! Let him die slowly!" Manfred said, kicking Leitham's sword under the bed.

Garsten's punch silenced Johanna screams. He lifted her and laid her out on the bed.

"Rope," Manfred said.

Garsten tied her hands and legs.

Manfred clenched his teeth. "Now lift her down."

Garsten bundled her over his shoulder, while Manfred

searched for a coat.

"You bastard," Leitham groaned.

Manfred ignored Leitham, cut a length of material from a shift, and bandaged it tight around his wound. He gritted his teeth as pain jabbed his leg. With a riding coat draped over his arm, he bent closer to Leitham. "I keep my promises," Manfred hissed as he limped away.

* * *

"Bring her inside," Manfred said, wincing as he dismounted.

Johanna groaned as Garsten lifted her off his horse and carried her into the house. He laid her down on the floor.

"Upstairs!" Manfred snapped.

"Where's my money?"

"You will have it. But I can't lift her with my leg."

Garsten lifted her with a grunt and clambered up the stairs.

"Yes, the room straight ahead."

After struggling to open the door, Garsten staggered in and threw her down on the bed. Manfred followed moments later with a pail. Water splashed over the edge as he set it on the floor.

Johanna writhed on the bed, mumbling. The beaded sweat stuck to her hair and sallow skin.

Garsten untied the straps of Leitham's great coat and slipped it off her quivering frame. He removed his dagger and eyed the contours of her body through her nightdress. "Now," Garsten slavered, caressing her breasts with the blade, "give me my money. Or I'll have my money's worth with this angel."

"Don't touch her again." The bastard had fear in him as he broke away from Manfred's gaze. "Now help me move the bed."

They pushed the bed toward the window, and Manfred tested the floor. A floorboard moved under his weight. "Your money is in there."

Garsten tested the spot. "Stand by the door, Captain."

Manfred backed away.

Using his dagger, Garsten pried up the floorboard and threw it to the side. He lifted out a sack cloth and tested its weight. His grin disappeared as he counted the money. "There's not even fifty here!"

"It's enough. Take it and leave."

235

"One hundred!" Garsten's eyes narrowed, and his jaw jutted forward, marking his brutality. "That was the agreement!" He used the blade to rip a part of Johanna's nightdress. The brute snorted at her feeble attempts to push him away.

"Take the horses."

"I was goin' to take them anyway." He ripped a little more of her night dress.

Manfred jerked forward, his body strained, trembling in desperation.

"Move again, and I'll fuckin' open her."

"Take what you want from the house—anything you want."

Garsten sneered. "I don't want your baubles and trinkets. You owe me, and I'll take fifteen minutes with the witch."

"It's not going to happen."

"Ah." He pointed at Hugo's leg. "You shouldn't be threatenin' me, Captain."

"With one leg, I could kill you five times before you took a second breath."

Garsten punched Johanna and knocked her out cold.

Manfred drew his sword. "The money's no use to you when you're dead! Make your choice!"

Garsten's beady eyes locked on Manfred. "Take your whore." He spat on Johanna. "And the devil can take you both to hell."

Manfred stood aside as Garsten backed out of the room. The scowling Garsten swaggered out, and Manfred slammed the door shut.

Below, the crash of Garsten's destruction and curses filtered up. But still Manfred waited at the window until at last Garsten mounted his horse. With the other horse tied behind and packed up with his valuables, Garsten hollered, "Best hope I don't run into you again, Captain!" He then slipped away into the night.

Using the sword as a crutch, Manfred hobbled over to the bedside drawer and removed a tinder box. He sparked the firestone using the flint. The tinder smoldered in the box until he used the delicate flame to light a candle. He fished out more candles and placed them about the room. They burned uneasily with the circulating draft.

In another drawer, he sorted through Sarah's nightdresses until he found the one he wanted. He lifted it out and unfolded it, holding it up to the candlelight. He caressed the material and buried his face into its white folds. He laid the nightdress out on the bed and then lifted the pail of water closer. Johanna, still unconscious, lay on her side.

He dragged a stool to the bed and sat down beside her, gently turning her onto her back. He touched her forehead. She burned with fever. He leaned closer to catch her shallow breaths. He wiped Garsten's spittle from her ripped nightdress, and then wiggled his hand through the slit of the frayed material. Her midriff was cold and soft. His hand rose and fell almost imperceptibly which each shallow breath. He ripped her nightdress and exposed her pale form, gasping at her slender fragility. Her perfection lay glorious and true beneath him. His eyes caressed every contour as he wrung out the cloth and ran it over her body. With each stroke, he trembled.

"Purged and purified, I will anoint thee. Purged and purified, I will anoint thee," he said with each sweep of his hand. He tossed the rags of her nightdress to the floor and slipped Sarah's over her head. Johanna moaned as her head slumped forward and back. "Sarah," tears welled as he stroked her hair, "my love..." He wiped her brow with the cloth.

Johanna's eyelids cracked opened. "Richard?"

"Shush." He caressed her cheek.

"Richard!"

"Be still, my love." He kissed her forehead. "It is I, Manfred." He stroked her hair. "Sarah, be not afraid."

"Madness!"

"Sarah, we will overcome this tragedy together," Manfred said, whispering.

"Let me go!"

Manfred groaned. He clawed at his face. "Like before!"

"Where is Daniel, tell me?"

"He was my *son!*" His features contorted monstrously "But you kept him from me! You cast me asunder, and I lost him!" He gripped her hand. "I loved you, and he didn't! How can love ever be wrong?"

Johanna tried to break from his grip, but he squeezed tighter still, and she cried out in pain.

"You left me alone! You murdered me, Sarah!" He took one

hand away to wipe his eyes.

Johanna struck him. "Release me!" She threw the bed covers off and gasped in horror.

"Your nightdress, Sarah. The one you wore that night."

"Please…let me go!"

"You want to leave me again!" Manfred said, rising from the edge of the bed.

"Let me go!" She sobbed. "I love Richard as you loved her. Let me go back to him!"

"As you wish." One punch rocked her head back, and she swooned flat onto the bed. "When I saw him that day, I was so proud," Manfred muttered. "I cradled his head even as his flesh slowly corrupted…I…*Davenport killed him*! Your bastard of a brother!"

Manfred reached down for Garsten's rope and bound her hands. "You are a coward, Sarah." The other and longer length of rope that Garsten had used to bind her ankles he threw over the central beam. "You'll never have power over me again." He placed the stool underneath the noose.

"Please…" Blood lapped about her mouth from a missing front tooth. "I am not her."

He dragged her across the bed.

"God as my witness…I am innocent!"

He struck her again, and she went limp. Dragging her up, he lifted her onto the stool.

"Johanna...I am Johanna."

Manfred put her head through the noose. He gripped her jaw and jutted his neck forward, his face inches from hers.

She cried out in terror.

"I lusted after you! You crept inside me and tormented me!" Manfred fell to his knees still holding her legs; his teeth violently shuddering in his maw. "But…I never violated you! I resisted!" He knocked the stool away, and she whimpered as her body dropped. He fought to keep her legs still and tried to drown out the terrible sounds of her choking. He smothered his face against her legs and cried out as he pulled her body down with all his strength. He held her tight until the final convulsions of mortality melted away from her frame.

In the feverish gloom, he held onto her cold, mortifying body, repeating the same word over and over. "Saved...Saved...Saved..."

Chapter 50 – Restoration

Five Years Later…

Henry Massie followed the guard through a warren of corridors and a multitude of doors before reaching the far wing. This gaol was as unpleasant as any in England he'd come across. But here, there came no shouts or pleading, nor talking or begging from the dark cells, just an unearthly quiet.

They stopped at a cell door, and the guard picked through the bunch of keys. After a few attempts, he forced the door open, explaining how the damp made the wood swell.

A stink assaulted him and almost made him sorry for the trip. But when the guard's torch illumined the darkness, his heart wept for the poor soul who shielded his eyes against the light. *"Es kann nicht sien?* Daniel Davenport." Massie said to the guard.

The guard shrugged. *"Ja, sehet, welch ein Mensch. Davenport."* He pointed at the wretch.

Massie brought the kerchief to his nose. "Bring him out!"

The guard stared back perplexed.

"Bringen ihn aus."

The guard led the shuffling figure into the daylight. The skeletal figure was indeed Daniel Davenport. Or what was left of him. His matted hair and beard couldn't completely hide his pale gaunt face, which had aged.

"Do you remember me, Captain?"

Davenport leaned against the wall to support himself. A glimmer of a recognition flitted in his eyes.

"Yes…I remember you," Daniel croaked, and then slid down the wall onto the floor.

"You're free, Davenport. Free to leave."

Daniel rubbed his shoulder, seemingly insensible to the announcement.

"I said you are free."

"How long?"

"Five years."

Daniel shook his head. "Why?"

Massie crouched down. "I asked you same question all those years ago. I never forgot your story, Davenport. Cromwell is dead and the Long Parliament has been restored by Monck. The Restoration of His Majesty is imminent."

"Five years? But you didn't answer my question."

"I'm here because of a promise I made to Lord Rochester. In spite of everything, God rest his soul, he never forgot your sacrifice at Worcester. And now the king is at The Hague, preparing to leave for England. It's time for you to go home, Daniel."

Daniel shook his head.

"Stop torturing yourself and go in peace."

"Peace?" Daniel snorted. "Long ago we parted company. Find me Hugo."

"Go home to your family."

"He murdered her," Daniel groaned, "and you could have stopped him."

"Go back to Taunton. She may still live."

"More fool you for believing that. There are no miracles, spymaster. Find him for me."

"He could be anywhere. Maybe he is dead and beyond your justice?" Massie clasped Daniel's shoulder. "Go back to your home. It is what she would want." He placed some coins on the ground beside him. "Enough for food and better rags, I think." He then gave the guard his share. "Where your life leads you from here lies with you. I wish you peace, Daniel Davenport."

"I will find him," Daniel called to him as he walked away. "Until the ends of the earth, spymaster!"

* * *

Daniel had hoped the evening would bring a cool breeze. But it was hot and sticky, and the people he'd met on the road droned on about the dearth of rain and the dying crops.

When finally he'd met someone who could answer his question, he was told, sure as not, he'd find the constable at The Archer Inn, for he was there most evenings. Daniel knew the place well enough, but it had not been an inn he'd frequented. He remembered it as a rough, hoary place full of old soldiers talking about fighting on the continent. It was not a place for music or merriment—just drinking and reminiscing.

It was no more comfortable inside The Archer as a blast of hot, musty air hit him when he walked in. The patrons didn't even bother to raise their heads. The innkeeper was slumped over the bar snoring. And the rest of the locals sat hunched over their beers with an apathetic lethargy.

Daniel cast an eye over the room. The constable sat alone in the corner; his finger tracing the rim of his ale cup. Daniel lifted a stool and sat down at the table.

Startled, the constable growled at the trespasser. It took a second before his mouth dropped. "I thought you were dead."

Daniel rubbed his shoulder, trying to resuscitate it back to life. "I need to know."

The constable swigged down a mouthful and rubbed his mouth. "Aye…It's a sad story, Daniel."

"I know she's dead. I felt it in my bones. But I need to know."

The constable sighed. "After he left with you, I went to Disbrowe and told him everything. He sent another Commissioner to Taunton and Hardy released her."

"Released her! She lives?"

The constable hesitated, and Daniel sank back onto the stool. "I'm sorry…"

"Tell me."

"Hardy told me Hugo would be relieved of his commission and investigated."

"Released, but without protection," Daniel said, banging the table.

"It's not true!" the constable flared up. "We decided it would be best if Johanna stayed with Richard. Two of Hardy's soldiers were also there the night he took her."

"The commissioner's men? How could one man best three?"

"Garsten helped him. Both guards were murdered, and it was a miracle Richard survived his wounds."

"Miracle?" Daniel frowned. "But no miracle for Johanna!"

The patrons glanced over uneasily, and the innkeeper woke with a start.

The constable slumped forward. "They snatched her away…It took us a week to find her."

"Tell me."

"He hanged her." The constable wiped his eyes. "We found her at his estate. I'm sorry, Daniel."

The picture of Robert flashed into Daniel's mind; his bulging eyes and blue face. "Johanna." He rested his head on the table. *Hung up…and alone. If only Hugo would still live. Lord, if only he still drew breath. Let it be so!* "Where is he, Constable?"

"Would you rather not know…" His voice choked. "Where…Johanna is?"

"I can't…I can't go to her, Vincent," Daniel said, almost apologizing. "Where is he, Constable?"

"He disappeared. Hardy searched for two years, but nothing. Hugo's property was confiscated by the government." The constable waved the innkeeper over, and he brought ale for Daniel. "What now?"

"I need money. I will sell the cottage, and then I will find him and kill him if he still lives."

"I can help you."

"You helped enough. Didn't you?" Daniel hauled up to leave.

The constable jumped up from his stool. "Wait, Daniel."

Daniel stopped, folding his arms.

"It was left on the bed—a verse, more gibberish than sense. But perhaps it has some meaning?"

"Show it to me."

"I can tell you: The heroes Drake and Howard, the tyrant's bane…" The constable closed his eyes. "Did play upon a gouted wretch, plucked by the heels the monster thwarted by prowess, and the Fleet did limp away."

"The Armada of Philip—"

"You see—gibber."

"I have it at home, if you need to check the hand?"

"In which month was the Armada defeated?"

"Ah." The constable scratched his head. "I can't recall." He banged his cup on the table. "Which month did we beat the Spanish dogs from our shores?"

That woke the patrons, and one ancient rose and hushed them. "I was a boy of six years, and I can still remember the bells."

The others nodded as if they also remembered.

"The year was 1588 and the month? End of July or beginnin' of August."

The men gave a half-hearted cheer, and the innkeeper raised his hands. "Then it was good enough to kill a Spaniard instead of our own."

The constable shook Daniel's hand. "Before you go...she's at the cottage."

"Good bye, Constable."

Daniel hurried out and left the others to their toasts. A long forgotten memory came back to him. The old well that straddled John's land, and the day they dangled Manfred over it by his ankles. "The clinging boy who wouldn't leave his brother's side even when teased and...beaten." It was a message for him, and Daniel would oblige.

* * *

Daniel sipped his drink. The locals had tolerated his presence to begin with, assuming him a traveler passing through, who would soon be on his way. That had been six days ago, and now their forbearance wore thin. Their whispers altered to cold stares, but Daniel hardly noticed for his mind was engrossed with Hugo. Truly, Daniel had no future past his confrontation with him. Life had become a misery with Hugo's shadow stalking his every moment since he'd followed him to Zeeland. It had to end one way or another, for Hugo had consumed his life.

For six days he'd visited the well—from morning to night—praying Hugo would appear. Was it another game? Or perhaps he'd escaped his justice after all? Daniel had studied the verse ad infinitum, and he had grown to hate the childish, cantankerous scrawl almost as much as the murderer who wrote it. Still, after hours of interpreting the text, he had found no other meaning.

The anniversary of the victory had come and passed without an appearance. Was Hugo watching him from afar, mocking his stupidity? Maybe, but Daniel was resolved to continue his watch, irrespective of the locals' feelings.

He set off early. All was quiet as usual. The well, long since dried up, had always been there, so John had said. John had told him, as they played about it during the long summer afternoons, the great wizard Merlin drank from it, and the water had dried up.

The meadows were damp from the morning dew, and the vapor was beginning to rise as the sun appeared from behind the morning clouds. Daniel sat against the stone and rubbed his shoulder. "The old wound," he groaned. The scars of Worcester had always run deep, but in his younger days the physical pain had been bearable. Now, to even lift a sword was agony. Still, it would be the last time anyway.

He stood and peered into the dark of the well. As before, it was still bottomless and black. He checked the surrounding grass, sifting through it for clues of his presence. Nothing.

Another afternoon ran away, and Daniel raised his head to the heavens, more dispirited than ever. "Even now he controls me."

The swish of the tall grass startled him. He scrutinized the approaching stranger. It was the image of himself when he had stared in horror at his reflection just before leaving Cologne. "It cannot be him," Daniel muttered.

The vagrant wore a rough woolen cloak that trailed through the grass. A monk? The man's head was bowed, but his thick unkempt beard and long, matted, silver hair with threads of black running through it struck Daniel. He pulled his sword, but the stranger continued toward him, unconcerned.

Ten yards from Daniel, the stranger raised his gaunt, bony face and fixed his eye on him.

"It has become a pilgrimage of sorts for me, year after year, hoping you would return. A fitting arena? I'm sure you remember how you both tortured me. Let's finish it, Daniel."

Daniel gripped his sword tight. His thoughts flew to Johanna. If only she could have been here. Or was she watching from on high? Or just bones resting in a box? "Children will always weed out the weak and needy. But I see your depravity has caught up with you. Arm yourself."

Hugo threw his cloak to the ground and drew his sword. The elaborate hilt sparkled in the sunlight. "After I saved Johanna, I had nothing left to live for. You were dead, and I longed to experience her salvation time after time, so sweet it was." Hugo raised his arms to the heavens. "You failed me, and you failed Johanna. You should thank me for saving her. I have come through the fire purified."

"What you are," Daniel said, "is an abomination. You are a murderer of innocent woman!"

"I prayed that had you lived. Oh, Daniel, she was a whore who writhed on her knees before me. But she couldn't bewitch me, though she begged."

"When you murdered her, you a murdered a spark of such goodness! All the potential for goodness and love in her, you destroyed."

"She begged me for salvation!"

"All those she would have loved and helped. The experiences she would have had. A thousand threads cut."

"To see you now, oh, you cannot believe the ecstasy. I will bring you through the fire with me, Daniel!"

"With your brother's wife?"

Hugo charged Daniel; his scream a demented clarion call, and his face twisted into a terrifying nightmare. His wild swings were uncontrolled in their fury.

Daniel blocked each attack—the thrusts and slices turned aside.

Panting, Hugo stepped back. His eyes rolled, and the froth of his spittle leapt from his maw with each exhalation. "You consider yourself better than I? After what you did to me!"

Daniel circled him, drawing in closer. "I know the truth. I didn't kill John. The shot took him from behind. Unnatural, coward!"

A flashing madness gripped Hugo's eyes. "I shot him! I murdered him!" he screamed. "He was always in my way!"

Hugo thrust low toward Daniel's leg. Daniel arched his sword down sharply and parried Hugo's thrust to the side. Hugo stumbled forward, and before he regained balance, Daniel's kick to the face leveled him flat out. Dazed, Hugo crawled to his knees. Daniel steered the blade against his throat.

"Vengeance is mine! You told me!"

Trembling, Hugo grasped the blade and pressed it harder against his throat. The blood trickled down his neck. Hate and madness leapt from of his eyes. "Yes, finish it!"

"*You* are guilty! *You* alone! For John! And for your bastard son!"

"She was a witch! She tried to tempt me, seduce me. Soft and

246

naked, the whore writhed on the bed before me! Cut me, you cur!"

"*You!*" Daniel said, shaking with rage, "are responsible for the death of your bastard's mother as well!"

"Kill me! Do it, you coward!"

Disgust and loathing for the creature before him welled up within Daniel. "I will repay, so said the Lord."

Hugo groaned like a wounded animal and fell back before him.

"I am not *you*!" Daniel cried out. "I will not soil my blade on one such as *you*."

Daniel staggered back as hellish curses spewed from Hugo.

"I am finished with *you*!"

Hugo shrieked and writhed on the ground as if the furies had already taken him.

Daniel tuned away from him, fell on his knees and wept. His body shuddered in the agony of his broken soul. He let the sword slip from his grasp and lifted his eyes to the heavens. "Johanna! God, forgive me!"

The pain took his breath away. A sword was stuck through him. Blood on steel. Daniel slumped forward into the grass.

EPILOGUE

Ecce homo. No, more animal than man, who lay unconscious in his own filth and dereliction. A creature of the darkness that skulked in the shadows during the daylight hours, and who was pursued in the night by his sins' nightmares.

It had been Sister Margaret who had first informed him of a soul possessed of madness from the drink and the burden of a guilty conscience. She had taken him in at the almshouse on Shoe Lane. Only after many days had she been able to say for certain that the vagrant had been a rebel, and many more days to confirm his name and identity. Obviously, Captain Davenport had failed to find him, and it now fell to Massie to take care of Hugo.

Henry Massie had thought about a trial, but why bother? This one wasn't worth the time and the expense. He had taken great satisfaction from his work over the past couple of years. Many prominent Parliamentarians had been brought before the king's justice, and rightly so. Trials were for cleansing and for resolution: beneficial both for the good people of England and for the perpetrator. Yet, after observing Manfred Hugo over the past weeks, he had come to the conviction that Hugo didn't deserve a trial. A rabid dog was put down before its madness spread. And so it would be a kindness to put Hugo out of his misery.

Yes, a trial was out of the question. No one should ever hear of the attempt on the king's life in Cologne. No one would ever hear of Hugo's plan to force a captain of the Lifeguard to assassinate his king. Hugo would slip from the world as if he had never been. A man with nothing, with no one left behind, would sink away into oblivion. He never was.

Massie removed the blade from his doublet and kneeled in front of Hugo. He almost fell back before the reek but steeled himself to his duty.

"Per istam sanctam Unctionem—"

Hugo groaned.

"—et suam piissimam misericordiam adiuvet te Dominus—"

Hugo stirred and his eyes flickered.

248

"—gratia Spiritus Sancti, ut a peccatis liberatum te salvet atque propitious—"

Hugo's eyes flashed in the gloom. "Devil's whores—"

Massie plunged the blade into his throat. The gush of blood warmed his hand as Hugo's final intake of air rattled in his throat.

"—allevet. Amen."

About The Author

D S Allen was born in County Antrim, N. Ireland. He grew up and lived for many years in the beautiful town of Whitehead. It lies nestled on the east coast overlooking Belfast Lough. On a clear day it is possible to see the sunny shores of Scotland. He am currently a teacher and a writer. He has also written a children's book series called, The Adventures of George and Flanagan: The Headmaster's Cave & The Bone Whisperer. www.dsallen.org.

Printed in Great Britain
by Amazon